Ca~~~~
Shop

Also by Kiki Swinson

Wifey

I'm Still Wifey

Life After Wifey

Playing Dirty

Notorious

Sleeping with the Enemy
(with Wahida Clark)

Published by Kensington Publishing Corporation

The Candy Shop

Kiki Swinson

Kensington Publishing Corp.
http://www.kensingtonbooks.com

DAFINA BOOKS are published by

Kensington Publishing Corp.
119 West 40th Street
New York, NY 10018

All Kensington Titles, Imprints, and Distributed Lines are available at special quantity discounts for bulk purchases for sales promotion, premiums, fund-raising, educational or in-stitutional use. Special book excerpts or customized printings can also be created to fit specific needs. For details, write or phone the office of the Kensington special sales manager: Kensington Publishing Corp., 119 West 40th Street, New York, NY 10018. attn: Special Sales Department. Phone: 1-800-221-2647.

Dafina Books and the Dafina logo Reg. U.S. Pat. & TM Off.

ISBN-13: 978-0-7582-3891-7
ISBN-10: 0-7582-3891-6

First mass market printing: January 2010

10 9 8

Printed in the United States of America

Dedication

I've got to dedicate this book to my loyal fan, Denyse Meade & her aunt Jackie Bailey from Boston, MA. To know that you got your aunt to drive you all the way down to Maryland, so you can meet me at one of my signings, will be something I'll never forget. Thanks for making me your #1 author!!!

Acknowledgments

It has only been the power of God & my Lord & Savior Jesus Christ that I have been able to persevere through as many of the trials I've had in my life. So, I thank Him.

To my publisher, Crystal Lacey Winslow, author of the latest book, **Sex, Sin & Brooklyn**, all I need to say is that you have been nothing but good to me, that's why I'm not going anywhere. So, let's shake some shit up & shut all the haters down! Oh & thanks for that huge package you sent in the mail for my baby! What can I say? You truly went all out!

To my new baby girl Kamryn, you are so beautiful, mommy! So, to be able to wake up to you every morning is a true blessing. To my other two spoiled brats, Shaquira & Lil J, I love you both so very much, which is why I try to give you the world. So, all I'm asking in return is that you two continue to make me proud. To my husband Karl, thanks for giving me a beautiful little girl! She's the best gift a mother can ask for. Grandma Clara, I love you!

To Mom, **Da' Diva**, you are truly a talent in itself. Now, go ahead and finish that book, so the world can get a taste of that creative juice you got flowing.

Dad, I love you so much! Sunshine Swinson-Torry, you truly make me proud to have you as my sister. You've graduated from college & now you're doing the damn thing at your new job. Girl, get that paper! To my brothers Eugene & Jamon **"Fro"** Swinson, keep your heads up & know that I love you guys too.

To my favorite cousin, Xymara Hines, hey b@#%h!

(smile). Girl, you know you're gonna always be my home girl, cousin or not! That's just how you and I roll! Kiss my god-daughter Zahria for me! (Hey ma ma!) Duke Woodley, even though your butt is living up in Maryland, you're still my favorite cousin too. I really do appreciate those long talks we always have. Laughing & joking back and forth with you has always been a sense of therapy for me. So, thanks for always keeping a smile on my face.

To my favorite aunt, Karen **"Sunshine"** Johnson, once again you gave me the seal of approval to move forward with this book, & one thing I know about you is that when you say something is hot—it's hot! I love you! Thank you too Essence (over @ QVC)!

To my best friend Letitia Carrington, girl, you and I are so much alike it's funny. But what's really special about our friendship is the fact that you never judge me & always got my back. I love you **L.T.**! (smile). And to you, Mr. Herman Carrington, I've gotta thank you for keeping it real with me when I'm going thru the motions. The way you break things down to me through that Bible is awesome! And not only that, I wanna thank you for treating me like family. You know you're the man, right? Give me some of that Longshoreman money! (smile).

Malika Foster, having you in my life means more to me than you'll ever know. You saw how I cried like a baby when you drove all the way down to Virginia to spend time with me at my baby shower. I mean, it seems like every time I need you for something, you're there. So, just know that I'm not trading you for nothing in the world. Thanks for being down for me! I love you girl! I love you too, Aunt Nancy & Hope!

To my home girl, Yolanda Hutt—**Yoki**, damn what

can I say about you? You are the shit, witcha' fly-ass self! You know can't nobody fuck witcha'! Hey Tia . . . . even though you're Shaquira's best friend, you're still like a daughter to me. You too, Shayla!

Dominique Mitchell, you know I can't forget about my half-sister. Even though we don't see much of each other nowadays, I still love you. Not only that, you did a hellava job raising Chandra. I mean, look at her! The girl's in college right now! Ma, you did your thang! To my big brother Joe Cameron, I see you're still holding me down! Come on, let's go into business together so we can make this a family affair! Hey Tiffany Hoyt—**Tip,** you are my girl! And I love you to death!

Ms. Kellie, I know God has put you in my life for various reasons. And there's one that sticks out above others, & that's that loving and encouraging spirit you have. Plus, you know how to get dem' prayers up! God knows I need 'em, I love you . . . Ms. One! Vandelette Ware—Pookie, girl, you are a bad sister too! And don't let body tell you different. To my spiritual mother Joyce Stancil, I love you!

Hey Rosalee Evans, you know you're still my homey! Thanks for always supporting me. Aunt Brenda & Uncle Mike Byrd, I love you both!

To my cousins Ant & Gee, I love ya'll too. Gee, I hear you & Pam got another baby on the way!

To my cousins Nikki & Toya, down in Georgia. I'm coming down there so make room! Also, congrats to you Toya, on your newborn baby. To Sharney, I truly value your constructive criticism, so when you say you would like to see certain changes in my book, I don't hesitate to do it. Thanks for all your input.

To my girl Amaleka McCall, you are a truly talented writer, so please don't stop at **A Twisted Tale of**

Karma, we wanna read something else by you. Oh yeah, your wedding pictures were beautiful. Hey Treasure E. Blue, your joint **A Street Girl Named Desire** is about to drop, so these other authors better look out! (smile).

To Kwan, author of **Hoodlum, Eve & Hood Rat,** thanks once again for the love. And one day I will return the favor! To the staff & my #1 supporters @ Waldenbooks in Military Circle Mall like: Linda, Ron, Patrick & Annette. You guys really have put me on the map & I owe you tremendously. That's why I'll do a signing for you at the drop of a dime. I love you guys!

To my home girl, **D.J. Deja' @ 103 JAMZ,** thanks for putting me on the air to broadcast to the world about my books. You are the bomb, girl! To my peoples: Kimberlie Flemings from Charlotte, NC., Iona Christian from Brooklyn, N. Y., Paula **Nikki** Bell (in Georgia), Yoni Wyatt, Chiquita Coleman, Sherry Cherry, Joan Chis-holm, Dana Brown, & my home girl, Delphine **Dee Dee** Johnson, Melissa White, Naomi T. Barnes, Shawntae Gatling, Chekesha Carter, Michelle Brent, Ina Mcgriff, my hair stylist Amii @ Salon Plaza (in Norfolk), Michelle @Hair Visions (in Berkeley), my girl "V" @ Exotic Glamour Hair Care (in Norfolk), Twiggy, April & Trina @ Jazzy Hair & Nails, Jeremiah & Ms. Kathy @ Hair Art, congrats to you Gayette on your new salon @ X -tremes, Shirelle Davis @ Styles Unlimited, Sharlette & all the other stylists @ Precision Kutts (on Baker Rd.), the twins @ Extreme Salon (on Princess Anne Road in Norfolk), Earnestine & Jackie @ E & J Selective Salon (in Norfolk), to all the hairstylists @ Mahogany Styles (on Kempsville Road), Michelle & Lady Bug @ Visions (on Turnpike Road), all you ladies have done nothing but show me love from the very beginning, so I want to thank you!

To all my peoples on lock: Charles "Silk" Dunn (FCI Elkton), Andrew King (USP Canaan), Leshawn Pullie & Lil Bill (in Petersburg Camp), Kevin Jones–aka- Ron (Petersburg), & my nephew's father Ervin "E" Smith. Keep your head up, because there is a light at the end of the tunnel!

Chapter 1

My Death Wish

My heart and my feet moved at the speed of lightning as I made a desperate attempt to elude this dealer name Papoose. I just beat him for his whole stash of dope. The sandwich bag I had clutched in my right hand had to contain at least one hundred caps of heroin. This was a fresh batch. I saw him stashing it behind the bushes of the run-down and boarded-up abandoned house I once lived in, called the Candy Shop. I used to trick with him a lot a while back for half of bundles of his most lethal dope—and methadone pills when I was trying to kick the habit—but that was before I got all strung-out looking. His twenty-something-year old, nice body-having, hip-hop-loving ass, looking like the R&B singer Tyrese, wouldn't have me now if I tried to give him some pussy or head for free. That's just how bad shit is for me right now. Yeah, I know I look like a fucking zombie, but I haven't always looked like this. I remember when I used to have niggas salivating over me and always telling me how much I reminded them of the actress Lisa Raye. But believe me when I tell you that we don't look that much alike. The only thing she and I have in common is that we both look like we're half-breeds with long hair. Plus, we're fly as hell with thick thighs, a tiny waist and a huge, round ass. My husband use to love when I would walk around the house, wearing nothing but a white tank top and a lace thong. His dick would always grow three inches from the sight of the strap of my panties getting lost between my booty cheeks—which was a major turn-on for me—so I'd always bend over and tell him to spread my ass apart and bury his tongue deep inside me. Those were definitely the days and I would give anything to go back to that life. But, I know that's only wishful thinking, considering how long I've been trapped out here in these streets.

It's been three years, as a matter of fact, with constant episodes of me chipping away at my life and having no place to go at the end of the day. And where I lay my head at night all depends on how the dice are rolled. I've seen nights where I've stayed at my best friend's apartment. And then, when the rent got behind and the eviction notice was posted on the front door, I found refuge with a couple of dudes. Now, it didn't last long, of course, but I made the best out of every situation. And the only thing I could give them in exchange for giving me a place to stay was allowing them to suck and fuck me in every orifice my body had to offer. So far, I've been doing heroin for a lot longer than I've been homeless and have been really fortunate not to have ever caught a dope charge. So trust me, I am going to try to keep it that way unless they fucked around and run up on me right after I make my score. And of course, if that happens, I know I am going to be in hot shit! Other than that, I am taking the bitter with the sweet because this world I created for myself isn't anything to play with. The other dope fiends I get high with out here are vicious as hell. They will turn on you for a ten-dollar cap of dope in a heartbeat, especially if their dirty asses is ill. So, it isn't a secret that everybody has to watch their own backs. Too bad I didn't plan out my escape a little more thoroughly because if I had, I wouldn't be running for my life as we speak.

"Bitch! I'm gon' kill you when I catch you!" I heard him yell from just a few feet away from me with an enormous amount of rage.

Hearing the tone of his voice—and the speed at which he was running—made me well aware that it was a matter of time before I would be begging him for mercy. So, naturally I wanted to pick up my speed but for some reason, my feet wouldn't allow me. And then all of a sudden, it began to seem like I was running in slow motion. And as I looked around me for an escape route, I noticed how all eyes were on me. It was very late—two o'clock in the morning to be exact—so the eyes beaming from the sidelines of this dimly-lit street belonged to the local crack heads and dope fiends who have migrated to this part of town. Seeing another fiend running for their life, and trying to keep a dope dealer from killing 'em, is nothing unusual. This type of shit happens day in and out, especially when dope addicts like me need a fix and can't find any other alternatives to copping a pill of dope. A normal hustle for addicts like me would be to go on a boosting spree and try to find any kind of merchandise with value. A family member's house would be an ideal place to start, unless they know your situation and wouldn't trust you to be alone in any part of their house. So, the next best thing is to try to find valuable items outside of their home, or anybody else's home, for that matter. But, if that plan goes up in flames then you're going to either have to run up in a department store, or get gully and get down on your knees and serve up the best head your mouth can perform.

Now you may not get nothing more than five or ten dollars for your services, so just look at it in a way that you didn't have five or ten dollars to start with and count your lucky stars that you're on your way to the dope man. But when all of these options run out, that's when we result to finding ways to clip the dealers for their package without them knowing it, which is like playing a game of Russian roulette. If you want to know the truth, it's more like a suicide attempt on our own lives. Sometimes we come out on top and sometimes we don't. The times we don't mount up to a serious beatdown or even worse, which is exactly what I am about to experience if I don't find a diversion in the next twenty seconds. Believe it or not, this nigga is gaining on me. I had a good fifty-feet head start on him, but he quickly made up that distance in speed and now he is on my ass. So, again, I am looking for a way to dodge this maniac. And right when I was about to cross over from one block to the next, I felt a hard blow hit me in the back of my head and the force from it sent me tumbling face first into the pavement. The very second I hit the ground, my face felt like it had exploded. And in the midst of it, I know I heard my jaw bone crack.

But at this point I couldn't be concerned about it,

because something much worse was about to happen; especially knowing that upon my fall, the bag of dope flew right out of my hand and every pill scattered all over the ground.

"Oh, bitch, you're dead now!" Papoose screamed and then he kicked me as hard as he could in my side with his Timberland boots.

The intense pain from the blow of his boots sent me out of this world. And before I could digest the excruciating pain that impacted my side, he began to kick me in the same spot over and over. And then he began to stomp me in my back. I tried pleading for my life, but he acted as if he didn't hear me. So, all I could do was scream and yell for help.

"Bitch, ain't nobody gon' help you. You gon' die tonight for trying to steal my shit."

"Papoose, I am so sorry" I cried out. "I promise, I'll pay you back."

"Bitch, how the fuck you gon' pay me back? You ain't got no mutha' fucking money!" He screamed as his anger escalated and the beating got more severe. "You ain't nothing but a homeless dope fiend." He continued and before I even realized it, he took out his burner and cocked the hammer.

Right then and there, my life flashed before me and all I could do was think about how I even allowed myself to get to this point. My ex-husband's and my daughter's faces appeared in my mind and I knew now that I had really fucked up my life. But what was really screwed up was that I knew deep down inside that I was at the end of my rope, and the only energy I had left in my body was to call out my ex-husband's and daughter's names. So, as this moment got dimmer and dimmer for me, I cried out, "Eric . . . Kimora . . ."

Chapter 2

My First Shot of Candy

February 14, 2003

"Eric . . . Kimora . . . breakfast is ready," I yelled into the hallway from the entrance way of the kitchen and moments later, they both appeared before me with big, empty stomachs. My husband Eric kissed me upon arrival.

My daughter Kimora, however, dashed right by me and took a seat in her favorite chair at the kitchen table. She made it very clear that her sights were set only on filling her belly. So, I let her be and served her a plate of her favorite pancakes with link sausages. Eric had the same and a side of scrambled eggs with cheese. I, on the other hand, made myself a cup of hot tea since I didn't have much of an appetite. And after I took a seat at the kitchen table next to Kimora, Eric felt the need to remind me about tonight's plans for dinner.

"Don't forget, we got to be at my parent's house by six."

I took a sip of my tea and assured him that I wouldn't miss tonight's dinner for the world.

"Have you decided which dress you're going to wear?"

"Not yet. But, I am leaning more toward the lavender one."

"Mommy, I think you should wear the red one. It's much prettier than the other one. And besides, it makes you look really sexy," Kimora commented between chews.

"How do you know what looks sexy?" Eric wondered aloud as he looked directly at Kimora.

"I just know," She told him.

I smiled proudly and glanced over at Eric, only to hear him say, "How in the world can a five-year-old child make judgment on what's sexy?"

"Had it ever occurred to you that she may have gotten it from you?"

"Yeah, Daddy," Kimora agreed.

"Enough with the talking while you've got food in your mouth."

"Yeah baby, don't do that," I said, agreeing with Eric. And then I looked down at my wristwatch. "My God, how times flies," I continued as I took one last sip of tea from my coffee mug.

Two seconds later I stood up from my chair, so immediately Eric wanted to know where I was rushing off to.

"Yeah, Mommy, you just sat down," Kimora added.

"I know. But, I've got to get to work a little early this morning."

"What's the occasion?" Eric wanted to know.

"It's nothing, really. Just need to help a few of my staff set up for the Valentine's Day cocktail party we're having for our teachers after school this evening."

"So, what time is this party over?" His questions continued.

"By six. But, I'll be out of there way before then," I assured him as I walked over toward the kitchen sink to dispose of my coffee mug.

"Do you think it would be wise for you to get dressed at work, instead of coming all the way back home?"

"No," I said, nodding my head. "I'll get back here in more than enough time to get dressed. And besides, after the long day I'm expecting to have today, I'd prefer to come home and wind down with a hot shower before I even attempt to get dressed and join your parents for dinner."

"Suit yourself. Just don't drink too many cocktails," he concluded.

I smiled with a cheesy expression and assured him that I wouldn't.

And as I began to make my way out of the kitchen, I reached over and kissed them both and told them to have a nice day.

Upon my arrival at work, which is the only prestigious performing arts school in the Tidewater area, at which I'm an assistant principal, I noticed my secretary, Teresa Daniels—who also happens to be my best friend—gathering some items from the trunk of her car. Immediately after I parked my vehicle, I got out and approached her. "Need some help?" I asked.

"Yeah. Grab that brown bag right there." She instructed me as she wrestled with three bags of her own.

"Damn!" I said the instant I grabbed ahold of the paper bag.

"It's heavy, huh?" Teresa commented and then she closed the trunk of her car.

"You damn right it is. What do you have buried under these napkins and paper plates?"

"Liquor and sodas for the party."

"Did you have enough money for everything?"

"Yes, I did. As a matter of fact, I've got about forty bucks left," she continued while we both headed towards the entrance of the school.

"Well, you know what to do with it."

"What? Keep it."

I chuckled and said, "No, silly! You've got to put it back."

"No one's gonna miss it."

"I will. So, put it back and while you're at it, write a receipt for the portion you used."

"I know. I know," Teresa said sighing heavily.

Now by this time, we were both in the teacher's lounge area. So, I sat my bag down, took a deep breath and said, "I feel like I just had me a little workout."

"Me too," Teresa agreed as she began to empty the contents of the bag onto the table.

"What time should we start setting up?" I wanted to know.

"Well, I was thinking the best thing to do, would be to set up the decorations now. And then immediately after school lets out, we could pull out the food, the drinks and the party favors."

"Okay. We can do that," I said to Teresa and began to help her arrange and set up the decorations. It only took her and I less than thirty minutes to put everything into place, which meant we still had a little time to B.S. around before the students arrived.

So, back in my office I took a seat behind my desk while Teresa found herself a resting place on my lounge chair. And like always, we never seem to run out of topics to talk about.

"What's on the agenda for tonight?" I asked her.

"Darren is suppose to come by around nine o'clock, so we'll probably order a pizza, watch a few movies, and fuck each other's brains out."

"That's it?"

"Yeah, as far as I know," she replied nonchalantly.

"But, don't you think you deserve so much better?" I asked, simultaneously searching her face for definite signs of hurt. Now she has her ways of being brutally honest with me but these last few months, she hasn't.

Believe me, I know her like a book. She and I have been friends for over thirteen years now. We met fresh out of high school at a party some mutual friends of ours had, and hit it off instantly. Through our entire friendship, she and I only squabbled on two occasions. Neither episode was a major issue because we tried to be as non-confrontational as possible. She has become more docile than anything. Not to mention, her petite frame and passive school girl image don't help her at all. She looks like and puts you in the mind of Toni Braxton, but with a tiny bit of fire in her heart. Lately she has been dealing with her issues by sweeping them under the rug and hoping that they'd go away. I stay on her constantly about this guy, Darren. He is such a complete loser. He never takes her anywhere because he's always crying broke. And to make matters worse, his ass is married. So, you know they have absolutely nothing invested, which is why I am always trying to introduce her to other eligible bachelors. But nothing ever seems to come out of it. So, all I can do is wish her the best.

"At times, I do," she finally replied. "But, he and I have been together for so long, that I just can't see myself with no one else."

"How long has it been since you've been seeing him?"

"Four years."

"And in those four years, how many times has he promised to leave his wife?"

"Over a dozen."

"So, you know what that means, right?"

She sighed and said, "Yes, I do."

"Well, then, you better start acting like it," I warned her, using a sincere and loving tone. And before I was able to carry on with my words of wisdom, my office phone began to ring. "Excuse me a minute," I said to her. "This is Mrs. Simmons," I continued, speaking into the receiver of the phone.

"Good morning, Faith."

"Good morning, Steve," I replied in an unenthusiastic manner to a man who happens to be my boss. He is actually the principal of the entire school and an asshole, I might add. Always on my back about nonsense, which makes me wonder if he ever gets any pussy at home.

"Did I catch you at a bad time?" he asked me.

"Oh no! How can I help you?" I continued with a smug expression on my face.

But before he could go into explanation mode,

Teresa folded her arms across her chest and whispered very softly, "What does he want now?"

Wondering the exact same thing, I threw my left hand into the air and shook my head with uncertainty. Quiet as it is kept, this cracker stresses me the hell out. And the bugged-out thing about him is that, he is always coming out of left field with some of the pettiest shit a person could muster up. It has become a natural reaction for me to brace myself whenever he and I come in contact with each other.

"I was hoping you had a chance to get your hands on the SOL scores," he finally said.

"No. Not yet."

"Can I ask why?"

"Well, because the school board's administrative office hasn't posted the reports as of yet."

"Oh . . . well, I'm afraid they have."

"When?"

"This morning. You and I were both were emailed the results."

"Oh, really."

"Yes. So, I'm going to need you to have Teresa download and print out the entire report and have it on my desk within the hour."

"I'll let her know."

"Has she made it in yet?"

"Yes, she has."

"All right, well when she's done, I would like for you to meet me in my office shortly thereafter for a brief meeting."

"Okay," I told him and then we ended our call.

"What the hell does he want now?" Teresa didn't hesitate to ask.

"He wants me to have you to download and print

out the entire SOL report and put it on his desk
within the next fifty-nine minutes."

"When did the report come out?"

"A few minutes ago."

"Well, why the hell does he wants me to do it?
Doesn't he have a secretary of his own?"

"Yeah, but you know how he is. So, just do it for me."

Teresa stood up from my lounge chair and said,
"Trust me, I'm only doing it for you."

"Thanks, girl."

"Don't mention it. I just wish I could tell your fat-
ass boss to go to hell without suffering the repercus-
sions of getting fired."

I burst into laughter and told Teresa to calm down.

"Oh, I'm calm. I'm just frustrated at how he's
always trying to carry you. I mean, he's always riding
you behind dumb shit! And he's probably doing it because he's intimidated by you and scared that you're
gonna snatch his job up from underneath him. But, if
I were you, I wouldn't let that bastard faze me one bit."

"Believe me, I'm not," I assured her in five words
or less. And then I had to usher her out of my office
because she had a job to do, and it was my duty to relieve her so she could do it.

Shortly after Teresa printed the SOL report, Mr.
Baker and I had our meeting as planned, which of
course ended on a sour note and I got the bad end of
the stick, because the SOL scores for our entire
school weren't up to his standards. Now, I had to
have a meeting with my teachers and make them feel
the remnants of the wrath I just encountered in

Steve's office. It was just a classic case of the domino effect. So, it was nothing personal.

Finally, my work day ended, and I was truly looking forward to the Valentine's Day cocktail party. Winding down with a cold fruity cocktail was all I could think about. Teresa, along with a few other teachers and staff members, came together in our lounge area to celebrate this occasion as well. But, for some reason or another, Teresa did not seem to be enjoying herself. It was obvious her mind was somewhere else. The way she cradled her drink in her hand told it all.

So, immediately after I poured myself a hefty one on the rocks, I joined her in the far right corner of the room.

"What's with the long face?" I asked her, the moment I approached her. She took a sip of her cocktail and said, "I am so sick of my life and everything in it."

"What happened now?"

"I just got a call from Darren."

"What did he say?"

"He told me that he couldn't see me anymore and that it was over."

"Why are you sad, Teresa? Him breaking it off with you is a good thing. He did not deserve to have you in his life. So, it's truly a blessing in disguise."

"I know that. But, I just can not get past the way he makes me feel when we're together."

"Well, you're gonna have to. Because, believe you me, that son of a bitch is going to get over you really quick."

"I sure wish my heart could believe that."

"It will. Just give it time."

"But, what do I do in the meantime?" She pressed on after she took another sip of her drink.

"Count your blessings and move on with your life."

"Easy for you to say." She commented and then she abruptly stood up to leave.

"Where are you going?" I got concerned.

"To the ladies' room, to let off some steam."

"Wait, don't go in there. Come on; let's go to my office, so you can have a little more privacy." I insisted and immediately lead her in that direction.

"Where are you two off to?" One of my teachers asked us as we walked by.

"To take a walk. We'll be right back," I told her.

On our way to my office, Teresa made a detour to her desk to retrieve her purse. But she did not allow a second to pass before she was back on the path to join me in my office. Now once we had arrived, I closed and locked the door while she took a seat on my lounge chair and sat her drink down on the floor next to her feet.

"Do you want to set your glass down on my desk?"

"No. It's fine," she replied and then she dove head first into her handbag and began to ramble in it rapidly.

"What are you looking for?" I wondered aloud, as I took a seat on the edge of my desk.

"My candy," she told me, revealing a folded dollar bill and an altered straw, made to be used as an instrument to snort any powdered form of drug.

In a demanding tone I said, "Wait, hold up," as I stood up on my feet.

Teresa looked up at me in a puzzled manner and said, "What?"

"What the hell you mean, what?" I snapped. "I thought you stopped using that stuff."

"I did."

"When?" I replied, standing directly before her.

"A few weeks ago." She started explaining herself as she began unfolding the dollar bill filled with a mixture of cocaine and heroin. "But, shortly thereafter shit started caving in all around me, so I went back to it," she continued.

In disbelief, I continued to stand there, mouth wide open and unable to say a word. Meanwhile, she placed the open bill in the palm of one hand and the straw in the other hand. Then she began to gather all of the powdery substance to the center of the bill, until she had it in one straight line. Moments later, she inserted one end of the straw into the drug and the other end into her nose. What she did next put the icing on the cake, because when she pulled her head back and ejected the straw from her nose, the residue from the drugs found refuge around the entire right nostril of her nose.

"Woooo . . . ! This shit is a missile!" she blurted out.

"Shssssh, be quiet before somebody hears you. And wipe your nose, while you're at it."

Taking heed to my minor demands, she sat the dollar bill and straw down next to her on the chair, wiped her nose clean and said, "You need to lighten up!"

"No. You need to get it together."

"Why are you acting like you've never seen me get high before?"

"Is that the impression I'm giving you?" I asked sarcastically.

"Hey, look Faith, I don't want to argue. So, please don't beat me up about this," Teresa expressed and then she laid her head back against the headrest of the chair.

"Don't want me to blow your high, huh?"

"That's the whole idea," she mumbled loud enough for me to hear.

Feeling at odds with what I was witnessing hit a major nerve right in the temple of my forehead, so naturally I wanted to react. But, then my conscience started eating away at me, which made me realize that I was using the wrong approach. And in knowing this, I decided to take two steps backwards.

Now, as I was doing this, Teresa mustered up enough energy to open up her eyes to see what it was that I was doing. And at that point I said, "Are you okay?"

"Oh yeah, I'm good."

"Are you sure?" I pressed on.

"Hell yeah, I'm sure. This shit I got pumping through me ain't nothing but the truth. I mean, it'll blow your fucking mind and it'll have you forget about all your problems."

"So, I've heard," I commented nonchalantly.

"No, I'm being serious here." She began to explain as she sat straight up, grabbing the dollar bill in hand. "You would be truly amazed at how this shit will make you feel."

"You've mentioned that to me before." I had to remind her.

"Yeah, I know. And I've tried to get you to test the waters too, but you keep getting cold feet on me."

"Look, just put that up before somebody comes knocking on my door."

"Oh, cut it out. Nobody's going to come looking for us and you know it. So, stop being so uptight and get on over here and try some of this good stuff. I promise you, you're going to love it." She tried convincing me.

Before I made an attempt to reject her offer as I've done a few times in the pass, she pressed the issue more by saying, "Come on girl, do it for me."

"No, thanks." I finally told her and then I took another sip of my cocktail.

"Come on, please," she insisted. "I promise, it's going to relieve you from all that stress Steve constantly piles on top of you."

"What are you trying to do, turn me into an addict?"

"No, I'm not. All I want you to do is try it one time. And if you don't like it, then that's fine. Plus, I promise I'll never ask you to mess with it again."

Feeling the pressure from Teresa started mounting around me pretty quickly because on one hand, she was right. Steve is constantly stressing me the hell out. I am also beginning to dislike my job. Plus, my life at home isn't all that great. My husband Eric always seems to find fault in everything I do. And the fact that he looks for me to be this perfect trophy wife really put a strain on our relationship. The only thing that keeps me sane is my daughter Kimora. Looking into her face every single day is the only reason why I continue to press forward.

Other than that, I'd be in a slump. So, I guess Teresa might be right for once. Maybe taking a hit of this drug one time will do the trick for me. Who knows, I may not even like it. But, I'll never know until I try it.

"Hey, what's up? Are you going to try it or not?" she asked once again.

I hesitated at first. But then I said, "Okay. I'll do it, just this one time."

Teresa stood up on her feet, smiling and said, "That's the spirit!"

So, within moments of the excitement Teresa put on display, I found myself lying at the hands of her mercy. She instructed me to sit back in my chair while she did the initial prepping. All was left for me to do was to snort the drug in its entirety. And as soon as I did just that, my left nostril started burning intensely. And as the feeling became more and more unbearable, I scrambled to my feet in effort to retrieve some tissue paper from my tissue box, placed at the far right corner of my desk. Seeing this, Teresa knew exactly what I was experiencing, so she took the liberty to grab a small piece of tissue paper for me and dipped a fraction of it into my drink. Three seconds later, she handed me the partially wet and discolored tissue paper and said, "Here, just stick this in your nose. It'll soothe the burning sensation and help drain most of the powder down into your mouth."

Following her instructions once again, I found that this little technique worked. It also didn't take long for the drugs to take affect, because at one point I began to feel cheerful and excited. And then all of a sudden, my heart started beating a lot faster than usual which, of course, scared the hell out of me. So, I looked into Teresa's face and said, "I've got to go."

"Where are you going?" she wanted to know.

"I don't know," I began to tell her as I raced for my office door. "I've just got to get out of here and do something because my heart is running a mile a minute." I continued grabbing ahold of the doorknob.

"Okay, we can go outside and take a walk. But, wait for me," Teresa suggested as she struggled to dispose of both the dollar bill and the straw. So, once that was done, we both headed directly outside into the parking lot, only to end up taking a stroll around the school's track. Luckily for me, I decided to wear my comfortable loafers today. Because if I hadn't, I would not have lasted a quarter of a mile in my normal four-inch heels. Teresa, on the other hand, chose to take it easy after the second lap and elected to watch me from the bleachers on the sidelines, but I kept it moving because I had an instant burst of energy to burn, and that's what I did. We stayed outside for about forty-five minutes. And then, once I realized that my heart rate had begun to slow down, I retired my walking shoes. Soon there after, Teresa and I returned to the party and had a few more drinks to mellow us out. The transition went smoothly and I felt like I was on top of the world. It's a high that'll make you feel like you can do anything. The effects of the drug also made me feel carefree and that nothing in this world could upset me right now. So, I loved every minute of it. And loved it to the point that I followed Teresa all the way home to get high some more, which was the start of my demise.

Chapter 3

No Turning Back

The street lights caught up with me before I had the chance to make it home, which is when I realized that it had to be late. And when I looked down at my wrist-watch and noticed that it was eight-thirty, I panicked because I knew that I had missed my in-laws' dinner engagement. Not to mention, how angry Eric is going to be when we come face to face. I also know that there is absolutely no way that I can come up with a good enough lie for him to understand why I was absent tonight. So, it was a no-brainer that I was going to get a tongue-lashing the moment I entered into our home. And to prevent from prolonging the inevitable, I pressed down on the accelerator to give my car more gas and headed home.

Now when I walked into the house, it was unusually quiet. So, I called out Eric and Kimora's names but got no answer; which was kind of strange, considering it was almost nine o'clock at night. So, my first reaction prompted me to go through the entire house to look for them, but I chose to check the garage for Eric's car instead. And when I opened up the hallway door that led to the garage and noticed that his car wasn't there, I let out a sigh of relief. Having him detect that something wasn't quite right with me wasn't a conversation I was ready to embrace.

Knowing him and his clever mind, it wouldn't be hard for him to figure out that I was under the influence of drugs. And the only way I would be able to shake it off is by getting some rest. So, before I went up to my room to retire for the night, I picked up the telephone and called him. I could not have him and Kimora barging in on me and destroying my high, so pinpointing his whereabouts was very critical for me at this point. And fortunately enough, he answered his cellular phone on the second ring.

"Hey baby, where are you?" I asked him in a cheerful manner, only to feel out his mood.

"I'm still at my parents. Why?" he replied, his tone never changing.

"Well, because I'm home and you're not. So, I wanted to know where you were."

"The question is, where were you?" he continued, his voice remaining idle.

"At work. You know I had to conduct a couple of meetings with a few of my teachers," I lied, knowing very well I was hanging out with my best friend Teresa at her apartment, snorting more of the heroin and cocaine she mixed together in that dollar bill.

Today was my very first day experimenting with the drug and I must say that it relaxed the hell out of you. On one hand, I felt real cheesy and ashamed. But after all the stress I'd been experiencing on my job, I saw no other resolution but this. To be perfectly honest, I've exhausted every resource I had within my grasp and nothing ever seemed to work. So, if anybody has their own opinion about the recent choices I've made in my life, then they need to keep it to themselves. Quiet as it is kept, I've been living out my entire life trying to please other people and I'm tired of it. From this point on, I am going to live my life according to the way I see fit. Screw everybody else and their expectations of me. It is time to do me.

"Yes, I was aware of that. But, it's Valentine's Day and you promised me that you were going to meet here at my parents' house right after you tied everything up at work."

"I know, and I'm sorry. So, I promise I'll make it up to you."

"Don't bother," he retorted in a nonchalant manner.

"But, I want to," I began to whine.

"Hey, listen, I've got to go."

"Okay, but where is Kimora?"

"She's in the kitchen with Grandma and Grandpa, eating ice cream and cake."

"Well, what time are you two heading home?"

"Probably within the next hour or so."

I sighed heavily and said, "All right. Well, I'm going to get ready for bed, then."

"Suit yourself," he commented and then he hung up.

The moment I realized that there was nothing but dead air between my telephone line and his, I pressed down on the flash button and placed the receiver back into the base holder, since there was no use in me calling him back. I mean, who would I be kidding? He didn't want to talk to me. So, I am going to leave well enough alone and head on up to my bedroom. Giving my body the rest that it needs is better suited for me at this moment. And that's exactly what I am going to do.

When I woke up the next morning to an empty bed, I immediately called Eric's name. But once again I got no answer and was forced to get out of bed and look for him. I looked in Kimora's bedroom first and noticed that she hadn't slept in it at all. So, I headed downstairs to the living room area and still they were nowhere in sight. Then something told me to check the garage for Eric's car, so I did. And of course, it wasn't there. So, I got back on the telephone and dialed all seven digits of his cellular phone number but for some odd reason, he didn't answer. Which led me to dial the number to his parents' house and his mother answered.

"Hello," she said.

"Good morning, Mrs. Kathy."

"Good morning to you, too."

"Is Eric there?" I didn't hesitate to ask.

"No, honey, he just left to take Kimora to school."

"How long ago was that? Because I just tried to call him on his mobile."

"Probably about fifteen minutes ago. He said he was going to head on to work as soon as he dropped her off."

"Oh, really," I answered with a chuckle.

"Yep, that's what he told me before he left."

"Okay. Well, thank you," I replied in a mild manner, trying not to let on how upset I was. But, Mrs. Kathy sensed it anyway and said, "What's going on with you two? And why didn't you show up for the

dinner last night? Your father-in-law cooked up a
storm 'round here yesterday."

"Mrs. Kathy, I am truly sorry that I didn't make it.
But, I got caught up at work yesterday with a long
and intense meeting with all of my teachers. And as
far as Eric is concerned, he's just going through the
motions right now because I was unable to make it
out to your dinner party last night."

"Well, since you had to work, then I guess I'll forgive you," she insisted and chuckled.

"Oh thanks, Mrs. Kathy. You're a sweetheart!"

"And so are you. That's why you're my favorite
daughter-in-law."

"Oh, stop it. You're making me blush."

"Well, blush on," Mrs. Kathy continued with
laughter.

I laughed a little as well and then I asked her what
foods did Mr. Charles prepare for last night's dinner?

"Oh honey, that man whipped up a beautiful pot
roast smothered in brown gravy, onions, carrots and
potatoes. He also baked his famous macaroni and
cheese, some corn bread. And he cooked a big pot of
collard greens."

"Hmmm . . . hmmm. All that sure sounds good."

"It was. But, don't worry. 'Cause, we've got plenty
left."

"Will you make me a plate?"

"I most certainly will."

"Okay, well, I'll swing by there this evening."

"What time?"

"Right after work. So, have my plate ready."

"And I'll be waiting."

"All right. Well, I'll see you later," I told her.

"Okay. Now, you be safe."

"I will," I assured her.

"Okay. Bye."

"Bye bye."

Immediately after I hung up with Mrs. Kathy, I stormed back upstairs to get ready for work. And while I was showering, all I could think about was how immature Eric had become over the last couple of years. Our little issue wasn't serious enough for him not to have wanted to come home and face me. He didn't even extend the courtesy of telling me that he was going to spend the night at his parents' place. What an asshole! Always wanting to have his way. And if he doesn't get it, he'll shut down on me, which makes me wonder what he would've done if he knew I was out getting high last night? And to be honest, I really don't want to think about it. So, I guess this little secret of mine will be taken straight to my grave.

Chapter 4

X-Treme Chaos

When I arrived at work, I noticed that Teresa had not made it in as of yet. So, I went on to perform my normal everyday duties. Meeting and greeting the students as they exited the school bus was how I start of my day.

And after the school buses leave, I am in the hallways, making sure everyone gets to their classes on time. So, today when all that was done, I headed back to my office. But halfway there, I was intercepted by my eleventh-grade school counselor, Kimberly Lawson. She's a full-figured Hispanic woman, who looks to be in her late thirties. She's been working here at the school for a least seven years now. And the children love her to death. Everyone is always raving about what a good counselor she is, and I must say that I agree with them one hundred percent. Now, it is very rare that she and I have one-on-one conversations, so

I am very curious to know what it is she wants to talk to me about. And that's why I invited her to join me in my office.

"Have a seat," I said the moment we entered into my office.

"Thank you," she replied.

"You're welcome. Now, what can I do for you?" I asked her right after I took a seat.

"Well, I want to talk to you about an incident that happened here on school grounds a couple of days ago, involving your secretary, Teresa."

"What happened?" I asked in an eager manner.

"Well, I feel kind of awkward saying this to you, knowing how close she is to you; but as a woman in my position, I felt the need to tell you that I saw her sitting in her car, day before yesterday, during lunch time, sniffing some kind of narcotics."

"And where were you?"

"I went out for lunch that particular day. And when I returned, there she was sitting there with her head down, pushing that straw up her nose as I walked by."

"Did you say anything to her?"

"No, I didn't. I was too embarrassed to approach her."

"Have you told anyone else about this?"

"No one but my husband," she began to say. "I mean, I had to tell somebody."

"Well, that was fine. But, do me a favor."

"Sure. Anything."

"Let's keep this between you and me. I mean, I don't want this conversation to leave this office. Okay?"

"Okay."

"Well, in the meantime, I will have a serious discussion about this with Teresa, because that type of behavior will not be tolerated in any way, form or fashion!" I assured her.

Now, before Mrs. Lawson got up to leave, she wanted to know if I would also do her a favor. So, I said of course and asked her what was the favor?

"When you decide to speak with her in regards to this matter, would you be so kind as not to mention who you got this information from?"

"Oh, sure. No, problem," I told her.

"Well, thank you."

"No, thank you."

She stood up from her chair and said, "Don't mention it. Now, let me get back to my office before I miss my nine o'clock conference call."

"All right. And thanks again for coming to me with this first."

Mrs. Lawson smiled and said, "You're welcome."

Teresa finally made it into work around ten o'clock. And as soon as we made eye contact, she knew from my expression that I wasn't at all happy about her being tardy. So, she rushed into my office with an explanation in hand.

"Please don't be mad." She started off saying, closing my office door behind her. "But, the reason why I'm late is because I was up all night going through some changes with that nigga Darren."

"Look, Teresa, I don't give a damn about the changes you and Darren are going through. You've got a job to do. And part of it is to be to work on time. Now, please don't let me have this conversation with you again!" I replied in a harsh tone.

Surprised by my approach, she said, "Well damn, what's wrong with you?"

"Well, first of all, I woke up to an empty bed this

morning because my husband decided that he wasn't going to come home last night, because I didn't make it to his parents' dinner party. And then when I come to work, I get a visit by one of my staff, who informs me that they witnessed you sniffing dope a couple of days ago in your car, during your lunch break. So, when I heard this, I became furious because you know better. And if this person would've taken this to Mr. Baker, your ass would be getting your walking papers right about now. So, you better count your lucky stars and never let that shit happen again. Because next time, you may not be so lucky. You got me?"

"Yeah."

"Okay, now tell me what happened last night that kept you from getting to work on time?"

"Don't be mad, but I sat outside Darren's house all night, waiting for him to come home, so I could talk to him since he won't answer any of my phone calls."

"You mean to tell me that this man has you so fucked up in the head, that you sat outside his house all night long, waiting on him to come home, for the simple fact that he refuses to answer any of your calls?"

Teresa nodded her head and gave me a cheesy smile.

"So, what did you accomplish from all of that?"

"Nothing."

"Did you get a chance to see him?"

"Nope."

"How long did you sit outside his house?"

"Until about four in the morning."

"Well, what makes you think that he wasn't home already?"

"Because his car wasn't there. But, his wife's car was."

"Well, did it ever occur to you that they were probably hanging out together?"

"Yeah, it did cross my mind."

"Well, let me ask you this."

"Shoot."

"Tell me, what you would have done if he had pulled up in his car with his wife?"

"I would've gotten out of my car and confronted him."

"But, why? I mean, didn't he tell you it was over?"

"Yeah. But, I need some closure. I mean, I do deserve that."

"For what?" I commented with frustration. "That man is married. So, that means he doesn't owe you a thing."

"Yeah, I know that. But, it's the least he can do."

"Look, Teresa, just get over it and move on. Because it's obvious that he's trying to make things work at home."

"But, what if all of this is coming from his wife?"

"I don't understand what you mean."

Teresa took a deep breath and said, "What I'm saying is, what if his wife told him that if he didn't break it off with me, she would divorce him?"

"It shouldn't matter if it came from him or her. The fact remains that he told you out of his own mouth that he doesn't want to be involved with you anymore. So, just leave well enough alone!"

"Look, Faith, I understand what you're saying. But, my heart believes that there's more to that story than he's telling me."

Frustration with Teresa's non-acceptance issues was beginning to weigh heavily on me, so instead of continuously trying to convince her to see the writing on the wall, I literally threw my hands up and said, "Okay, look, do whatcha' want to do. I'm done with the whole thing. But, the next time you decide to stay out all night to go on one of your stalking adventures, please make sure you call me bright and early if there's a chance you're going to be late coming into work."

"All right," she replied. And then she stood up to leave. But before she had a chance to make her exit, I said, "Oh and another thing . . ."

She turned around and gave me her full attention. "What's up?"

So, I said, "You're a grown woman, so I don't care what you do on your own time. But, we need to be clear about you not getting high here at work any more."

"Oh, I'm clear on that. It won't happen again."

"Okay. Good. You can go now." I replied, giving her a stern look. And as much as it hurt me to do it, I would not have done her any justice if I would have been a little more lenient. I just can't tell her the shit she wants to hear. It's not in my character to do so. And the good thing about it, is that she knows this and doesn't expect me to be any other way; which is why we have an understanding. Other than that, she and I have a very close bond. I just hope she doesn't lose sight of that and continues on doing what she's supposed to do the moment she punches that time clock. Because if she doesn't and messes around and lets somebody else catch her pushing that straw up her nose, she will take that fall on her own. I mean it!

Chapter 5

Taking Da' Bitter
Wit' Da' Sweet

As promised, I stopped by my in-laws place on my way home. And to my surprise, I saw Eric's vehicle parked in the driveway, directly behind his mother's minivan. So, I braced myself for the unknown and proceeded toward the house. Mrs. Kathy, who happens to resemble the late actress who played Louise Jefferson, on the sitcom *The Jeffersons* greeted me with a warm hug and a smile. "Come on in, darling."

I kissed her on the left cheek and said, "How are you doing?"

"Well, my sugar has been rising a little these last few days, but other than that, I'm fine."

"Have you been taking your diabetes medication?"

"Yes, I have. But, I still have a weakness for moist chocolate cake and butter pecan ice cream."

"If you know like I know, you'll leave that stuff alone, before it kills you."

"Oh hush, girl. You sound just like your father-in-law."

"Where is he, anyway?"

"Sitting in the den with Eric."

"Where's Kimora?"

"She's back there too. So, come on," Mrs. Kathy insisted, as she led me into that direction.

And as soon as she made my presence known, I smiled and greeted both my husband and my father-in-law, who seemed like they were engrossed in their conversation. But, of course they spoke back. And as I made my way further into the den area, I noticed that Kimora was sound asleep on the sofa next to Eric, so I quietly crept over to her and gave her a kiss on her forehead.

"Please don't wake her," Eric begged me in an ir-ritated manner.

"I'm not," I assured him and then I took a few steps back from him and her both. Judging by his facial expression, it was obvious that he didn't want me too close to him. And since he was very polite with his words, I gave him exactly what he wanted. But as I stood there and looked at him, I was becom-ing furious by the second. So, I let out an exasperated sigh and asked him if I could speak to him alone in private? He immediately obliged and accompanied me outside on the back patio. And not even a second after we were alone, he wanted to know what it was that I wanted to speak with him about.

"Well, for starters I want to know why you refused to come home last night?" I began to tell him. "Be-cause if it had anything to do with me not showing up here last night for dinner, then you're being very immature and blowing this whole thing out of proportion."

"Faith, please don't stand here and lecture me. You, of all people, knew how important it was for you to be here to celebrate Valentine's Day with me and my family last night. But instead, you chose to be at work."

"Oh Eric, please don't play the work card on me. You knew I had a mandatory meeting to attend."

"Yes. And I also know that you attended the after work cocktail party, too."

"You're absolutely right. But, it was work related," I lied

"Bullshit, Faith! That party wasn't work related and you know it. So, stop it with the damn lies!" he replied as the pitch of his voice got louder.

"Look, I'm not lying. And please stop raising your voice."

"You know what; I can't stand here and listen to this nonsense anymore," he continued as he attempted to storm back into the house. But, I stopped him in his tracks by grabbing ahold of his arm, which probably wasn't a good idea because he looked back at me with the ugliest expression he could muster up and said, "Let me go, please!"

"Well, are you going to stand here so we can finish our conversation?" I asked.

"I'm not in the mood to talk anymore. So, let me go."

"But, why are you always running away when I want us to have a discussion?"

"Because you're always catching me at the wrong times."

"You know what Eric, you are so pathetic!"

"Tell me something I don't know," he replied sarcastically.

I struck back at him and said, "And you wonder why we can't ever resolve our issues." And then I released his arm.

I stood there and watched him walk back into his parents' house as if nothing had transpired between he and I which, of course, made me cringe. But instead of flying off the handle and making a scene, I marched back into the house and made my way into the kitchen, where I found Mrs. Kathy wiping down her kitchen countertops. "Need some help?" I asked.

"Oh no, honey. I'm fine," She insisted.

"So, what's on the menu for tonight?" I wondered aloud.

"Leftovers."

"Oh yeah, where's my plate?"

"It's in the fridge."

"Where exactly?' I asked her as I scanned the entire refrigerator with my eyes.

"It's on the second shelf, behind the yellow salad bowl."

"Oh, okay. I see it now." I informed her, relieving the container the instant I closed the refrigerator door behind me.

"Wanna warm it up?"

"No. I'm going to take it home with me and warm it up later."

"You sure?"

"Yes, ma'am. I'm sure," I replied in a manner of assurance. So, she handed me a plastic bag to carry the dish in while we continued our little chat. We talked for at least another twenty minutes before I threw in the towel.

Engaging in a conversation about what stores had sales this week, wasn't exactly what I would deem to be a juicy topic. So, I kissed her and called it a night. And on my way out, I asked Eric if he wanted me to carry Kimora home with me, but he insisted on bringing her himself. I let him have his way and left.

Teresa had been weighing heavily on my mind from the minute I left work today, so I got her on the phone immediately after I settled in at home.

"How are you doing?" I asked her, expressing concern.

Responding to my question, she said, "I'm okay."

But, the weight of her tone told me differently. So, I questioned her sincerity. "Are you sure? Because you don't sound like you are."

"I'm just tired. That's all."

"Have you eaten?"

"Yeah, I stopped by Subway on the way home and picked me up a sandwich."

"How was it?"

"It was good."

"So, what have you been doing since you got home?"

"Nothing but watch a little TV. But, that's about it."

"Have you tried to call Darren?"

"Yeah. And I just found out he changed his number."

"And how do you feel about that?"

"I feel hurt and betrayed."

"Do you need me to come over and sit with you for a while?"

"No, I'll be fine . . . ," She began saying, but her voice faded out as if she had been distracted. "Wait, hold on," she continued, and sat the receiver of the phone down on a hard surface. And then a minute later she picked the telephone back up and said, "That's my brother Eugene. So, let me call you back."

"He's there at your apartment?" I questioned her.

"Yeah, him and his friend Lamont stopped by to see me. But, they aren't gonna be here very long, so I'm gonna call you right back."

"Okay, you do that," I encouraged her. But, I know if I sat up and waited for her call, then I would be waiting in vain. Because you see, her brother was there with her. And the only reason why he was there, was because he recruits different dealers to come by her place to supply her with drugs. So, when that guy Lamont is done replenishing her supply container, she is going to go into seclusion and I will not hear from her until the morning, which is why I am going to tune in to these *Good Times* re-runs and call it a night myself.

Eric finally brought his dumb ass home around eight o'clock. He still had nothing to say to me, which was fine. My main concern at that point was to get Kimora into bed. And that's exactly what I did.

Chapter 6

Time to Re-up

Now, I have a ritual every Saturday, whereas I will make plans to spend the entire day with my family. We always start the morning off with a nice hot breakfast at IHOP or Denny's. And then we would either check out a movie or do some shopping at the mall. But you see, Teresa had another set of plans in store for me. So, when I received the call from her this morning, and heard the urgency in her voice, I knew that I was going to have to deviate from my plans a little bit.

And after I assured her that I would be at her place within the next thirty minutes, she sounded somewhat relieved and told me that she'd be waiting.

Now when I broke the sudden change of plans to Eric, he immediately blew up about it. So, there was no point in me trying to convince him to act a little more rational. He is a little too stubborn for that. And besides, my best friends needs me, so I've got to be there for her.

On my way out, Eric met me at the front door with an ultimatum in hand. "If you walk out of this house, don't expect me and Kimora to be here when you come back."

I stood there with an expression of disbelief. I mean, I couldn't believe that he would stoop this low. So, I asked him, "Why are you trying to blow this out of proportion?"

"Why are you always putting outside affairs before your family?" he retaliated.

"Look, I know it seems that way. But, the truth of the matter is that you and Kimora mean more to me than anything."

"Well, prove it!"

"Eric, don't do this."

"Don't do what?" he replied aggressively. "Just admit it! You don't have time for us anymore."

"Eric, please stop. Because it's not like that."

"Oh, it's like that. And it's been this way ever since you took that position as an assistant principal. Always working late hours, and you're hardly ever home to sit down and eat dinner with us."

"Eric, it's a performing arts school, and we discussed the fact that I was going to be working long hours before I even took the job."

"Yes, we did. But, I didn't think it was going to be like this."

"Look Eric, I see your frustration, but can we talk about this when I get back?"

"No, we can't."

"And why not?"

"Because I won't be here when you get back," he

replied and then he walked off in the direction of Kimora's bedroom.

It took everything within me not to run down the hall behind him, but when I realized that he was pulling one of his stunts, I opened up the front door and left. I figured it was too early to start the day off with drama.

Fully dressed in a pair of flannel pajamas, Teresa was definitely glad to see me. Her eyes lit up when she opened up the front door to her apartment. So, after I was let in, I asked her what was going on? "Come in the living room so we can talk," she replied in a nervous manner as she led me into that direction.

Now when I entered into the living room area, I wasn't expecting to see Teresa's brother Eugene lounging on her sofa. But, what was really bizarre was the fact that he was pretty banged-up looking. And then, not too far from him, sat Lamont. A very young looking guy, who had to be in his early twenties. But, he had the body frame of a linebacker. So, I cordially spoke to him and he nodded back. Now when I set my sights back on Eugene, I couldn't help but wonder out loud about the black eye and the scratches on his face. And that's when Teresa went into her spiel about their dilemma. "I got some coke and heroin from somebody," she tried to explain but was interrupted.

"That somebody is me!" Lamont interjected in a cocky manner, which of course scared the hell out of me because I wasn't expecting him to say anything. Nervously, Teresa opened her mouth and tried to finish her story but Lamont wouldn't let her get a word in edgewise. "Look Ms. Lady," he said, looking directly at me. "These two muthafuckas right here got some smack from me over a week ago, and promised to pay me my dough by Friday. And when I came over here yesterday to collect, this ole bitch right here tried to give me some ole sob-ass story that didn't even concern me. So, I told her that if she didn't get my money by this morning, then I was going to fuck her and her brother up. And I guess they thought I was playing, because when I got here an hour ago and they told me they didn't have my dough, I had to smack the shit outta her and rough him up a little bit."

Trying to digest all of this chaos was like trying to swallow a horse pill, but somehow I managed to cope. Holding my composure was another hurdle I needed to cross. So, I took a deep breath and very calmly asked him how much money did these two owe him.

"Two hundred."

Baffled at his response, I said, "Two hundred!"

"Yeah, they owe me a hundred for the coke and a hundred for the dope."

Before I made another comment to this guy Lamont, who was obviously at his wit's end, I turned to the direction in which Teresa was standing and asked her how much money did she have to her name. And her response to my question was, "Girl, I don't have a penny." So, I looked over to Eugene and asked him the same exact question and his answer was almost identical. "I ain't got no money either," he said.

"So, what are y'all going to do?" I asked, my voice screeching.

"Well, I was hoping you could loan us the money, that's why I called you to come over here."

Frustrated with their lack of concern for their well-being, I lashed out and said, "But, I don't have that much money on me!"

"Well, somebody better come up wit' something," Lamont belted out with anger.

Feeling the effects of his roar, Teresa nervously moved a little closer to me and asked me exactly how much money did I have on me?

"I really don't know," I replied, sticking my hand into my purse to retrieve my wallet. "But, I know that it's no where near the two hundred you need," I continued, as I pulled my wallet out and began to look in it.

"So, how much do you have?" She asked me once again, peering over my shoulders and directly into my hands.

"I've got one hundred and thirty-one dollars," I was finally able to say and then I held the money out to her.

"Don't give it to her," Lamont's voice roared again. "Pass that dough right on over here to me," he demanded.

So, I did. But at the same time wanted to know where he stood with her and Eugene.

"Oh, they a'ight for now," he began saying, "But, I'll be back tomorrow for the other hundred," he continued, as he stuffed the money into his pants pockets.

"What other hundred?" I protested. "I just gave you a hundred and thirty-one dollars."

Going into his left pants pocket and then revealing a plastic bag of powder-filled capsules, he said, "Yeah, I know. But, that thirty-one dollars was added interest, since it took these morons longer to pay me."

"Come on now, Lamont! That's not cool!" I commented.

"I'm sorry you feel that way. But, they know that if that was somebody else's shit they had, they would've been paying more interest than that. But, just to show you that I ain't as fucked up as you think, I am gon' give y'all a pill of coke and dope free of charge, so y'all can loosen' up 'round here." He smiled, throwing the two capsules into my direction. I wasn't in the mood to play catch, so I let the pills fall to the floor. Seeing everything play before her and reacting off my actions, Teresa fell to her knees and gathered both of the pills from off the floor, and then she scrambled to get back up to on her feet, clutching the drugs tightly in the palm of her hands. "Good looking out!" she managed to say, trying to catch her breath. "I will definitely have the rest of your money by tomorrow," she continued, trying to assure him.

Lamont laughed aloud once again and said, "Yeah, you better. 'Cause if you don't, I ain't gon' be so nice the next time."

"Don't worry. We're gonna have it. Just give us 'til about six o'clock," Teresa suggested.

"A'ight," he agreed and then he made his way out of her apartment.

The moment he disappeared beyond the front door, Teresa rushed over to lock it behind him. "Don't want him changing his mind and coming back," she commented with a cheap little smile.

Meanwhile, Eugene jumped to his feet. It immediately became apparent that his sudden burst of energy was fueled by a craving to get high off the drugs Lamont had just left. And like a true fiend, he rushed up to Teresa and said, "Want me to get the plate and the razor blade?"

"Yeah, go ahead," she encouraged him and off he went.

I stood in the same spot and watched these two in awe as they paraded around here with their heads stuck up in the clouds, acting like they did not just get their damn heads banged up by that nigga they owed money to. So, as I continued to watch in dismay, Teresa finally realized that I was still in the presence of her apartment and said, "Oh, damn! You so quiet, that I forgot you was in here."

"No shit!" I replied sarcastically.

Teresa giggled at my comment. So, I looked into her eyes and asked her was she all right?

"Hell yeah, I'm all right! You just saved me and my brother from getting another ass whipping!"

"But, why put yourself in dangerous situations like that? I mean, you and Eugene could've gotten seriously hurt by that guy."

"Oh girl, snap out of it! We're all right," she replied and then she grabbed ahold of my hand and said, "Now, come on in the room with us, so you can get that monkey off your back."

Now, I don't know why, but I allowed her to lead me into her bedroom where Eugene was already posted up on the edge of her bed with his eye all black and blue, waiting patiently to catch his next high. Poor thang! He was truly in another world. And you know what? I was too, right after I snorted a good amount of that white candy. It literally blew my fucking mind.

A couple of hours after the speed ball—which was a combination of the two drugs—had begun to wear off, I was starting to come to grips with what I had just done. But, by then the damage was already done; not to mention, I had damn near scratched my arms off. But anyway, as I drifted back into reality, one part of me instantly embraced the whole idea of pushing the straw up my nose. I mean, why not? I was under a lot of stress. Shit, between the drama I had earlier at home with Eric, and the drama I walked into here, was enough for me to go off into wonderland.

But then, after you come down off your high, your mind begins to play games with you and causes you to have mixed emotions. One minute you'll be all happy and then all of a sudden, you'll start feeling guilty and ashamed of what of you just did, which in turn makes you want to get high all over again. But, unfortunately for us, there was nothing else to get high off of. So, I laid back on Teresa's bed and waited for my senses to get back on track.

Meanwhile, Eugene realized that there was no longer a need for him to be in the presence of either myself or Teresa, since the plate was completely empty. So, he grabbed his jacket and said, "Yo, I'm out."

"Where you going?" Teresa wanted to know.

"To the block, to make some moves."

"You coming back?"

"Yeah."

"What time? 'Cause you know we got to get up the rest of the money we owe to Lamont by tomorrow."

"I know. I know. I'm gon' handle it. Just let me go out here and grind for a couple of niggas and we gon' be a'ight."

Teresa sighed with frustration and said, "That's what you said the last time. And look what happened."

"Well, this time it ain't gon' be like that," he assured her and then he left.

"What was that all about?" I began to inquire.

"Whatcha' mean?" Teresa asked, as she began to straighten up her bedroom.

"What kind of grind is he getting ready to go on, that's going to enable him to get up that other hundred dollars?"

"Oh, he's going to run for a couple of the street dealers who be getting their hustle on out there in Norfolk. And then at the end of the day, they'll pay him."

"What do you mean by 'run'?" My questions continued.

"Running is when street dealers find young boys or fiends to go out and get other fiends to come and buy their drugs. And when you help the dealer sell his entire package or get them enough sales, then they'll pay you with cash or give you drugs."

"Why do the dealers need people like your brother to get other addicts to buy their stuff?"

"Because it's so much competition out there and when you got a true dope fiend on your payroll, telling others how good your shit is, believe me—niggas will buy it."

"Oh, really."

"Yes, ma'am. A dope fiend will believe another dope fiend before they believe the nigga who's selling the drugs."

"Why is that?"

"Well you got to look at it like this," she began to explain, "a dealer will lie to you in a heartbeat about how good their shit is, just to get rid of it. But, a fiend ain't gon' lie. They know when a nigga's shit is garbage and they'll tell you if you ask 'em."

"Well, it sure sounds like you've made a few trips down that road."

"Shit! I didn't have a choice. Can't always trust Eugene to go out and buy my stuff."

"Why not?"

"Because he has burnt me too many times."

"But, you're his sister, so why would he do that?"

"Girl, please! Eugene is a dope fiend first and my

brother second, so he's gon' treat me like a stranger from the streets when it comes to those drugs."

"Has he ever stolen anything from you?"

"Yeah. He's got me for a few dollars a couple of times, but that's it."

Teresa continued to educate me about the life she and her brother led. It was pretty interesting, I might add. But, an eye-opener nevertheless.

I took every last detail in, not even realizing that I would need it later on down the road.

Chapter 7

Caught Her Slippin'

Just when I thought Monday was going to be the start of a good week, I get a call at eleven a.m. from Mr. Baker, asking me if I would come to his office immediately for a meeting. So, I did. But, got the surprise of my life the moment I walked through the doorway to his office.

There awaiting my arrival was Katherine Montoya, who happened to be the director of Human Resources. Sitting alongside of her was one of my newly hired ninth-grade English teachers by the name of Sandra Early. So, instantly my mind started wondering what was going to be the gist of this meeting we were about to have. And then without warning, the shit hit the fan.

"Faith," Mr. Baker began saying, after I greeted everyone and took a seat in a chair placed directly beside Mrs. Early's. "I called you into this meeting because this matter that we're about to discuss will effect you in several ways."

"Oh really!" I wondered aloud, as my heart began to pick up speed.

"Yes, it will. That's why Katherine and I decided to inform you before hand."

"Well, tell me what's going on?"

Mr. Baker hesitated a bit and then he said, "Being that this is a very complicated situation and Mrs. Early knows about it firsthand, I am going let her take the floor and tell you about our problem."

"Okay," I replied, shifting my attention directly towards Mrs. Early. "I'm all ears." I told her.

Before she uttered a single word, she sat up in her chair and cleared her throat. It was becoming obvious that this matter was very difficult for her to talk about. But eventually, she mustered up enough courage to speak and when she did, I gave her my undivided attention.

"Well, not too long after the first bell rang this morning, I took a quick bathroom break and stumbled across your secretary, Teresa, snorting drugs in one of the bathroom stalls."

My heart started racing a mile a minute, which made me act defensively. So, I immediately interjected, "What makes you so sure that she was in that bathroom stall, snorting drugs?"

"Because as I entered into the bathroom, I heard a loud snorting noise, but I didn't think anything of it until I heard it a couple more times. So, when I asked her was she all right, I must've startled her because she started fumbling with a folded dollar bill and then she accidentally dropped it to the floor, and that's when a white powdery substance spilled all around her feet."

"How did you manage to see her fumble with the dollar bill?" My questions kept coming.

"Because I was peeping at her through the open space on the side of the door. And then when she looked up at me, as if I was invading in on her privacy, I took a couple of steps back and that's when I noticed that she had spilled the drugs onto the floor."

"What did you say to her after all this happened?"

"I apologized to her for imposing and then I left out of the bathroom."

"So, you didn't ask her what it was she was doing?"

"Well, it was obvious. So, I didn't think it would be necessary."

"What was obvious?" I pressed on.

"That she was using drugs."

"Did you actually see her using drugs?"

"No, I didn't. But, I heard her."

"So, you're telling me you know first hand of what it sounds like when someone is using drugs?" I asked her in a sarcastic manner.

"Now Faith, that will be enough." Mr. Baker jumped to Mrs. Early's defense. "You're interrogating her as if she's the one whose being accused."

"Well, please allow me to apologize for my aggressive nature. But, I just cannot sit here and listen to this accusation when she did not actually witness Teresa using drugs. I mean, come on, Steve, this is a serious allegation, which could cost her her job. So, it's imperative that we investigate this thing thoroughly before we make any hasty decisions."

"And we will." Katherine spoke up. "That's why I'm here."

"So, what's your plan?" I asked.

"Well, since you know that this school has a zero tolerance for the sale or use of illegal drugs, I am here to enforce that rule, which has given me no other choice but to test Ms. Daniels."

"And when do you plan to do that?"

"Immediately, after we call her into this meeting and inform her of our findings."

"What will happen if she declines to take the drug test?"

"You know the rules, Faith." Steve interjected. "She will be terminated."

Knowing that Teresa's fate lay in the hands of these two crackers made me sick to my stomach. And what was so fucked up about all of this was that I couldn't do anything about it. My hands were completely tied.

But, something within me wanted to try my hand anyway, so I sat back in my chair, took a deep breath and asked Katherine would she allow me to administer the test? And her answer to me was, "Absolutely, not! That's my job."

Shocked by her candor, I was at a loss for words. It was like home girl had shut me down and I couldn't say shit about it. I did, however, have my way when I asked them both if I would be able to sit in on the meeting when they addressed this situation with Teresa. So, as we all waited for her to show up, all I could feel in my heart was pain for her, knowing she had no idea that she was about to be fired. I mean, this was this girl's livelihood and now it's getting ready to go up in smoke, without any notice. I just hope she remains diplomatic throughout this whole ordeal. Acting belligerent would only add fuel to the fire.

Now, it only took Teresa several minutes to join us, but before she did, I thought it would be a good idea for Mrs. Early to be excused from the meeting. Having the two in the room at the same time would only exacerbate the problem. Not only that, it would be very unethical to have Mrs. Early witness Katherine and Steve reprimand Teresa. And it wouldn't sit right with me, either. So, after Teresa entered into Steve's office and took a seat, I gave her the *"you're in big trouble"* look. And I don't know if she understood it, but I figured she would soon find out.

"How is everybody?" she asked after taking a seat.

We all said, "Fine." But, immediately after, Steve pulled no punches and went straight for the kill. "Ms. Daniels, we've all called you into this meeting because of some disturbing allegations involving some misconduct on your behalf. So, we all felt that it was necessary to have you come in and shed light on this matter."

Going into a defensive mode, Teresa said, "What matter? What disturbing allegations?"

"I was informed this morning by one of the teachers that you were using illegal drugs while you were in the ladies' bathroom."

Teresa chuckled and said, "Who, Mrs. Early?"

"So, you don't deny it?" Mr. Baker asked.

"Of course, I deny it," she struck back. "Mrs. Early doesn't know what the hell she's talking about!"

"So, what were you doing?" Katherine interjected.

"Minding my business."

"Well, we're sure of that. But, you need to be a little more specific," Katherine continued.

"I wasn't using drugs, if that's what you're wondering."

"Then what were you doing?" Mr. Baker wanted to know.

Teresa fell silent after Steve asked her the exact same question as Katherine did. And then she looked to me, as if I could help her, but I couldn't. So, I looked away from her. I couldn't stand the sight of seeing her so defenseless. She looked so pitiful. But, Steve wasn't into the pity-party scene, so he asked her again, "What were you doing in the bathroom stall of the ladies' room, when Mrs. Early approached you and asked if you were all right?"

Feeling the pressure mounting all around her, Teresa looked directly at Steve and said, "I was minding my business."

"So you're still denying that you were using illegal drugs?" His questions continued.

"Yes, I am."

"So, you wouldn't mind taking a drug test for us, then?"

"Am I going to be the only one being tested?" Teresa asked sarcastically.

"But, of course." Steve replied.

"And why is that?"

"Because you're the only person who has been brought before us with allegations of using drugs," he continued.

"Well, I just don't think it's fair!"

"What don't you think is fair?" Katherine asked her.

"I don't think it's fair that y'all have singled me

out. I mean, if you're gonna test one person, then you might as well test everybody who works here."

Bomb!, was what I felt when my heart landed in the pit of my stomach. I couldn't believe what Teresa had just said. What in the hell was she doing? Because it definitely sounded like she wasn't trying to take the fall by herself. And knowing that I had gotten high with her all day Saturday, which was only two days ago, would make me a likely candidate for a positive urine analysis. So, as bad as I wanted ask her what kind of game she was playing, I remained calm and held my composure.

"Well, I'm sorry, Ms. Daniels," Katherine said, "but we have to follow a strict code and since you're the only one who has been accused of violating it, then we have to enforce the policies and procedures."

"Well, I'm sorry too, 'cause I am not taking that test."

"If you don't take it, then we're going to have to dismiss you."

"So, you mean to tell me that you're going to fire me?"

"Yes, that's exactly what we mean." Katherine replied, giving Teresa a slight smirk.

"Y'all can't fire me because someone told you I was using drugs."

"You're absolutely right," Mr. Baker said. "But, since you're not fully cooperating with us so that we can investigate this matter thoroughly, then you leave us no choice."

"You're telling me you're not gonna use any other recourse to resolve this?"

"I'm afraid not," Mr. Baker told her.

Teresa stood up from her chair and said, "I bet if

I was the one who would've come running into your damn office, accusing one of your own of doing the same thing, you and this stuck-up-ass cracker over here would not have did shit! But since I'm black, y'all are trying to make an example out of me. But trust me, it ain't gon' fly, 'cause I am going to have both of y'all asses in court."

"If you're finished, then you can leave now," Mr. Baker told her.

"Oh, I'm leaving. But you ain't seen the last of me," she assured him and then she walked out of the office and slammed the door behind herself.

Witnessing every word thrown back and forth across the room had me speechless. I honestly couldn't believe how Teresa handled this whole situation. And then to use the race card really threw me for a fucking loop. So, as I got up to leave, I attempted to apologize to both Steve and Katherine for Teresa's racial outburst. But he cut me off in mid-sentence and said, "There's no need to apologize for her antics. Just do us all a favor by helping her pack her things and escorting her off the school grounds."

"Will do," I assured him and then I proceeded to leave.

In the midst of trying to cope with all of the chaos, I managed to get back to my office without losing my cool. And as I was about to take a seat behind my desk, Teresa pops her head through the doorway.

"Why didn't you tell me those crackers was trying to railroad my ass?" she asked me in a sarcastic manner.

"If you stop being so damn loud and bring

your butt into my office, then I'll tell you exactly what happened."

Very eager to hear what I had to say, she walked in and closed the door behind herself. And when she walked over to my desk and stood there as if I owed her something, I let her have it.

"First of all, why in the hell are you standing there like you're a victim?"

"Because I am. Remember, I'm the one who just got fired!"

"But, you did that shit to yourself." I lashed back. "I told you not to do that shit here at work. But you did it again, anyway. So, what the hell am I supposed to do when someone goes and rats you out to Steve? The shit was out of my hands."

"Well, the least you could've done was take up for me. I mean, you didn't say not one damn word the whole entire time!"

"What in the hell could I have possibly said in your defense?"

"You could've argued against the idea of them drug testing me."

"I did."

"When?"

"Right before Steve called your ass into his office," I began to explain. "As a matter of fact, we were going toe to toe behind your silly ass, if you want to know the truth. But they weren't trying to hear shit I had to say, especially after Mrs. Early had already been sitting in his office for about thirty minutes prior to my arrival. But, what gets me is the fact that you didn't even tell me that you had the run-in with Mrs. Early this morning. So, how the hell do you think I felt, when I'm the last person to find out about it?"

"I didn't say anything to you because I didn't think that she realized what I was doing."

"Well, she did."

"Well, do you think I can appeal their decision?"

"You can try. But, I don't think it's going to work."

"So, when do they expect me to be out of here?"

"As soon as possible."

Teresa shook her head in disbelief and started carrying on like her life was about to come to an end. "Faith, what the fuck am I going to do? I've got bills!"

"Don't we all," I commented nonchalantly.

"But you ain't got shit to worry about because you still have a job."

"Well, after that stunt you pulled earlier in Steve's office, I'm surprised that I still have a damn job!"

"Whatcha' talking about?"

"I'm talking about that statement you made to Steve and Katherine, about how they need to test everybody who worked here. I mean, what part of the game was that? Shit, you know I would've been dead meat if they would've decided to test me."

"Believe me, I wasn't thinking about you when I made that comment. I was just grasping for straws and tried to get them to see that they were discriminating against me. That's all."

"Well, I'm sorry your plan didn't work. But, do me a favor."

"What's that?" she wanted to know.

"Don't you ever put me on the spot like that again."

"Well, I told you I didn't mean for it to come out the way that it did. And so that you know, it won't happen again."

"Thank you very much," I replied, literally about to bite my bottom lip off from being so frustrated with this whole ordeal.

Minutes after our discussion had ended, I helped her pack up her things and walked her out to her car. But, before she left, I assured her that I would be stopping by her place a little later to check up on her.

Later that day rumors started circulating rapidly about Teresa being terminated. A few of the teachers—with whom I had become very close with over the years—approached me, wanting to know the details. So, I told them in so many words that Teresa elected to quit. I only said this to save her the embarrassment.

Chapter 8

Taking No Shorts

When I made it to work the next morning, I found out from a memo placed on my desk that I was going to go through some of the same events that happened the day before. This didn't sit right with me at all. And I began to feel sick to my stomach. But, before I started overreacting, I made a call to Steve's office. He answered on the first ring.

"Good morning, Steve. How are you?"

"I'm okay. What about yourself?"

"I'm fine. But, I have a quick question."

"Shoot," he replied, giving me the go ahead.

"Well, I got this memo in my hand and I see that we're going to start implementing random drug testing. So, my question to you is, if we're going to start doing this, then why does everyone have to submit a urine sample today?"

"Because I spoke with the superintendent about

yesterday's fiasco and he and I just want to make sure that nothing like that ever happens again."

"Are you planning to test everyone today?"

"Everyone who showed up."

"So, when will it start?"

"Some of the staff have already completed the drug screening. So, Katherine and I are looking to wrap things up by noon today."

"She's here."

"Yes, she's here. As a matter of fact, she's in the teacher's lounge, helping Mr. Barino take the urine samples. So, when you're ready, stop by there so they can get you all squared away."

"I have to take it too?"

"Yes, of course. Everyone does. I even had to take it."

"Well, after I take care some of this stuff on my desk, I'll swing by there too."

"Sounds good," Mr. Baker commented and then the line went dead.

After I put the telephone down I became a nervous wreck, thinking about all sorts of things. The first thing on the top of my list was the fact that I knew my drug screening was going to come back positive. And when it does, I am going to be without a job. My career is going to go right down the fucking drain! Now, how fucking stupid could I have been to let Teresa pull me into her trap? This shit is all her damn fault. Because if she would've listened to me and kept that getting-high shit at home, then she would still have a job and I wouldn't be on the verge of losing mine. See what friends will do for you! They will fuck your life up if you let 'em, which is exactly what's about to happen to me.

While I was going through one of my self-persecution episodes, I got a knock on my office door. "Who is it?" I asked.

"It's Kimberly," She answered.

Since it was only Mrs. Lawson, the school's counselor, I didn't hesitate to give her the okay to enter into my office. And from the moment she entered into my immediate circle, she could sense that something wasn't quite right with me so she said, "I don't like the long face. So, smile."

"What's there to smile about, when I just lost my secretary and Steve is about to turn this place upside down?"

"You must be talking about that memo everybody got this morning."

"Yes, that's exactly what I'm talking about. I mean, what message is he trying to send by saying that his decision to implement the random drug testing derives from the unfortunate incident that occurred yesterday?"

"You know what, when I read that part I had the same reaction as you. Because in all honesty, he knew he didn't have the right to give any of us the slightest inclination of what went on with Teresa's situation."

"You damn right he didn't! And when I spoke with him a few minutes ago, I wanted to mention it to him, but it was too early to bump heads with him."

"How is Teresa doing anyway?" Kimberly shifted the subject.

"Under the circumstances, she's doing okay."

"What are her plans? Is she going to start looking for new employment?"

"She said she's going to chill out for the rest of this week and maybe catch up on some things she's been putting off. But, next week she's going to start her job search."

"Well, I sure hope she finds something."

"She will because I'm going to give her an excellent job reference."

"Will she be able to get any unemployment benefits?"

"No, she sure won't."

"That's sad."

"Yeah, it is. But, she'll be all right."

"Whatcha' think about Mr. Baker ordering everyone to take the drug test?"

"Personally I think he's just using his authority to shake everyone up."

"Do you think he's going to be able to sift out anybody else?"

"I'm not sure. But, I do know that if he does, then he's gonna walk around here like he really did something major."

"Have you given your urine sample yet?"

"Not yet. Have you?"

"Yes. I just came from doing it."

"How long did it take?"

"Not long." She began to explain. "Katherine gives you a urine specimen cup with your name on it and sends you in the bathroom. And once you're done, she'll place it in a clear bag and store it in a locked box, like a first-aid kit."

"How did you feel once you were notified that you had to take that test?"

"It really didn't bother me. Why?"

"I just asked."

"Well, how do you feel about it?" Kimberly asked me in somewhat of a suspicious manner.

"I just feel like Steve has an agenda."

"What type of an agenda?"

Before I could get a chance to convey my feelings about this whole matter, my telephone started ringing. And guess who it was? Ole Katherine herself, calling me from the teacher's lounge. So naturally I got a bad taste in my mouth. But what was more over powering was the urge for me to find out what it was that she wanted.

"Excuse me one minute," I told Kimberly. And then I went straight into professional mode with Katherine by asking her, "How can I help you?"

"I was just wondering when you would be available to come down to the teacher's lounge to give a urine sample?"

"With everything I've got going on, I can't really say right now."

"Well, Mr. Barino and I just realized that there's only a few more staff members who haven't given their urine samples, but they assured us that they'll be coming in shortly. So, in retrospect, I was hoping that you could come on down in the next thirty minutes or so, so we can get you in and out and wrap this up."

Katherine was really trying to turn the heat up on my ass, but right now wasn't the time to let her see me sweat. So, I remained calm and said, "As soon as I'm done with what I've got going on here in my office, then I'll be down there."

Not really happy by my response, Katherine said, "Okay."

As I was about to hang up my telephone, I noticed Kimberly getting up from her chair. And after looking at her for only seven or eight seconds, something within me sparked up an idea. So, I immediately asked her to sit back down, while I got up the gumption to bring my idea to the forefront.

"What's up?" She wanted to know.

"Listen, I'm about to ask you something that may put you in an awkward position, and it may even offend you. But, I'm in a tight jam and you're the only person who can help me right now."

"What is it?" she asked with concern.

"Listen, Kimberly, you have to promise me that what I'm about to tell you will stay within the walls of this office."

With the utmost sincerity she said, "Okay. I promise."

I looked straight into her eyes and gave her an earful.

"Kimberly I smoke marijuana," I lied, downplaying my use of drugs. "So, if I submit a sample of my urine for testing, then it's bound to come back positive. And you know what's going to happen from there. So, I was wondering if you would do me this life-saving favor and allow me to use a sample of your own urine. And before you answer me, just know that I would do anything for it."

"Oh, my God! I mean, I don't know what to say." Kimberly replied, as if she was at a loss for words.

"Just say yes," I responded desperately.

"But, I can't."

"Why not?"

"Look, Faith, as bad as I want to help you, I just won't allow myself to get into anything like that and jeopardize my job."

"But, no one will know."

"I'm sorry Faith, but I can't take that chance," she said firmly and then she stood up to leave. "But, I do wish you the best," she continued and then she made her exit.

Watching my only candidate for job security walk out of my office was very devastating. Plus, I was wondering did I make the biggest mistake of my life by divulging that type of information to her, even though I lied a bit?

Damn, I feel foolish! But, I am beginning to feel more embarrassed than anything, knowing she could hold this over my head. So, what the fuck am I going to do now? Just sit here in my office and pray to God that Katherine forgets that I haven't taken the drug test yet? Wishful thinking on my part, I know. So the only other thing I can think about doing is crawling under a freaking rock somewhere. There, I wouldn't have to worry about any of the bullshit going on here. But, I know that's a long shot, too. So, I might as well brace myself and face the music, because I am about to go down a bumpy road.

Locked away in my office, I sat behind my desk and watched the clock on my wall as the hands moved one behind the other. And it was weird because on a normal day, time never seemed go by this fast. But, I figured it couldn't be nothing but my mind playing tricks on me. So, I grabbed a handful of tissue paper from the box placed on the edge of my desk and wiped away the sweat pellets around my forehead. Meanwhile, I got another call. But, this time I was somewhat hesitant to answer, so I let it ring. And after a while it stopped. So, I exhaled and tried to calm my nerves, but that was short lived when I received a knock on my office door.

"Faith, are you in there?" Katherine yelled through the door.

Hearing her voice made me not want to answer, but my back was up against the wall, so I figured that I didn't have a choice. "Yeah, give me a minute," I finally answered and stood to my feet. But before I opened up the door, I scattered paperwork all across my desk just to make it look like I've been really busy.

"Come on in," I said.

"Well, I wasn't trying to stay," she began to say. "I was just wondering if I could get you to follow me on down to the lounge, because you're the only one left who hasn't the drug screening."

"You mean now?"

"Yes, because we're trying to wrap things up. And you're the only one we're waiting on."

Feeling the pressure mounting around me once again, I wanted so badly to tell her to stick that test up her ass, but I couldn't. So, instead I agreed to follow her. I mean, what other choice did I have? Because she had no intentions of letting me off the hook whatsoever. That's just the way this cracker operated.

Now once we were in the teacher's lounge, I was handed the cup and sent to the bathroom like Kimberly had mentioned. And when I was done, Katherine bagged up my specimen and locked it away in a gray metal box. So, I began to wonder aloud when she would have the results of the test and she said, "Well, when I leave here, I'm gonna head over to our medical center and drop all of these samples off. So, I will have the results no later than tomorrow morning."

"Really," I said.

"Yes. And see, it actually only take a matter of minutes to test urine for signs of drug use. But, since we don't have the proper equipment to test the samples with, we have to take it to the lab at our medical center."

"Well, have fun." I told her and then I left the lounge area.

I headed back to my office, feeling sick to my stomach. And since I knew that there was no way that I would be able to function properly for the rest of the day, I called Steve and told him that I wasn't feeling well and that I would be taking the rest of the day off. And when he said that would be fine, I hauled ass straight to my house nonstop.

Chapter 9

A Nervous
Fucking Wreck

Thank God it was too early in the day for Eric to be home, because right now I really need to be alone. So, once I settled in, I picked up my telephone and called Teresa, who seemed like she was kind of out of it. It was my guess that she was high. But since she was somewhat responsive about some of my issues that I had to get off my chest, I continued to keep her on the phone.

"What are you doing?" I asked.

"I'm just relaxing."

"Been dipping in that candy jar, huh?"

"Just a little."

"Well, guess what that candy is about to do for me?"

"What?"

"Take my damn job!"

"Take your job!" she said with uncertainty. "Take it how?"

"I had to take the fucking drug test this morning."

"You're kidding, right?"

"Hell no! I'm not kidding! Because as soon as I walked into my office this morning I've got a damn memo sitting on my desk, telling me that every teacher and staff member must take a fucking drug test today."

"Get the fuck out of here!" Teresa screamed. "So, what did you do?"

"What do you mean, what did I do? I couldn't do shit but give Katherine a damn urine sample."

"She was there?"

"Yeah, that bitch was there. And she worried me to death."

"So, who wrote the memo?"

"Steve wrote it. And knowing how sneaky that bastard is, he probably had his dumb-ass secretary type it up yesterday, right after our meeting."

"I believe that too. But, did he take the drug test himself?"

"He said he did. But, I couldn't tell you for sure."

"He probably didn't, wit' his fat ass!"

"You're probably right. But, whether he did or didn't, I'm the one whose going to be getting my walking papers tomorrow."

"Don't let 'em fire you! Just quit on their ass! Shit, you'll have a better chance at getting another job if you did it that way. 'Cause if you hold out and let them get rid of you, then you're gonna be out back."

"Well, you know what? At this point it really doesn't matter, because I've already given them my urine sample. So, even if I decided to quit, they're gonna to find out about my drug use anyway."

"Well, what are you going to do?" Teresa wanted to know.

"I'm not sure. But, I guess all I can do is wait."

"Are you going to go into work tomorrow?"

"Do you think I should?"

"I wouldn't. Shit, let 'em call you so they can save you the embarrassment."

"You've got a point there. But, I've already experienced an embarrassing moment today."

"What happened?"

"You will not believe this, but because I was under so much pressure this morning, I played myself by asking Kimberly Lawson to let me get a sample of her urine, so I could use it to take my drug screening. And of course, she told me no, after I poured my fucking heart out to her. But, what's really bothering me right now is the fact that she can hold this confession of mine over my head."

"You got that right! But, what in the hell possessed you to even set yourself up to ask her something like that? She ain't your friend, for real!"

"I know. But, when I kept getting phone calls from Katherine telling me that she's trying to wrap the drug testing up, I got a little desperate."

"Well, you should've told Katherine to stick that drug test up her ass and quit!"

"Well, it's too late for that. What I need to do now is figure out how I'm going to tell my husband why I got fired from my job, and hope that he doesn't try to divorce me behind it."

"Girl, that man ain't going nowhere. He loves you."

"Well, he hasn't been acting like it lately."

"That's because you haven't been able to spend a lot of time with him."

"Well, after tomorrow, that won't be an issue anymore."

"And that may be true, but I wouldn't tell him I got fired."

"Why not?"

"Because he's going to want to know what happened."

"So, what would you tell him?"

"Just tell him you quit because it was putting a strain on y'all marriage."

"Yes. That's exactly what I'll tell him. He'll believe that."

"Well, then you've got your answers. Now, all you've got to do is let this whole thing play out."

"Easy for you to say."

"You're right about that." Teresa chuckled. "So, whatcha' getting ready to get into?"

"Nothing. I'm just gonna lay back and watch some TV."

"Stop acting like an old lady and come on over here, so I can cheer you up."

"And do what? Get high?"

"You might as well. I mean, what the fuck you got to lose? Your job is already up in smoke."

"You got a point there."

"Well, come on over then, so I can help you take your mind off that bullshit!"

"All right. I'll be over in about thirty minutes."

"Okay."

Chapter 10

My 1st Mistake

To save myself from the embarrassment of Steve and Katherine walking me off the job, I called Steve at home bright and early this morning and told him I wouldn't be in to work today because I was still feeling a little under the weather. He told me that it must be something going around the office, because he wasn't feeling that well either, so he wouldn't be going in himself. I immediately told him to take it easy and that I hoped to see him tomorrow. He extended the same courtesy and then we said our goodbyes.

Immediately after I we hung up, I thought that it would be a good idea for me to run by the school and pack up my things before any of the staff got there. So, I figured that in order for this to be possible, I would need to leave my house right then. And that's exactly what I did. Kimora and Eric were still asleep, so I didn't bother to wake either of them. And besides, it was a little after six a.m., so if I would've woke Eric up, he would've wanted to know why I was leaving the house so early and I really didn't have the time that it would take to explain my motives to him, which is why I got out of there as quickly as possible.

When I arrived at the school, I noticed only one car there. But, it belonged to our head janitor, Mr. Clemons, so I was cool. He was no threat to me.

And knowing how he operated, he was probably in the back of the school, hanging out in the boiler room. And if that was the case, he wouldn't even realize I was there, not that it mattered any.

When I entered into my office, I wasted little or no time at all throwing my things into the storage box I brought along with me. And surprisingly, it didn't take long at all for me to get everything organized and packed away. But to be honest, I think it had something to do with my heart beating out of control and the adrenaline pumping inside of me. The fear of letting one of my teachers see me with my things was something I was really trying to avoid. So, after I cleared everything and closed my office door behind me, I headed back out to my car. And right when I was getting ready to pile all my things into the trunk, Steve came driving up and parked his vehicle right next to mine. Now, I just got off the phone with this man not even forty-five minutes ago and he told me that he wasn't going to come into work today, so why the fuck was he here? And I knew the only way I was going to get the answer to that question was by waiting for him to get out of the car, and I was not looking forward to that because he was going to want to know why I was packing my shit in the trunk of my car. So, without further delay, I shoved everything into my car and quickly closed the trunk afterwards. But unfortunately for me, this bastard got an eyeful and went into question mode as soon as his fat ass got out of his car.

"What's going on? I thought you were under the weather," he said.

"Oh, I am," I began to say. "I just needed to come up here and get a few things, so I can have something to do while I'm home. But, what about you? Because you did mention that you were under the weather yourself."

"I am. But I got a phone call from Katherine and she's going to meet me up here in the next hour or so, so we can sort out a few things."

"Well, have fun!" I told him and proceeded to the driver's side of my car. But, before I could even get within a few feet of it, Steve continued by saying, "Why didn't you tell me you had a drug problem too?"

I stopped in my tracks, but my heart sped forward as I turned around to face him. Every part of me wanted to crumble to pieces, because I figured, how in the world was I going to face this question head on? But, then I realized that I was only in his company, so my respect and dignity wouldn't be affected at all. Katherine was the only person who had the power to rip that part of me to shreds and since she was not here to humiliate me, the hell with both of their asses. My shit was already packed, so what could they do to me? Nothing! And when I finally got my thoughts together I said, "I beg your pardon!"

"I asked you why didn't you tell me you had a drug problem too?"

"I'm sorry, Steve but I'm not following you," I replied sarcastically.

"Faith, let's cut to the chase," he said walking closer in my direction. "Your drug screening came back positive."

Trying to shield myself from degradation, I went into a state of denial and responded by saying, "There must be some kind of mistake."

"Faith, let's not do this."

"Let's not do what?" I replied nonchalantly.

"Come on, let's take this into my office," he urged me.

"Steve, I'm not up for going into your office right now. So, whatever it is we need to discuss, let's do it right here."

"But, what we need to discuss wouldn't be appropriate to do it here."

"Steve, just spill it out," I demanded.

Steve looked into my eyes and said, "You know I'm going to have to let you go," then he paused for a moment and said, "but I will allow you to give me a letter of resignation if you fax it to my office this morning."

I stood there speechless. My mouth wouldn't move. So, Steve continued on to say, "Now, is that feasible enough for you?"

Humiliated to the tenth power, I somehow held my head up and said, "I can handle that."

"Well, that's great!" he said, patting me on my shoulder. "Because I really didn't want to fire you."

"Everything's okay," I assured him.

"Well, I'm glad to hear that. But, let me say this."

"Go ahead, I'm listening.

"You're a very bright and intelligent young woman. And with your credentials, you can go so very far, so please don't let those drugs take over your life."

"It's just marijuana. And I only do it sparingly."

"Faith, I don't care what it is. Just don't let it take your life from you."

Respecting what Steve had to say, I took it in and pondered on it for a moment, but then all of a sudden I realized that I had bigger fish to fry. Finding a way to tell my husband that I no longer have a job was one and trying to recondition myself to accept what I can't change was the other. So, everything else was water under the bridge.

Now before Steve walked off, he told me he had a couple of other people he had to send packing. So, I said, "Wait, there's more?"

"Yes, there is."

"Who?"

"Let's just say that Mr. Evans, the biology teacher; and Mrs. Templeton, the music teacher, aren't as righteous as they appear to be."

Stunned by Steve's response, my eyes protruded instantly. But, I refused to make a comment. It would've been very hypocritical of me if I did. So, with little effort on my part, I just shook my head in disbelief and waved him a goodbye.

Chapter 11

Taking It to Another Level

It had been a week since I became unemployed and I had to admit that it didn't feel half bad. Speaking of which, I showed Eric the resignation letter I faxed it to Steve. So, there was a little convincing on my part that it was solely my decision to make this transition. And telling him that my decision to leave had a lot to do with the strain our marriage was under, was like putting icing on the cake. So, trust me, he ate it up. But during the day while he was at work, I made it a habit to hang out at Teresa's place. Now, there was always something unusual going on over there and believe me, today was no different.

"Girl, you aren't gonna believe what I am about to tell you," she said the moment she opened up her front door to me.

"What's going on now?" I asked.

Teresa closed the front door behind me and as we began to walk into the direction of her living room, she grabbed my hand and placed in the center of her stomach. So, I stopped in my tracks and said, "Don't tell me you're pregnant."

Her face lit up like a Christmas tree. "Yep, I sure am."

"So, what are you going to do?" I wondered.

"I'ma keep it." She replied with certainty.

When we reached the living room, she sat down and I took a seat next to her. And the whole time, all she was doing was rambling on about how happy she was and that she was sure this baby would bring her and Darren back together. So, I stepped in and said, "Don't set yourself up to get your feelings hurt."

"My feelings aren't going to get hurt." She replied in a cocky manner.

"They will if you think Darren is going to leave his wife and come back to you, because you say you're pregnant."

"He ain't gotta leave this wife. I don't mind sharing."

"Girl, you need to wake up and leave that lady's husband alone," I began to tell her, "All you really need to be concerned about is that he takes care of that baby."

"Oh trust me, he will."

"So, when are you going to break the news to him?"

"I've been trying to call him all morning, but he's still not accepting my phone calls. So, I left him a message and told him that he needed to call me because it was very important. But, if he doesn't, I'm going to go right back 'round his house and show the fuck out!"

"And what is that going to solve?"

"All I'm trying to do is get some attention."

I laughed and shook my head. "Well, you'll definitely get some attention that way," I assured her and then I immediately changed the subject. "You got some blow?"

"You know I do," she said, all excited, as she attempted to retrieve a plastic baggie from her front jean pockets. "I just got this delivered right before you got here." She continued.

"Why is it so brown?"

"That's because it's all heroin."

"I'm not doing that shit by itself," I protested.

"Stop fretting! I still got a little bit of coke left over from last night."

"Well, get it. 'Cause, I'm ready to get fucked up!" I announced in a cheery kind of way, taking off my jacket to get a little more comfortable.

Minutes later, Teresa had everything situated on top of the coffee table in front of us. Now from the looks of the bag of dope, and all the items such as the plate, the razor blade, a straw, the cotton balls, the beer bottle cap filled with tap water, the cigarette lighter and the syringe, I can only assume that Teresa was about to do some type of surgery on herself. I was literally baffled at the contents of the cigarette lighter and the syringe. So, I asked her, "What is all this shit for?"

"Oh, don't worry! I ain't gon' try to put you on to this. That's why I placed a straw on the table."

"When did you start shooting up?"

"I've been doing it on and off for about two mouths now. Trust me, it ain't no biggie."

"Isn't that dangerous?"

"Yeah, if you don't know what you're doing. But, I've gotten plenty of practice by doing it with Eugene."

"Are you going to mix it?"

"No, ma'am!" she began to say, as I watched her draw the water up into the syringe, "I'm gonna do straight dope this time."

Curious about what she was going to do next, I watched her next moves very closely as she dumped a small amount of heroin into the other end of the syringe. Next, she shook up the syringe, dissolving all of the drug into the water and then she shot it out of the other end into the bottle top. Seconds later, she picked up the cigarette lighter and lit the bottom of the top with a small flame for about six seconds, and then stuck a small piece of cotton ball into the top. "What's that cotton for?" I wanted to know.

"I'm using it as a filter, so I won't pull up any of the trash from the dope or the bottle top into the syringe," she replied, drawing up all the liquid through the needle. "Here we go," she continued as she pushed the tip of the needle into a bulging vein located in the crease of her arm.

Seeing the blood trickle back up into the needle scared the hell out of me, so I said, "You're bleeding!"

"Don't worry, I'm okay," she assured me.

Moments later, she injected the blood-mixed drug into her arm. And as it began to travel through her veins, she slowly closed her eyes and laid her head back against the head rest of the sofa. Now, watching her go through this major transition had me at a loss for words. I honestly did not know whether to leave her alone or shake her to death, just to make sure she was still alive. And once I realized that she was off into a zone, I left well enough alone and started on my journey to my next high.

Unlike Teresa, I felt like sniffing the drugs would be a lot safer, which was exactly what I did and I had a fucking blast, once it hit me. And from that point, I drifted off into la-la land.

Teresa and I used up the entire gram of heroin, along with the rest of the coke she had saved from the day before, so we were high as fucking kites. But, by the time our kite started descending, Teresa started ranting and raving and crying her poor little heart out. She was completely falling apart on me as she began to vent about how fucked up her life is. Truthfully speaking, I still had somewhat of a buzz going on, so I wasn't feeling the fact that she was blowing my high. So, I said, "Hey, can you calm down! You're fucking up my high!"

"I'm sorry, girl," she apologized. "But, if I don't get to talk to Darren by nightfall I am going to go crazy!"

"Girl, you are not going to go crazy."

"Yes, I am." She began to explain. "You have no idea what that man has done to me." She continued as the tears began to fall from her eyes.

"Well, whatever it is, you need to shake it off because he's not going to come around."

"We'll see!" Teresa commented and abruptly got up from the sofa.

"Where are you going?" I asked.

"To his house," she replied, slipping on a pair of sneakers.

"Teresa please don't go over there," I begged her.

"You know what? Fuck that! This nigga has been avoiding me for far too long. And right now, I got some shit I need to get off of my chest."

Before I could continue trying to talk her out of bum-rushing Darren's house, she had already grabbed her car keys and headed out the front door. The last words I heard her say was, "I'll be right back."

Realizing how serious she was, I knew I couldn't just sit here and let her go off on her own and do God knows what. So, I jumped to my feet and followed her. Truth be told, I wanted to make a U-turn and carry my red ass home. But, under the circumstances, I decided against it. Who knows? I maybe able to talk her out of walking up to his front door and making a fool out of herself.

During the drive I tried several attempts to call her on her cellular phone, but she refused to answer it. Since I couldn't make contact with her this way, I continued to tail her in my car. We ended up in a beautiful upscale neighborhood in the Great Neck area of Virginia Beach. The houses here had to be at least $600,000 or better. And to get here, it only took us twenty minutes, so we were there in a flash.

Teresa was able to get there a few minutes before me, because of the lead she had on me. So, by the time I was able to park my car directly behind hers, she was already out of the car and on her way up to Darren's front door. It seemed like everything was going in fast motion and there was no way for me to stop any of it, which seemed like a disadvantage on my part. And seeing her bang on his door really threw me for a loop, so I reacted by getting out of my car and then I tried to yell out her name. But it was too late. A woman had already opened up the front door.

Curious to see what this woman looked like, I walked up a little closer and stood at the edge of the driveway as Teresa began to introduce herself. The woman—whom I assumed to be Darren's wife—was very average looking. She stood at about five feet, two inches. So, she was very short. Her hair was straight and long, like mine. She wore it in a straight, layered cut, and I must say that it fit her very well. But, her body frame was in desperate need of an overhaul. She had to be at least ninety pounds soaking wet. So, it was apparent that home girl didn't spend a lot of time in the kitchen. And it also became clear to me that this Darren character had a huge fetish for small women, because Teresa was definitely on the petite side but she was thicker and plus, she has a shape with hers.

Meanwhile as they were going through their introduction, two small children, who looked to be around the ages of three and four, peered around their mother's leg to get a glimpse of who it was she was talking to. Teresa also noticed them peeping at her, so she smiled at them and immediately went back into the reason for her visit. And then all of a sudden, the woman comes out onto her porch and closes the screen door behind her. So, Teresa moves back a little to give her some room and that's when the shit hit the fan!

"What the fuck you mean, you're pregnant by my husband?" I heard the woman say.

"Look Marie," I heard Teresa say, "I am not trying to upset you."

"It's too damn late!" the woman interjected.

"Well, I'm sorry. But, all I want to do is talk to Darren, because he needs to know what's going on."

"And I told you he wasn't here."

"Well, could you tell him that he needs to get in touch with me?"

"You damn right I'm going to tell him. But, I want to know from you, how long have you and him been seeing each other behind my back?"

"It's been a little over four years."

"Four years!" I heard Marie scream. "You mean to

tell me that you been fucking my husband for four god-damn years? And then, to top it off, your ass is pregnant? How fucking convenient!"

"Look Marie, I'm sorry . . ." Teresa tried to say but Marie cut her off in mid-sentence to say, "Listen, don't keep telling me you're sorry! I ain't trying to hear that bullshit right now. But, what I do want to know is, how far along are you?"

"Well, I just took the pregnancy test this morning, so it's too early to say. But, I'm guessing I'm about four or five weeks."

"Are you planning to keep this baby?"

"Yes, I am."

With a disgusted look Marie said, "So, what do you think you're going to get out of this?"

"I'm not looking to get anything. All I want to do is to let him know that I'm pregnant. And from that point, he can decide whether or not he wants to be this child's life."

"Oh, I can tell you right now that he is not going to be in that child's life, especially when he's got two right here living at home with him. And how do you know that, that baby is his, anyway?"

"Because he's the only man I've been sleeping with. I've never cheated on him."

"Cheated on him!" Marie said with rage. "You're standing here, acting like y'all are exclusive or something. You ain't his fucking wife! I am! So, don't be acting like you're the fucking victim here!"

Now before Teresa could get another word in edgewise, Darren drives up out of nowhere in his pearl white and gold-trimmed 2007 Lincoln Zephyr. And while he slowly cruised up the driveway, I purposely paid close attention to his facial expression and I must say that whatever he was thinking, it wasn't nothing nice.

"Oh, good, this bastard is here!" Marie said with her hand posted up on her hip. "Now, we can get all this shit straight!"

"We sho' can." Teresa agreed and turned in the direction of the driveway.

I stood back watched in silence, waiting patiently to see what was about to happen next.

"What the hell is going on here?" Darren asked the moment he got out and slammed the door to his car.

"That's what the fuck I'm trying to figure out!" Marie blurted out.

Darren walked closer to the front porch and Teresa just stood there, with the evilest expression she could muster up. She knew that he was going to come out of his bag with something. But, she had no idea to what degree it would be. And then out of nowhere he lunges back and smacks the hell out of her. "Get the hell off of my property!" he demanded.

Completely caught off guard by the sudden impact of his blow, Teresa stumbled a bit until she managed to regain her balance. But before I allowed her to retaliate, I ran over to where they all were standing and said, "What the hell is wrong with you? You are not suppose to be putting your damn hands on her!"

"You need to mind your fucking business!" He shouted back at me.

"She is my fucking business!" I told him. "Now, put your damn hands on her again and see what happens!"

"Just get off of my damn property before I call the police and get you arrested for trespassing."

"Well, while you're at it, tell 'em you smacked your ex-lover in her face too." I replied sarcastically.

Frustrated with my remark, he lashed back and said, "Oh fuck off and get off my property!"

"Come on, Teresa, let's go," I said grabbing ahold to her arm. "This shit right here ain't even worth it."

"Wait," Marie interjected. "Before she goes anywhere I need a couple of things cleared up."

"I ain't gonna clear up shit! 'Cause I don't got a motherfucking thing to hide. Now, if you want to ask me some questions after they leave, then I'll talk to you. Other than that, I ain't got nothing to say."

"Look Darren, I'm sorry, but that's not about to go down because this lady came all the way over here to tell me that you been fucking with her for over four years now. So, you will stand here, in front of her, and tell me whether the shit is true or not."

"I told you, I don't got shit to say."

"You are going to tell me something!" Marie replied her voice screeching. "Because she's saying she's five weeks pregnant with your baby."

"She's lying!" Darren's voice roared. "It's not my baby."

Teresa broke the mold. "It is your baby, you piece of shit! So, why don't cha' go on and tell your wife about the many nights stayed over my apartment til' about two o'clock in the morning."

"Yeah Darren, tell me about those nights." Marie insisted.

Darren stood there frozen solid, not knowing how to respond to Teresa's comment. So, Teresa broke the ice and said, "What happened to all that mouth you had? What, you scared to tell your wife about all those times you were trying to get me pregnant? But, I told you I wasn't ready for that type of commitment, unless you left your wife. And you said, in due time you was."

"Oh, he did! Huh?" Marie said.

"Yep. He sho' did. That's why I kept seeing his no-good ass!"

"What's wrong Darren? You don't have anything to say?" Marie asked him.

"Nope. I sure don't," he commented and then he stormed off into the house.

"Go ahead and run you, fucking coward!" Teresa shouted. "But, you ain't seen the last of me! 'Cause as soon as I have this baby, I am gonna drag your short ass in court for child support. And trust me, I am going to stick you for every dime I can."

"Come on girl, let's go." I told her and grabbed ahold to her arm once again. But, she showed a little resistance. So, I continued by saying, "Look, I know you're hurt by what he said. But, you are not going to get nothing resolved by just standing here. So, come on."

"Yeah, you're right. But, I ain't gon' be satisfied until I do this." She replied and then she reached down on the ground to pick up one of several bricks that was used to landscape the flowers beds around the front lawn.

Frantically, Marie asked Teresa what was she going to do with the brick? But, Teresa totally ignored her and rushed over towards Darren's car and smashed the windshield with as much force as she could muster. It was truly a mind-blowing experience. And the only thing that came to my mind was getting the hell out of there.

"Oh my God! Darren come here!" Marie yelled at the top of her voice after witnessing Teresa slam the brick through the windshield, shattering the entire glass.

"Come on, girl. We've got to go!" I said hysterically.

"No, I'm not going anywhere. I'm gonna wait for that sorry motherfucker to come outside and face me." Teresa replied in a cocky manner.

"You know what?" I began to say. "You can stand here all you want to. But, I am leaving, because this nigga is crazy! And I am not trying to get into a fist fight with him behind you fucking up his car!" I continued and then I marched directly to my car.

But, before I could get in the driver's seat really good, Darren came rushing out of this house and headed straight towards Teresa with a loaded .38 revolver. Now, I didn't know whether to pull off and leave or try to intervene. My mind went totally blank and I became numb. But, my eyes didn't blink not once as I witnessed him grab her by her throat and jam the barrel of the gun in the right side of her temple.

"Bitch! Do you know that I will kill you behind my shit!" He roared.

"Well, go head!" Teresa barked back. "I ain't got shit to live for anyway."

"No, Darren, please put the gun down!" His wife pleaded, as she stood next to him. "The kids are watching you from their bedroom windows."

"Nah, fuck that! I'm sick of this dope fiend bitch!"

"Call me what you want, nigga! 'Cause your goofy ass get down too!" Teresa fired back.

"He what?" Marie said in a raspy tone.

"Oh, I'm sorry! But, I forgot to tell you that your husband is a certified sniff addict himself."

"Shut, up bitch!" he continued as he buried the barrel deeper in the side of her head.

And seeing this, I had to do something. So, I got on my cellular phone and dialed 911. The operator wanted me to stay on the phone until a police officer arrived, but I hung up. And instead of waiting in the car I got up the gumption to go and try to defuse the situation on my own.

"Darren," I said the second I approached him, "the police are on their way. So, you might want to put that gun away before they get here. Because if you don't, they are going to arrest you and put you in jail."

"I ain't doing a motherfucking thing! This bitch came on my property and bust out my damn wind-shield, so she's going to jail."

"But, remember, you assaulted her first."

"That's because she invaded in on my space and tried to poison my wife's mind."

"Look, I know you're upset. But, you're gonna have to take that gun out of her face and let her go."

"Yes, Darren, please let her go." Marie begged him once again.

And after a few more minutes of struggling with the idea to do just that, he finally decided to let Teresa go. And when he released her from his grip, I grabbed her by her arm and began to pull her in the direction of her car.

Relieved but somehow a little frustrated, I said, "Come on, let's get out of here before the police pull up."

"Yeah, you better get that bitch out of here, before I kill her."

"Oh, nigga, shut up! You won't about to do shit to me and you know it!" Teresa screamed to the top of her voice.

"Ahh, fuck off bitch!"

"Yeah, go ahead and show off for your wife," Teresa yelled aloud right before I pushed her inside of her car, "But just remember that my front door is always open when you want to powder your nose and fuck some good pussy!"

"Can you please leave?" his wife yelled back. "You see he's not paying your ass no mind."

"He will be, after I have this damn baby!" Teresa replied sarcastically.

But instead of allowing Darren to play into Teresa's trap, Marie grabbed him and began to walk him towards the house. Her eagerness to neutralize this situation prompted me to do the same. So, I reached through the car window and grabbed Teresa by her shirt to get her attention.

"Will you please pull it together so we can get out of here," I yelled.

"I hate that motherfucker!" She expressed the moment she looked into my face.

"I can see why. But, all that yelling back and forth through your car window is only making you look stupid. Now, I've had it up to here with all y'all damn drama, and I'm getting ready to leave. So, you can sit here if you want to. But, don't call me when the police get here and decide to arrest your ass for vandalism!" I told her and then I stepped off and walked to my car.

By the time I got in and closed the door behind myself, I heard her start up the ignition, revved the engine a bit and then she sped off. I did the same and sped right off behind her.

When we reached the end of the block, two police cars rode right by us, which made me very nervous. But to my surprise, they didn't even look our way. So, we both kept it moving.

* * *

I elected to not to return to Teresa's apartment, especially after everything I had just endured. And once she realized I had turned off into another direction, she got on her cellular phone and called me. I was very short with her, so our conversation ended quickly. But, I did get a chance to tell her that I would call her sometime later.

Chapter 12

Putting Salt in Da' Game

Even after all that chaos I allowed myself to be involved in yesterday between Darren and Teresa, I ended up letting her talk me into coming back to her place today. I didn't notice it yesterday, but she had some pretty rough looking scratches around the throat area of her neck. She was looking pretty rough herself, wearing the same exact outfit of clothing from the day before. The expression on her face was very vacant and the dry white ring around her mouth gave her the look of death. This was definitely not the Teresa I knew, so I commented, "Why the hell you walking around here looking like that?"

"Girl, I'm just going through something right now, but I'll be all right," she replied as we walked into the kitchen.

I took a seat at the table, while Teresa stood with her back against the kitchen sink. "What time did you got to bed last night?" I asked.

"Not until about around midnight."

"What were you doing?"

"Riding up and down Darren's block."

"For what?" I asked sarcastically.

"I only did it to see if I could catch him coming out of his house by himself."

I shook my head in disbelief and chuckled. "Teresa, you got some serious fucking problems."

"Tell me something I don't know."

"Well, you tell me why you wanted me over here so bad?"

Teresa grabbed a glass out of the dish rack and filled it with some tap water from the sink faucet, took a sip of it and then she said, "Because a bitch is trying to get high. But, I can't do shit if I ain't got no money."

"So, you called me over here to give you money to buy you some dope?"

"That was the idea. Shit, I've been sponsoring us all fucking week. And now I don't have a dime to my name."

"Look, I don't mind picking up the tab sometimes. But, don't you think you need to slow down a little bit, since you're going to keep the baby?"

"After the shit that happened yesterday, I'd be a fool to keep this baby!"

"So, when do you plan to terminate the pregnancy?"

"I called the abortion clinic in Norfolk this morning and made an appointment for next Saturday, at ten o'clock."

"How much will that cost?"

"Three hundred and twenty dollars."

"You've got that kind of money?"

"I will after I get my last check next week."

"So, what are you going to do about your bills?"

"I can't worry about that right now. I've got to get this taken care of first."

"Well, you need to be looking for another job while you're at it."

"Girl, I got about three more weeks before my bills are due again, so I'm gon' be all right," she replied, and then she drifted back to our prior conversation.

"But, never mind all that, let's get out of here so we can go make this run."

"Where are we going?"

"Downtown."

"Downtown where?"

"Where I get my shit from."

"Teresa, I am not taking my brand new Jaguar into nobody's ghetto to buy drugs. I will stick out like a sore thumb."

"Girl please, the niggas out there be driving better cars than yours," she commented and then she walked out of the kitchen and went into the hall closet to retrieve her jacket. And not even five seconds later, she was back in the kitchen and stood in the middle of the floor with her hand on her hip and asked me why I was still sitting there? And the rebuttal I used with her was, "Because I'm not driving my car."

"Well, all right. Then we'll take mine." She agreed and then we left.

* * *

Teresa had us in the heart of Norfolk's housing project called Grandy Park. This place was saturated with dealers and dope fiends on every corner. To see these dealers selling to these fiends out in the open like this, really blew my mind. But, what really threw me for a loop was when I rode by a guy and a girl and over heard them arguing with each other because she found out he had some dope and he didn't share it with her.

"Oh, dat's all right, you sneaky muthafucka!" I heard her yell. "You ain't have to share your shit wit' me, but it's all good. 'Cause as soon as I make my next score, I'm gon' put the duck on your ass, just like you did me!" she continued. But homeboy wasn't fazed by her idle threats. And neither was I, which was why I hurried up and rolled up the passenger side window.

Now as we approached the end of the strip, Teresa noticed her brother Eugene standing next to a light pole by a crowd of people, so she pulled her car over to the side of the curb and yelled out his name. It took him a second to figure out who was calling his name. But, once he realized that it was Teresa, he rushed right over to where we were parked. And as soon as he got within one foot of the car, Teresa and I got a quick whiff of his disgusting body odor, which was very unpleasant and I didn't hesitate to let it be known.

"Why do you smell like that?" I asked him in a blunt manner.

Eugene leaned against the driver side door with both elbows and said, "Smell like what?"

"Like you haven't taken a bath in a week."

"Oh, you're tripping! I don't smell that bad."

"You've got to be kidding, right?" I continued sarcastically.

Ignoring my comments, he waved me off with his hand and immediately asked Teresa what was up?

"How long you been out here?" she asked him.

"All day, why?"

"Because I wanna know who got the good shit out here."

"Whatcha' trying to get?"

"Well, you know I want some dope. But since Faith wants to speed ball, we gon' need some coke too."

"How much y'all trying to get?" he wanted to know.

"What can we get for a hundred dollars?" I asked.

"Five pills of dope and a fifty bag of powder."

"So, who got the best shit?" Teresa asked again.

"Dat' nigga Spanky got some banging-ass dope, 'cause a few of these muthafuckas 'round here done already OD'd off that shit! But, as far as that powder, I think dat' nigga Pie got some a'ight shit!"

"Whatcha' mean it's all right?"

"What I'm saying is, I ain't heard nobody throwing salt on his shit, so it's gotta' be a'ight."

"Well, here," I said, handing him two crisp fifty-dollar bills, "go ahead and get the stuff."

Eugene took the money from me and raced off in the direction of the first dealer, who I assumed was the guy who was selling the heroin.

And then when Eugene walked away from him, he ran over to the other side of the street and handed the second dealer money in exchange for his drugs. But, what was so different from this transaction, was that this guy handed Eugene a few dollars back and he slid it in his front pants pockets. So, I didn't hesitate to wonder what that was all about. And right before Eugene got a chance to make it back over to the car, I asked Teresa was she aware of what just happened?

"Whatcha' talking about?" she wondered.

"That guy just gave Eugene money and he stuck it in his pocket."

"When?"

"Just a few seconds ago."

"Nah, I didn't see that," she began to say, "my ass was looking at this fine-ass young boy over to my left."

"Well, I just saw him. So, he's got some explaining to do."

"Girl, don't even sweat it," she started saying, but was interrupted by the presence of her brother.

"Here we go, ladies," he said in a giddy way, handing Teresa five pills of heroin and a very small bag of powder.

I took the bag of coke out of Teresa's hand and took a closer look at it. And after I opened it and gave it a taste test, I looked back at Eugene and told him that it was fine, but couldn't hold my tongue about the size of it. "Why is the bag so small?" I asked him.

"That bag of powder ain't small. That's what niggas is giving you for fifty dollars."

"Well, if that's the case, then why did he give you some money back?" my questions continued.

"That's because I told him to give me a fifty bag for forty dollars."

"Well, you need to give me back my change!"

"Shit, how do I look like, giving you back the ten dollars when I went and copped the shit for y'all? I mean, that shit didn't even sound right coming outta your mouth."

"Yeah, Faith, he earned it. So, let 'em have it," Teresa interjected.

I rolled my eyes and sighed at the larceny he was feeding me. But, I did leave well enough alone, since

Teresa was siding with him. Dope fiend or not, that's her brother. So, I can't expect anything less.

Now after they exchanged a few more words, she started up her car and had us out of there and back to her apartment in less than twenty minutes flat. And once we were inside, Teresa went right to work on her needle fix. I refused to watch her jam the syringe into her arm this time around. So, I grabbed myself a plate from her kitchen and mixed both of my treats together with my straw and went for what I knew. And when everything was all said and done, me and Teresa were both lying around on the living room sofa, spaced the fuck out! And boy, what a feeling!

Chapter 13

Two Months Later

I'd been spending time at Teresa's house damn near everyday for the last two months. And of course Eric was not at all happy about it, especially after noticing how our checking account balance had dwindled a bit. According to our bank statement, I had made over $4,200 worth of ATM withdrawals. So, while I was preparing dinner in a pair of gray sweat pants and a pink tank top that revealed my belly button, Eric took a seat and laid the bank statement flat out on the table, and decided to question me about my frequent trips.

"I need you to explain something to me," He started off.

I turned around from the kitchen stove and said, "Sure. What's the matter?"

"Why have you been making frequent trips to the

ATM machine, and only making withdrawals in seventy-dollar increments?"

"Because I needed the money," I replied as the palms of my hands began to sweat.

"Needed for what?" he pressed on.

"Well, I been lending Teresa money to cover some of her bills. And I've been using the rest for gas and other miscellaneous things."

"Wait. You and I both have gas cards. So, when did you start using cash to fill up?"

"What's up with all the damn questions? Can't you just take my word for it?" I told him and turned back around to continue cooking.

"No, I will not take your word for it. Because these impulsive trips back and forth to the ATM is not something you used to do. And then to with-draw over $4,200 out in a matter of a month and a half, and have nothing to show for it, is not your make-up. So, I believe there's something you're not telling me."

My heart started beating uncontrollably after Eric continued to press the issue. But, I knew I had to play it cool, so I turned back around toward him and said, "You are really blowing this whole thing out of pro-portion."

"Well, just tell me where all that money went?"

"But, I've already told you."

"Faith, you're lying!" he replied, his voice escalat-ing.

"Please don't call me a liar! Because you have no idea what you're talking about," I struck back.

"Well then, what's this?" he continued as he pulled a folded envelope from the top pocket of his shirt and threw it across the table at me.

Immediately I became consumed by anxiety at the sight of this mystery envelope. And as bad as I wanted to see what it was he was talking about, my body wouldn't allow me to move an inch. So, I had no other choice but to stand there. But Eric wasn't buying into my hesitation, so he sought after another avenue to get me to talk. He got up from the chair, he grabbed the envelope from off the table and literally shoved it into my chest. "Here, take it and open it," he demanded.

Still somewhat apprehensive about what I was about to get into with Eric, I remain motionless and watched as the envelope fell from my chest.

"Oh, so you're not in the mood to open it?" he asked sarcastically as he grabbed the envelope from out of thin air.

"What is it?" I finally got up the gumption to ask.

Eric ripped the letter from the envelope out of it and opened it up directly in front of me. And before I knew it, I was faced with my biggest nightmare.

"Here. Read it out loud for me," he continued as he turned the piece of paper around so I could read the contents of it.

I quickly scanned the letter from top to bottom and as my mind began to retain every word typed in black ink, my heart started beating out of control. And to think that I was motionless before, I was completely paralyzed from head to toe. So, if I had any intentions of walking out of this kitchen before this whole thing blew up in my face, I would be shit out of luck.

"Read it!" he yelled.

"You read it," I struck back.

"No problem," he replied and turned the letter around to face him. "*Dear Faith Simmons,*" he read. *"This letter is to inform you that your urine drug screen came back positive, detecting drug use of cocaine and heroin.*

The results of this screening will be forwarded to your employer. If you have any questions or concerns, please contact our office immediately. Sincerely, Carolyn Ginn, Urgent Care-Lab Technician."

After Eric finished reading the last word from the letter, he looked back into my eyes and asked me if I had something to say?

Instead of responding, I nodded my head.

"Well, you may not have anything to say," he told me, "but, this letter definitely explains your frequent trips to the ATM machine. And not only that, I know why you can't stay away from Teresa's house."

"She's my best friend," I blurted out.

Totally ignoring what I had just said, he stood closer to me and said, "How long has this been going on?"

With a dumbfounded expression, I said, "What?"

"How long have you been using drugs?" he asked me again.

"I don't use drugs," I began to lie. "The results from that letter have to be a mistake."

"Cut it out, Faith!" Eric yelled to the top of his voice. "Stop with all the fucking lies! You have a drug problem and it's time that you face it."

"I don't have a drug problem," I responded nonchalantly and turned back around towards the stove.

Seeing my reaction, Eric stormed away from me and headed towards the entryway of the kitchen. But, then I heard him abruptly stop in his tracks and turn back around. "Now, I get it," he said. "It all makes sense."

"What makes sense?" I replied, turning slightly in his direction.

"You were forced to resign, weren't you?" he didn't hesitate to ask.

"No, I wasn't," I lied once more.

"You're lying, because I know how you loved working at that school. So, you would not have resigned on your own if your life depended on it."

"Well, I'm sorry to disappoint you, but no one forced me to resign," I began saying. "I told you, I did it so I could spend more time with you and Kimora."

"You're lying!" he roared once again.

"Can you hold it down before Kimora hears you?" I pleaded.

"You know what, Faith? I've got a better idea," he said, as he took a step closer to me. "I'm gonna do you and I both a favor, and leave."

I turned all the way around and asked him where was he going? And in a cruel manner he told me he was going to his parents' house and that he was also taking Kimora with him.

"She's not going anywhere!" I protested.

"Oh yes, the hell she is. And please don't try to stop me because if you do, then you will be sorry!" he warned me.

"What is that, a threat?" I snapped back.

"Take it anyway you want, Faith. And while you're at it, take it easy on our account because I will be watching it like a fucking hawk."

"I don't care what you do! But, just remember that a lot of the money belongs to me too."

"Correction, the money belongs to the both of us, so I will not allow you to waste it away on drugs for you and your friend."

"Look, you don't know anything about her, so please leave her out of it."

"Faith, I am not going to continue to argue with you about this shit. Just stay the hell out of the account!" he said, once again, and then he left the kitchen.

After Eric left the house, I hopped on the telephone and dialed up Teresa's number. And once she answered the line, I briefly gave her the rundown of the argument Eric and I had just had, but also told her that I would be stopping by to talk more in depth. She gave me the okay and we hung up.

Chapter 14

Picking Pockets

Teresa's front door was unlocked when I arrived, so I didn't hesitate to let myself in. And as soon as I closed and locked the door, I walked a few feet down the hallway and heard Teresa moaning and groaning. So, I figured she was entertaining a male companion in her bedroom and headed into the living room.

But, little did I know. Because never in my wildest dreams did I expect to walk into the living room and see Teresa kneeling down on the floor before Lamont, with his pants pulled down around his knees. Now, this was the same nigga who slapped her ass around a few times and whipped her brother's ass behind some money they owed him. So, to see her sucking on his dick like she really enjoyed it, fucked my mind up.

"Yeah, Tee, suck dis' dick good," he instructed her as he combed through her hair with his hands. "I wantcha' to show me how bad you want dis' dope I got in my back pocket."

Reacting off his comments, Teresa engulfed his entire dick into her mouth. I mean, she took the whole thing in her mouth like it was nothing. The shit shocked the hell out of me. This girl was a fucking pro. But, since I couldn't stand watching her perform lip service for her next high any longer, I took a few steps backwards into the hallway and tiptoed into her bedroom. I figured this was the better place for me. Because the way things were going on back in that living room, it was just a matter of time for him to bust off in her mouth and I knew my stomach wouldn't be able to take that kind of action. So, until the coast is clear, I will leave those two alone and give them as much privacy as needed.

The moaning and groaning lasted about five more minutes and then all of a sudden I started hearing bits and pieces of commotion, so I stood up from the bed and planted my left ear against the bedroom door. And before I knew it, the bedroom door came crashing in on me with the force of Teresa's weight. I instantly lost my balance and fell into her television set. "Ahh, shit!" I said moaning agony. "What the fuck is going on?" I yelled, trying to regain sight of my surroundings. And when I realized what was going on, it was too late.

Lamont was dead on top of Teresa's ass. "I'ma kill you, you dirty bitch!" he yelled as he smacked her back onto her bed. And before I could react, he jumped on top of her and started punching her in every area of her face and head. So, I jumped to my feet and rushed to her defense.

"Get off of her!" I screamed, pounding him in his back.

"Mind your business, bitch!" he told me. And then without any warning, he single-handedly grabbed me by my neck and tossed me backwards. He slung me right back in the direction I came from. Poor little me, I plunged right back into the television. But this time, when I collided into it, I pushed the entire set and the Surround Sound speakers crashing to the floor, with me on top of it. And boy, did I feel like I was between a rock and a hard place. Struggling to get back on my feet was a very hard task at this point. But, as I watched Lamont physically beat Teresa with every inch of strength he had, I became more and more reluctant to muster up enough energy to get back up and help her. So, I sat there in total shock as fear and anxiety consumed my entire body. But thankfully, the beating didn't last too much longer. Because Teresa was crying hysterically, using her arms to block as many blows as possible. And she was looking more and more helpless by the moment. So, when he got up from the bed and stood on his feet and said, "Try stealing from me again and see if I don't splatter your brains all over this muthafucking apartment."

"I told you, I was sorry," she sobbed.

"Fuck dat! Just don't try dat shit again," he said once more and then he looked over at me. "And if you ever put your muthafucking hands on me again, or get in the middle of some shit I'm trying to straighten out, I'm gon' splatter your shit too! You understand?"

Now, with the amount of fear I had throughout my body, it was by sheer luck that I was able to nod my head. And when he realized that I had acknowledged every word he had uttered, he turned back around towards Teresa and tossed two pills of dope at her. It landed on the bed near her legs and she didn't waste any time to pick them up.

"Dem two pills of dope right there ain't for you sucking my dick, 'cause your mouth game wasn't all that good," he said with a chuckle, "But, I am giving it to you for taking that ass beating like a man!" he continued and then he walked out of the bedroom.

Teresa looked over at me with the silliest-looking expression ever. It was apparent how she was feeling on the inside. So, I figured now wasn't the time to blast her about yet another stupid move she made. Instead, I got up from the floor and embraced her the moment I sat down next to her on the bed.

"How long have you been here?" she wanted to know.

"Since you first put his dick in your mouth."

"Girl, I am so sorry I got you mixed up in my shit again," she began to apologize.

"Don't worry about that. Just tell me what happened."

Clutching the two pills of dope tightly in her hands, she said, "Well, when I was giving him some head, I had one hand wrapped around his dick and my other hand trying to slide a few of them fifty-dollar bills he had sticking out of his front pockets. And the crazy part about it, is that I almost had 'em. But, my greed got the best of me. Because right when I was about to get that third bill, that's when he realized what I was doing and went the fuck off."

"Why do you put yourself in those dangerous situations?"

"I don't know."

"But, look at your face," I began to say, "Aren't you tired of getting your ass kicked by that nigga?"

"If I told you I was, you wouldn't believe me."

"And you're right about that," I replied, using my hand to brush her hair back away from her face.

"Do you know that I didn't even get to finish sucking his dick?" she told me with a half smile.

"Would you have wanted to after all that? I mean, look at you. You look a fucking mess, with all these cuts and bruises on your face."

"I know I do," she replied and put her head down.

"So, let me ask you, was all this worth it?"

"Nope."

"Can I ask you another question?"

"Go 'head," she insisted.

"What possessed you to make the arrangement of giving him a blow job for some fucking drugs?"

"Because I didn't have any money and I wanted to get high. I mean, it ain't like I haven't done it before."

Shocked by her candor, my reply to her was, "You've got to be joking, right?"

"No, I'm not. I trick with Lamont all the time when I can't pay him for his candy."

"Does he know you're pregnant?"

"No."

"But, why not?"

"Because it's none of business. And besides, he wouldn't care anyway."

"Is there a possibility that he could be the father?"

"Girl, nah! Every time I fuck him, we use a condom."

"Speaking of which, when are you going to get that abortion you keep hollering about?"

"Soon."

"Yeah, I'll believe it when I see it. And anyway, do you know that you can get him arrested for beating you up like this, especially since you're with child?"

"Do you know that nigga would have his boys run up in this motherfucker and blow my fucking head off, if I ever called the police on him?"

"Yes, I believe that, which is why you need to leave that bastard alone. Because the way he beat you a few minutes ago, he could seriously kill you and leave your body in here to rot for days."

"I wouldn't ever let it get that far."

"Don't fool yourself, Teresa," I began to say, "You have absolutely no control of that psycho mother-fucker, once he's fired up."

"I know that. That's why I'm only going to deal with him on a business level, from here on out."

"After today, you shouldn't want to deal with him at all."

"I'll be all right."

"Okay, if you say so," I replied in an aggravated manner.

Then I got up from the bed and walked over to the television set so I could pick it up off the floor, but the damn thing wouldn't budge. So, Teresa got up and lent me a hand. And once she put some of her strength behind it, it didn't take us long at all to get it and both speakers back on the stand.

"Damn, that TV was heavy!" I complained.

"You tell me," she commented.

"Do you think it still works?" I asked as she attempted to plug the cord back into the outlet.

Teresa pressed down on the remote control and waited for the television to turn on before she answered my question. "Yep. It still works." she finally answered.

"Good. Because I know if it was broke, you would've had me running you down to Circuit City as we speak."

Teresa laughed and said, "Come on, now. You're my girl, so I would not have shit on you like that."

"That's reassuring, considering the bullshit I had to endure earlier."

"Oh yeah, you're talking about that fucking letter that came to your house about the drug test."

"Yep. And not only that, he had our bank statement sprawled across the kitchen and started questioning me about all the withdrawals I made from the ATM machine, only taking out seventy dollars at a time."

"What did you say?"

"I told him I've been lending you money so you can get caught up on your bills. But, he wasn't buying that shit, especially after getting that bogus-ass letter in the fucking mail."

"So, what did he say?"

"He just kept pestering me to confess to having a drug problem. But, I wouldn't. So, he stormed out of the damn house, like he always does, and took Kimora with him."

"Did he say where he was going?"

"Girl, where else is he gonna go, but to his folks' house?"

"But, he's always running to his parents' house after y'all have an argument."

"I know. And this has been going on since we've been married."

"But, why?"

"I can't really say. But, I'm guessing he can't

handle the pressures that comes with married life. So, he runs home to his parents like it's his safe haven."

"It sounds like he's intimidated by you."

"I don't think he is now. But, his attitude did change a whole lot after I got promoted to the assistant principal position."

"So, what are you going to do now?"

"Do about what?"

"About cha' candy use?"

"I don't know. But, I do know that he's going to be watching our bank account like a hawk. So, whatever I do, it's gonna have to be at a minimum. Unless I use my credit cards for cash advances. Other than that, we're gonna have to be on a strict budget."

"Don't worry about all that, because we're going to be all right," she assured me and then she pulled both pills out of her shirt pocket. "Now, come on, so we can get get fucked up," she continued.

"Well, can we go to the kitchen and get you some ice for your face, first?"

Teresa smiled and said, "Yeah, we can do that."

Chapter 15

It Is What It Is

I had a feeling I wasn't going to find Eric home when I returned from Teresa's house later that evening, so I had already conditioned my mind that I was going to be sleeping alone tonight. However, I wasn't prepared to find a handwritten letter left on the kitchen table by Eric. And as I began to read the contents of it, I realized why he felt that it was so important for him to express himself on paper, rather than talk to me face to face.

Faith,

As you already know, I am over at my parents' house. And since I plan to be there for a short while, or at least until you can come clean with me about your addiction, I have packed a few items of my clothes, as well as Kimora's. I feel that by doing this, I leave you no other alternative but to decide what is more important: your family, or Teresa and those drugs. Trust me, I will not sit around and watch you tear your life apart. And I refuse to allow you to bring me and your daughter down with you. I have also decided to take my name off that joint account and withdraw all but one thousand bucks. So, do with it what you please. Now, you don't have to worry about me telling my parents about your drug habit because I'm not in the mood to share your embarrassment. I will, however, let them know that once again we are going through some very difficult changes, which is why I elected to leave the house for a few days. So, if you want me to stick to this story I suggest that you stay away from me until you can be honest about everything. That means, stay away from my parents' house too. If you want to speak with Kimora, I suggest you call. Other than that, leave me alone.

Sincerely Yours,
Eric

Boy, was my mind blown away after reading that awful letter. But, what was really devastating was the fact that he packed up some of his clothes, which was a clear indicator that he was really ticked off with me. But then again, doesn't he always get pissed off about something I do that he doesn't like, and fly over to his damn parents' house? So, this type of behavior is nothing out of the ordinary. He'll be back after his parents start to get on his damn nerves. But in the meantime, I need to figure out a strategy. Because I want to keep the peace in my household, but at the same time I am not ready to give up the peace of mind I get when I get high.

That's the only thing that keeps me sane. So, he and I am going to have to come to a common ground. And until then, I am gonna do me just a little while longer. That's just it!

Before I went to bed, I called my in-laws' house so I could tell Kimora goodnight. Mrs. Simmons answered the line and talked to me for a few minutes and then she passed the telephone to my baby. Kimora and I spoke briefly about how much fun she'd been having thus far and wondered if I was going to come by. But, I told her no. But, I did assure her that she would be seeing me in a couple of days so. She was extremely happy about that and gave me a kiss goodnight.

After my phone call ended with Kimora, I pressed down on the flash to get a clear line and dialed Teresa's home number. Surprisingly, she answered on the fifth ring.

"Hello," she finally said.

"Hey, what took you so long to answer the phone?" I asked her.

"Because, I was in the shower."

"Are you done?"

"Yeah, I'm drying off now," she told me, "so what's up?"

"Girl, you will not believe what I found when I got home this evening."

"What was it?"

"Eric wrote me a letter and left it out on the kitchen table, in clear view for me to find it as soon as I walked through the door."

"What did the letter say?"

"It just said that he's going to be at his parents'

house until I decide to be honest with him about my drug addiction. And for me to stay away from him."

"So, how does he expect for you to see Kimora?"

"He doesn't give a fuck about me seeing her. But, he did give me the okay to call."

"Oh, he's truly a fucking asshole!"

"You tell me."

"So, have you spoken with her?"

"Yeah. I just got off the phone with her a few minutes ago."

"How is she doing?"

"Well, she said she was having a ball. So, I'm cool with her being there."

"Did you speak to him?"

"Nope. His mother answered the phone. So, I spoke to her for a second and then she handed the phone to Kimora."

"Do you think he told her about y'all argument?"

"Well, he told me in the letter that he wasn't going to mention it to them because he didn't want to share my embarrassment."

"Do you believe him?"

"I figured if he did, then she would've said something in reference to it, 'cause one thing about Mrs. Simmons, she can't hold water."

Teresa laughed. "You know your mother-in-law, huh?"

"Like no other."

"So, whatcha' doing tomorrow?"

"Well, I need to fax out a few more resumes, so I can line a few jobs up. But, other than that, I'm free to do whatever."

"Wanna do me a favor?"

"What's that?"

"Wanna lend me the money so I can get that abortion I scheduled for this weekend?"

"Come on now, you know I am on a strict budget. And besides, you know you are not going to be able to pay me back."

"Yes, I will."

"When?"

"When I get a job."

"You've been hollering that same old line since the first time I lent you some money. And I haven't seen you fill out one application yet."

"That's because I can't get up in the morning. This morning sickness be killing me. And anyway, if I don't get it by this weekend, then I'm not gonna be able to get it at all."

"Well, I'll see what I can do."

"All right! Fair enough," Teresa replied and then we both jumped into another conversation. But, our chat didn't last long at all because of the unexpected guest that came knocking at her front door. So, she immediately told me to hold on while she went to see who it was. And then about twenty seconds later she came running back to the telephone.

"Girl, let me call you back," she told me abruptly.

"What's wrong?" I asked her. "And who is at your front door?"

"It's the police. So, let me call you back."

Now before I could go any further with this conversation, I realized Teresa had disconnected our call. So, there I was lying in my bed, with the receiver of the telephone cradled next to my ear, listening to dead air. And as bad as I wanted to call her back to see what was going on, I decided against it. I figured she would be back in touch with me as soon as the officers left.

* * *

Waiting on Teresa to call me back never happened. So, after waiting for nearly forty minutes, I pressed the re-dial button and waited patiently for her to answer the phone. But strangely enough, she didn't pick up. So, I hit the flash button and pressed the re-dial button once more. And again, she didn't pick up. Now, I couldn't help but wonder and begin to worry about why she wasn't able to answer her telephone. And then it occurred to me that maybe Darren took out a warrant on her and the police were there to arrest her on charges of vandalism. And knowing this could be possible, I hopped out of bed, threw on a pair of sweats, a T-shirt and a pair of sneakers, grabbed my keys and my handbag and headed out the front door. I really didn't know whether to go by the police station first or her apartment. But, as I began to drive, my instinct told me to ride by her apartment first and that's what I did.

Now when I reached her apartment complex, I noticed a police car pulling away from her building. But, as the officers cruised by me, I couldn't help but notice that their back seat was empty; which was a sigh of relief for me, but at the other end, my stomach was still battling an anxiety attack. So, I took a deep breath and proceeded on to her apartment. And when I approached her front door, it was somewhat ajar so I pushed it opened and said, "Teresa, where are you?"

"I'm in the living room," she replied, her voice barely audible.

Instantly feeling a sense of relief throughout my entire body, I closed the front door and rushed into the living room. And when I finally came face to face with her, my whole mood shifted back into first gear.

"What's wrong?" I immediately asked as I took a seat on the sofa next to her.

Looking like she had just taken yet another beat down, Teresa sat there with her eyes bloodshot red and her face saturated with falling tears, she opened up her mouth and said, "Eugene is dead!"

Not knowing if I heard her correctly, I said, "What?"

She wiped both of her eyes with the back of her hands and repeated herself. "Eugene is dead!"

"How?" I asked, my voice screeched.

"The police told me somebody shot him in his back two times. So, whoever he was running from was the one who killed him."

"Where did this happen?"

"In Norfolk, out by Grandy Park."

"You talking about that place where he usually hangs out at?"

Teresa nodded her head.

"Ahh man, that's crazy!" I began to say. "So, how long ago did this happen?"

Still sobbing, she said, "The police said it happened a little over an hour and a half ago, and that the homicide detectives are still at the scene, trying to get people to tell them exactly what happened."

"Tell me how did the police know you were related to him?"

"Somebody out there had to have told them, since Eugene wasn't the type to carry an ID card."

"Who do you think could've killed him?"

"I'm not sure. I mean, it could be anybody because my brother was a fool! He didn't give a damn about nobody. All he was concerned about was who he could jack for their shit! And it didn't matter if he got the shit stomped out of him, because he would get right back up and find his next victim."

"Well, whoever it was damn sure made an example out of him," I commented and then I got up from the sofa to get some tissue paper from the bathroom in the hallway.

And when I turned the corner to enter back into the living room, Teresa stood to her feet and said, "I'm going out there."

"Out where?" I asked her, even though I knew 'there' could have only meant Grandy Park.

"I wanna go out to Grandy Park and see if I can find out exactly what happened to my brother," she continued.

"Are you sure that's going to be a good idea?" I replied in a way, trying to dissuade her.

"Faith, going out to Grandy Park would be the only thing that'll keep me from going off the deep end right now. So, please take me."

"Okay. I'll take you," I said willingly and handed her the tissue paper.

Teresa and I both remained quiet during the entire drive to Grandy Park. The drive itself took shorter than normal. It probably had something to do with the fact that there was little or no traffic at all. But at this point, it really would not have mattered one way or another. Our main focus was to get there and that's exactly what we did. Now, when we arrived on the scene, Norfolk's police department was all over the place. They even had the entrance of the main strip blocked off. So, I was forced to park my car, get out and walk the rest of the way.

Teresa didn't mind at all. She figured it would be best to walk through the projects, since the streets were flooded with bystanders and those same people had to be talking.

"Come on, let's go this way," Teresa insisted as she led me alongside this run down apartment building with a dimly lit light pole. And after walking through one hundred yards of broken glass and dirty syringes, we ended up in the exact spot she intended for us to be in, which was among a crowd of both young and old residents who stood directly across the street from where Eugene was gunned down. The yellow tape was very noticeable and it was squared off around two light poles and two trees. Detectives and police officers were busy questioning people, while the forensic specialist scoured the entire area for anything that would link them to Eugene's killer. So, as we continued to stand there, two young, ghetto-looking chicks, who had to be in their early twenties, sparked up the conversation amongst themselves about what happened. They were talking very low, but it wasn't low enough. So, I got an earful.

"I know one thing, dat nigga Bing Bing better not show his face around here for a while, if he know what's good for him," the first girl said.

"Girl, that nigga don't give a fuck about no police!" the second girl said. "Especially, when it comes to some off-the-wall junkie trying to steal his shit."

"Oh trust me, dat nigga cares! Because as soon as he popped that fiend in his back with dem' two hot balls, his ass got the hell out of dodge," the second girl continued.

"Shit, you would've done the same thing," replied the first girl.

"I sho' would've, 'cause a bitch like me ain't trying to go to jail."

"And neither is that nigga Bing Bing. So, he better sit his ass down and chill out for a couple of days until this shit blows over."

"It wouldn't matter either way, because ain't nobody out here gon' tell dem crackers Bing Bing shot that dried up-ass dope fiend. Shit, dat' nigga had it coming to him anyway, after that switch-a-roo stunt he pulled on dat nigga Stinka last week," the second girl concluded.

"Oh yeah, I remember that," the first girl said, going off memory. "Stinka beat the shit out of him with that iron bat, for trying to switch three dummies for real dope."

"He sho' did. But, it didn't slow that junkie down one bit."

"It sho' didn't. And now his ass is gone."

"That's what that dope will do to you," the second girl summarized and then their voices faded out.

Now others in the crowd had their own version of what transpired but it was more hearsay than anything. And after Teresa and I figured that we had heard enough, it was time to move on.

"I know you heard everything those two hoes were saying about your brother?" I said as we maneuvered our way through the crowd.

Teresa sighed heavily and said, "Yeah, I heard them bitches running off at the mouth! That's why I walked away from their asses."

"Well, at least we know a guy named Bing Bing killed your brother."

"Yep. And all I got to do is let the police know too," she replied in a nonchalant manner as she continued to march her way out of the crowd.

"What are we getting ready to do now?"

Pointing directly at a tall, straggly-looking woman

who couldn't be but twenty feet away, Teresa said, "I'm going on there to talk to Zena."

"Who is she?" I asked, following her.

"Some chick Eugene use to bring to my apartment a while back."

"You think she saw what happened?"

"That's what I'm about to find out," she told me as she proceeded towards this lady.

Now when Teresa initially approached this woman, she had to jog her memory about where she knew her from. And when she realized who Teresa was, she opened up to her instantly. "Come follow me over here," she instructed Teresa in an inconspicuous manner and led us only a couple of feet from where she was initially standing. And without further ado, she said, "I know you came out here to find out what happened to your brother. So, I'm gon' be straight up with you, 'cause that was my partner and he didn't deserve to be shot like he did."

"Did you see him get killed?" Teresa didn't hesitate to ask her.

"Nah, I was around the corner, copping me some of that Predator dem New York boys got. But, I do know that it was a case of get back."

"Whatcha' mean?" Teresa wanted to know.

"Well, a couple days ago, Eugene snatched up one of Bing Bing's packs of dope and he would've gotten away with it, but one of these junkies 'round here ratted him out. So, I heard when Eugene came back out here to score a couple pills from this other nigga, Bing Bing ran up on him and shot him."

"So, how does this Bing Bing guy look?" Teresa pressed on.

"He's got like the average height for a man. But,

he's black as shit, with long dreads that he keeps in a pony tail." Zena said. "And you can catch him driving a white Dodge Magnum too."

"Do you know his real name?"

"Nah, baby girl. Mu'fucka's like me don't go around asking niggas what's their real name. Shit, all we care about is how good their product is."

"Where is Bing Bing from?"

"I'm not sure. But, I know he ain't from 'round here."

"Do you think somebody out here could've told the police what you just told me?"

"I doubt it. 'Cause these people out here ain't trying to get in some shit dat don't even concern dem."

"Well, how often does this Bing Bing guy come out here to hustle?"

"He comes out here damn near everyday. But, I doubt if he comes out here anytime soon, after what happened tonight," Zena concluded and then her attention was drawn in another direction. "Hold up a minute," she said as she looked beyond my shoulders. So, naturally Teresa and I both turned around to see what she was looking at. But, it was only another dope fiend chick, trying to get her attention. "You ready?" Zena yelled out.

"Yeah, come on," the other woman said.

So, Zena looked back at Teresa and I and said, "Hey look, I gotta make a quick run. But, I'll be right back."

Knowing good and well that this chick was lying out of both sides of her mouth, Teresa said okay anyway and watched her haul ass on across the street. It was evident that she was on a mission to get high and she wasn't going to let no one stand in the way of that. So, there was no point in us trying to get any more information out of her.

Now, as the police detectives began to disperse from the scene, so did the residents, which was our cue to get out of there as well.

When we arrived back at Teresa's apartment, I decided to spend the night at her place, so she wouldn't be alone. This was a trying time for her, so I want nothing else but to be there for her.

Chapter 16

The Following
Morning

The next morning Teresa and I met with the homicide detectives down at the coroner's office, to identify Eugene's body. The process didn't take long at all. So, after she filled out and signed the appropriate paperwork, she talked briefly with the detectives about the conversation she had with a very close friend of her brother's and the events that led up to her brother being killed. They took down her information and told her that they would follow up with that lead, and get back with her if anything comes of it. Teresa said fine and we all departed ways.

"How long do you think it's going to take for them to find that Bing Bing character?" I asked the moment we got into my car.

Teresa began to gaze out at window at God knows

what and said, "I don't know. I just really hope that they can catch him."

"Oh, don't worry! They will." I assured her.

"I sure hope so," she said with little enthusiasm.

So, I rubbed her across her shoulders in a circular motion and instead of dwelling on the what ifs, I switched up the conversation and asked her how was Eugene looking to her on that table?

Before she answered me she looked into my eyes, as if she was searching for the right words to say. And then after a brief sense of hesitation on her part, she finally came out and said, "He looked like he was asleep to me."

"I thought the same thing," I told her. "But, you could tell that he had a hard life," I continued.

"Hard ain't the word," she began to say. "That man has been through some shit in his life since he started fucking around with that needle. I mean, it's crazy, because he used to have a damn good job at the Ford plant before they did that big lay off. And it seems like after that happened, everything started falling apart on him."

"Oh yeah, I remember that because he lost his house and his car behind that."

"Yep. And do you remember that bitch he was married to named Stephanie?"

"Oh yeah, I remember her."

"Well, do you remember when she packed her shit up and took both of his kids from him, because money was getting low and he couldn't find another job?"

"Oh yeah, I remember all of that," I replied as I visualized how that whole incident went down. "And you know what?" I continued. "He wasn't right after she did that shit to him, too."

"Hell nah, he wasn't right. And I believe that's what sent him to the streets, too."

"Now, that I think about it, you're probably right. But, let me ask you this."

"Go 'head," she insisted.

"Have you called your mother and told her about Eugene getting shot?"

"Yeah, I called her right before you came by last night."

"And what did she say?"

"She really didn't have much to say."

"What do you mean by that?" I wondered aloud.

"Well, she's sort of been expecting for something like this to happen to him since he's drifted off into that lifestyle. So, it didn't come as no surprise to her when I told her. But, she did tell me that she'll be in town by tomorrow morning to take care of his funeral arrangements."

"What about your other relatives? Are they gonna fly here too?"

"Girl please, my other relatives could care less about my brother. They're probably glad he finally put himself out of his own misery."

"Damn, that's sad!"

"It sure is. And that's why I don't deal with none of their asses right now to this day," she expressed harshly as if she had a bad taste in her mouth.

"Well, what about your father?" my questions continued.

"My mom will probably bring him. But, he's so far gone now with his Alzheimer's that it's going to be impossible for him to even remember he had a damn son."

"Wait, I thought he was going through that dementia stage?"

"He was. But just recently, my mother called me and told me it progressed."

"Damn, I'm sorry to hear that."

"Don't be sorry, 'cause when that motherfucker was in his right mind, he used to terrorize the hell out of me and my brother while we were growing up. And I couldn't understand, for the life of me, why he treated us the way he did and never told us that he loved us."

"He was probably dealing with some issues of his own," I said in effort to downplay her father's behavior. But, as our conversation progressed, her facial expressions began to turn sour by the minute. So I took it upon myself to change the subject to something more pleasing to the ear, which worked, because Teresa calmed right on down.

So, far the police hadn't been able to apprehend this Bing Bing guy for killing Eugene and it was tearing Teresa apart. But, she did manage to put those feelings on the back burner and solely dealt with laying him to rest, which was a very sad occasion. And I guess shit had gotten too overwhelming for her because in the middle of the service, she fell out cold. So, me and a couple of her relatives had to get her some medical attention. She came back around not too long after the services had ended and cursed out a few of her family members, while the hurt she was suffering from was fresh on her mind.

Now, I tried to defuse a couple of her confrontations but after a while shit started getting redundant, so I figured what's the use and carried my ass home to my empty house. And yeah, that's right! It's been two weeks now and Eric is still camping it around his parents' house. I've made a couple of stops by there while he was there, but he refused to talk to me. He's still holding that letter he read about my positive drug screen, over my head. And until I come clean about my drug use and get some help for it, then there's nothing for us to talk about. So, I had to make it clear to him that he could stay around his parents' house as long as he wanted to but, Kimora will be returning home very shortly, so he'd better make some rational decisions before shit gets really ugly. And all the response I got out of him was a door slammed in my face. But, it was cool though, because I didn't expect anything else but that type of behavior coming from him.

That's just how he has been from day one. So, silly of me to think that he would ever change.

You would think that after all the shit Teresa went through with Eugene's death and all the shit I went through with my husband, that we would want to straighten out our lives. But, unfortunately, that just wasn't the case because we've been acting reckless and getting high like crazy. And I also began to lose sight of everything I deemed important in my life. My bank account and my credit cards are almost maxed out and I even lent out my brand new Jaguar to a couple of dealers, in exchange for huge amounts of heroin and coke. And every time it came time for those assholes to bring my car back, a problem would always come into play. Like the incident that happened two days ago, when I let this young guy named Papoose pay me $150 worth of coke and heroin to use my car for the whole day. But, the motherfucker didn't bring it back until almost forty-eight hours later and when I chewed his ass out about it, this bastard got in my face and threaten to smack the shit out of me if I didn't shut up. So, naturally I backed off and went on my merry way because this nigga seemed like he was crazy. And I was truly not in the mood to be getting my ass kicked behind disrespecting some ole young-ass punk. And besides, how in the hell was I going to explain to my husband how I got a black eye? Because either way it came out, he wouldn't understand. So, I did a good thing by walking away.

Speaking of which, Eric moved back into the house, but he made it his mission to make my stay there very uncomfortable and I found myself hanging out at Teresa's apartment more often than usual. I even spent the night over there a few times to avoid going home all fucked up. And today was no different. So, immediately after I took a couple of sniffs of the little bit of shit I had left, I looked over at Teresa, who was sitting in the love seat on the opposite side of the living room with the tip of the needle still injected into her arm and said, "Are you all right over there?"

"Oh, I'm straight," she said, her words slurring. "I'm just enjoying this feeling I'm getting from this shit and trying to figure out how I'm gon' get me some more of it."

"Is that why you haven't taken that needle out of your arm yet?"

"Boy, you learn fast," she commented, scratching

the left side of her face like the dope she had just shot into her veins was really taking effect.

So, instead of responding to her comment, I elected to lay my head back and close my eyelids because I had nothing else to say. But she did.

"I know one thing," she began to say, her words still slurring, "I sho' gotta get me a couple more pills of that penny candy, 'cause them young boys put their thing down with this shit today."

"But, I thought you were on that Predator kick?"

"I was, until I got a taste of this shit here."

"It is better, huh?"

"You motherfucking right! So, we gon' have to make another trip down to Grandy Park before that shit runs out."

"Now, how are we going to do that, when we don't have a fucking penny to our name?"

"Don't worry," she told me. "I've got just the right thing for that," she continued as she ejected the needle from her arm. And then she got up from the chair and headed down the hallway towards her bedroom. Two minutes later, she returned to the living room with a fairly new, black woman's leather jacket in her hands.

"How much you think we can get for this?" she asked me.

"I'm not sure," I replied with uncertainty.

"Well, let's go find out," she insisted.

But before I got up, I hesitated a bit and began to weigh the pros and the cons about what I was getting ready to get into. Now, I was high already from the shit I had just snorted. So, if I decided to run downtown with Teresa to cop some more of that penny candy she was talking about, then I was not going to be in any shape to go home. But, if I decided not to ride out with her, then I was gonna miss out on some good shit. And I wasn't trying to do that, so what was a girl to do?

"What you stalling for?" she asked me.

"I'm not stalling," I assured her.

"Well, let's go then," she continued.

Feeling the pressures of trying to stick by her side, I stood up from the sofa and followed her out the front door. And once we were outside, I elected to drive us to our destination because she was truly not in her right state of mind to drive us herself.

Chapter 17

The Ice Cream Man

As expected, the main strip in Grandy Park was packed from corner to corner with junkies, dope fiends, the dealers, and a few hoes lurking on the sidelines, trying to put their bid in for a nightcap in exchange for some cash or a couple pills of dope. So, there was nothing unusual about this scene. Now, once I got a parking spot, Teresa hopped out of the car with her leather jacket in hand and headed over towards this cute, young, fat guy whom everybody called the Ice Cream Man. And from the looks of this cat, I guessed they called him the Ice Cream Man for either his weight problem or all the jewelry he wore which, in my opinion, made him look like he was trying to be superior to all of these low-income housing residents out here. Or, for a better phrase, made him look like he was The Man around here. So, when Teresa walked up to him, she gave him a little bit of lip service and then she held up the jacket in front of him. But, for some reason, homeboy wasn't interested at all, so she folded the jacket up, tucked it under her arm and walked away. And as she attempted to cross the street, I heard him say, "Ay yo, Shorty, come back over here so I can holler at you for a minute."

And like a dog adhering to her master's command, Teresa turned back around and marched her ass right back over to where he was standing. Now, I couldn't make out what either of them were saying this time around but whatever it was drew their attention in my direction. So, I sat in my car with a bewildered expression and wondered to myself what the hell could they be talking about. And then, out of the blue, here came Teresa running over toward me.

"You are not going to believe what that nigga just asked me to do," she said the moment she approached me, sounding out of breath.

"You're probably right. But, what did he say?"

"He wants me to ask you if you would trick with him?"

"Are you fucking crazy! I'm not a ho!" I said with utter disgust. "I mean, how could you even fix your mouth to ask me some shit like that?"

"Look, I already told him you wouldn't go for no shit like that. But, he was like if I didn't make it happen, then he wasn't trying to make a trade."

"Well, I don't know what to tell you. Because I am not selling my pussy for a couple pills of his so-called penny candy!" I expressed with discontent.

"Oh, he was gon' give you more than a couple pills." She said with confidence. "As a matter of fact, he told me he'll give you $200 worth of dope if you'll be with him for one hour."

"Well, it ain't gon' happen, so let's go."

"Come on now, Faith," she began to beg me. "This is is the only way we're going to be able to get ahold to some of his shit."

"Well, you fuck him, then."

"But, he doesn't want me."

"Well, I'm sorry 'cause I'm not about to do it. Now, if you can't get him to buy that jacket right there, and get your silly ass in this car right now, then I am going to leave you."

Desperate to make the trade through any means necessary, Teresa said, "Hold up, wait a minute," and then she dashed back off in the direction of the Ice Cream Man. Now, I couldn't tell you what she had up her sleeve, but whatever it was, I knew I wasn't going to allow myself to take no part in it. I didn't give a damn if I used drugs or not, I refuse to let a young-ass drug dealer treat me like I was some gutter trash prostitute for some fucking dope. So, I'll leave that department up to Teresa, since she seems to enjoy it.

And while she was working her magic on home-boy, a couple of his watchout boys yelled out to alert him and everybody in the area doing something illegal, that a couple of undercover narcotics detectives came rolling through in civilian-like cars. So, naturally everyone panicked, including myself. And that's when it dawned on me whether I should pull off and leave Teresa's dumb ass out here where she belonged, or just sit there and act cool. So, as I was about to make my decision, I noticed how quickly that fat nigga handed her a tiny, black package and walked away from her. And as she began to walk back into the direction of the car, it became clearer by the second that, that package she carried couldn't be nothing else but that fat bastard's drugs.

Now, it took everything within me not to drive the fuck off, seeing as though the police were watching everything moving. So, what were the odds of them fucking with her, much less questioning me after they see her get into my car? And who knows, they could even fuck around and violate my constitutional rights by conducting an unauthorized search on me, as well as my car, because of the environment we were in. And I couldn't have that, especially not now. So, whatever I decide to do, I know I am going to have to play it very safe.

"Come on, let's go." Teresa instructed me the second she jumped into the passenger seat.

"Wait," I said, trying to hold my composure. "Did he just hand you a little black bag?"

"Yeah, so come on before the police comes over here and fuck with us," she replied as if she was getting a little impatient.

Now, I was on the verge of blowing her ass clean out of the water for that dumb-ass move she made that could put us both in jail. But, I held my tongue to prevent from making a scene, which of course would have opened a door for a major disaster, and then I got out of that place as quickly as possible.

On the way out, I saw two more police officers harassing a couple of guys at the end of the strip. And even though I felt a sense of relief that I was home free, I also knew that it only happened at the expense of those guys. So, as I approached highway I-264, Teresa reached down inside her pants and pulled out the black bag. And with the biggest smile she could muster up, she said, "I betcha' can't guess how much is in here?"

"Whatever it is, I sure hope it would've been worth you going to jail behind," I commented in a hasty and no-tolerance manner.

"Girl, those police officers weren't thinking about me," she began to explain. "All they come out there for is them niggas they see out there every day, which is why Ice Cream gave me his shit and told me to hold it."

"What do you mean, hold it?"

"Well, I'm supposed to be meeting him around the corner, so he can get this shit back. But, after the way he carried me, he can kiss my ass 'cause I ain't about to give him shit!"

"Oh my God, Teresa! That man is going to kill you when he catches up with your ass!"

"Please, he ain't gon' do shit! 'Cause if wasn't for me, the police would have been dead on his ass and locking him up as we speak. So, the nigga owes me."

"That's not how he's going to look at it, once he figures out you're not going to show up."

"Who cares," she replied as she opened up the bag. And then within seconds, her face lit up like a Christmas tree.

"Girl, we hit the mother fucking jackpot!" she continued.

"Yeah, so you think," I commented with little or no interest at all.

But, it didn't stop her from harping on how she planned to devour the entire package. "I am gonna have me a motherfucking ball with this shit here. And I ain't gon' come up for air until all of it is gone," she commented with pure excitement.

And instead of responding to her ridiculous comments, I chose to leave well enough alone because I figured, what's the use? She's a grown-ass woman who chooses to live her life in the danger zone. So, if she wants to keep getting her ass kicked behind taking people's shit, then that's exactly what was gonna continued to happen.

Later that night, I found out that the black bag Teresa walked away with contained forty-five caps of the Ice Cream Man's dope. So, you know she thought she was in paradise. I, on the other hand, played it safe and only sniffed a small quantity of it, since I didn't have any coke to mix it with. And I must say that it wasn't quite bad either. But, it did make a motherfucker nod off in the blink of an eye. That's just how powerful the shit was.

Chapter 18

If It Ain't One Thing It's Another

You will not believe it when I tell you that it only took Teresa and I three days to blow up all forty-five caps of that penny candy. So, you know we had not had one ounce of sleep for those entire three days. My body was tired and it was urgent that I take a bath immediately because my ass was kicking.

I mean, I'd never gone this long without washing my ass. This was not like me at all. And I'd noticed that when you're getting high, staying on top of your hygiene wasn't really that important. But, what was important was how you were going to cop your next high. And the way we studied our options was like how scientists studied the law of gravity. Now, I know that sounds really crazy, but believe you me, this shit was serious.

It was a Wednesday morning and I'd finally gotten up the nerve to go home and face my husband's wrath, after being gone for almost a week. And I knew it wasn't gonna to be pleasant, since he'd been trying to contact me the whole entire time. So, I suited up and was going to be prepared for whatever he threw my way.

Now as I approached the house, my heart started beating out of control. And when I stuck my keys into the front door and couldn't turn the lock after trying two times, my heart fell straight to the pit of my stomach.

"Wait a minute. What's going on here?" I said aloud with a puzzled look on my face.

And then as I was about to knock on the door, it opened and Eric was standing there with evilest expression he could muster up. So, as I was about to say something in reference to him changing the locks, he beat me to the punch. "Thought you were gonna be coming in, huh?"

"Of course, I did. I do live here," I replied sarcastically.

"Not anymore," he struck back.

"So, what, you put me out?"

"No, I didn't. You left."

"And how in the hell did you come up with that conclusion?"

"After you decided that you wanted to stay out for almost a week. And when I've tried to contact you you failed to take any of my calls, better yet even come home. So, what in the hell was I suppose to think?"

"Look, I don't want to discuss this mess out here for all the neighbors to be in my business," I began to say, as I moved forward to cross over the threshold of my front door.

"I'm sorry but you can't come in here," he told me in a cold-hearted manner as he stood directly in the path in which I was trying to travel.

"I beg your pardon!" I snapped, throwing my hands over my hips.

"Listen, Faith, please don't try to cause a scene" he warned me.

"Eric, I'm not trying to cause a scene. You are," I lashed back.

"Okay, listen I've gotta go," he said, taking a couple of step backwards, making room to close the front door.

"Oh, so you're just gonna close the door in my face?"

"That's the idea."

"You know what, Eric? You're acting really childish right now. So, you need to snap out of it and talk to me like an adult, because these games you're playing aren't funny anymore."

"Oh, so you think this is a game, huh?"

"Yes, I do."

"Well, let me be the first to tell you that my decision to change the locks and file for a legal separation is not a game," he started off. "I am sick of all your bullshit and everything you stand for. I mean, look at you."

"What's wrong with me?" I interjected.

"Haven't you looked in a mirror lately? Because, if you haven't, then let me be the first to say that you look like shit! And you smell like you haven't bathed in a whole week."

"Oh, bullshit! That's a fucking lie! You don't smell me and you know it."

"Trust me, Faith, I do. And believe it or not, it really hurts me to see you like this. But, what's so ugly about the whole thing is that you refuse to be honest with yourself and admit that you have a drug problem."

"That's because I don't."

"Come on now, Faith, who are you kidding here? I mean, tell me, what person stays out for five or six

days and don't come or call home? And when they do
show up, they look like roadkill."

"You got all the answers. So, you tell me."

"Nah, I don't have to tell you, because you already
know."

"Yeah, whatever Eric, because I'm really not in the
mood to hear all of that."

"Well, are you in the mood to hear about how
much your daughter misses you? And is always
asking me why you won't return our calls?"

"Where is she?"

"It's ten o'clock in the morning, so she can't be
anywhere else but school."

"What time are you going to pick her up?"

"I'm not. My mother is, since Kimora asked her
last night could she come and get her so they can go
out for ice cream."

"Well, what time is she bringing her home?"

"You don't need to be concerned about that. But,
what you need to be concerned about is calling Caro-
lina Finance Company and making some arrangements with them about when you intend to make
your two-month-overdue car payments."

Stuttering between every word, but trying to make
my explanation sound plausible, I said, "Wait, there
must be some kind of mistake. I don't owe them two
car payments because that company automatically
takes it out of the account."

"I know that, and so do they. But, the representative
told me that when they've tried to make the electronic
drafts from your account, it's always coming back in-
sufficient funds. So, I personally called your account
to check your balance and found out that you're in the
negative of ninety-eight dollars. Now, how can you ex-

plain that when I left you over one thousand dollars in that same account a little over a month and a half ago?"

"I refuse to explain anything to you, after the way you're carrying on."

"Well, I guess there's nothing else for us to talk about," he told me and proceeded to close the front door.

But, before he was able to close it fully, I stuck my foot in the door sill to block him from further closing it. And when he saw this, it really pissed him off to the point that he said, "If you don't move your foot right now, I am going to break the shit off!"

"Well, let me in the damn house!" I yelled with extreme rage. Because by this time, I was at my wit's end about how he was treating me. I mean, I knew he was going to be upset, but I didn't have any idea that he would put me out of my own house and file for a legal separation. Was he fucking losing his damn mind or something, because I owned this house just like he did, so I was not gonna just stand here and let him treat me like I was some fly-by-night piece of ass he just fucked last night. It just wasn't going to happen.

"Faith, if I have to tell you to leave once more, then you'll leave me no choice but to call the police and have you escorted off the premises."

"I don't give a fuck! Call 'em!" I dared him. "Because when they find out I live here too, then we'll see who gets the last laugh," I continued as the volume of my voice got louder.

"You're absolutely right! We will see who gets the last laugh after I tell them that I've got an emergency protective order against you."

"You got what?" I screamed even louder.

"You heard me. Now get off of the premises before I get you arrested!"

Hearing Eric utter the words "protective order" blew me clean out of the water. I couldn't do a thing but just stand there and look stupid. But, then I thought to myself, on what grounds was he able to get this order against me. So, I challenged the validity of his statement. "You know what?" I began to say, "I am having a hard time believing somebody gave you a fucking protective order against me."

"Well, believe it," he struck back as he pulled the document out of his back pocket and flashed it right before my eyes. "Now, get the fuck away from here and carry your ass back to your drug addict girl-friend's house, where you belong," he continued.

Becoming numb from the sight of the document and the words that were coming from Eric's mouth, wouldn't allow me to move one inch. I mean, this whole altercation with him had me thrown for a loop. And once again, he found a way to belittle the hell out of me. So, what was I to do? Just continue to stand there and have my ass arrested for trespassing on the premises of my own house. Nah, I didn't think so. So, I immediately convinced myself to suck it up because this whole ordeal would only be temporary. But, I did make one last attempt to try to salvage what life our marriage had left.

"Can I ask you a question?" I said.

"Yeah, go ahead," he insisted.

"Is there any way we can work this whole thing out?"

Before he answered me, he hesitated for a brief moment, but then he said, "Faith, I've tried so many times to get you to open your eyes and realize what you were doing to me and your daughter. But, you're so wrapped up in that world of yours that you can't even see how your lifestyle is effecting us. I mean, look at you. Your hair looks like shit. And you look like you haven't had a wink of sleep in days, which is a clear sign that you're on drugs. And I can't have you around us like that. So, until you admit that you have a drug problem and check yourself into a drug treatment center, then we have nothing else to discuss."

"Well, what's going to happen with us in the meantime?"

"Nothing," he replied in a nonchalant manner.

"Are you going to let me see Kimora?" I continued as my eyes began to become glassy.

"Not until you get yourself together."

"So, what about my things?"

"What things?"

"My clothes," I began to say. "I need my clothes."

"Oh yeah, you can get your clothes," he assured me.

"But, when?" I pressed the issue.

"You can get them now. Just let me open up the garage door."

"But, why do I have to go through the garage to get my things?"

"Because that's where I put everything after I packed them up," he replied.

But instead of me reacting in an unpleasant manner because of the response he gave me concerning the whereabouts of my things, I left well enough alone and backed out of the doorway. He closed the front door immediately after and by the time I walked over to the garage door he had it ajar, with him standing there, waiting to assist me.

"Is this everything?" I asked after I scanned every taped-up box in sight.

"Yep. It's everything you had in your closet," he replied as he reached down to pick up the first box.

"What about my jewelry box?"

"I packed that up too," he told me and as he struggled to carry the heavy box out of the garage.

Now, after making between seven or eight trips, Eric and I had every single box stored away in my car. But, when it was time for me to make my departure, I couldn't get him to tell me that he still loved me, to save his damn life. The only words I could get him to utter from his mouth were, "I hope you get a chance to straighten out your life before it's too late." And then he walked back into the garage and closed the door behind himself. So, to hear him say that made me feel even lower than I felt when I first found out he changed the locks on me. But, what could I do? Nothing but swallow my pride and carry my ass right back over Teresa's apartment, since I no longer had a leg to stand on here.

Teresa was trying to straighten up her nasty-ass apartment when I returned. So, when I came through the door with all my shit in tow, she had a ton of questions for my ass. In a sense, she was upset at how Eric was handling the situation with putting me out of a house he and I shared, the legal separation, and me not being able to see Kimora until I got some help with my addiction. And of course, I shared her sentiments. But, at the same time, she was happy that I was able to come back to her place and be her roommate, since she had always lived alone. So, I was very grateful that she was allowing me to be here until I could straighten shit out at home. Whenever that would be, of course.

Chapter 19

Karma Is a Bitch

Just when I thought everything was going to be okay, then I get slapped with a dose of reality. Now, here I am, living with my best friend and have been doing it for nearly four months. Bills are piling up around here like crazy and just this morning, she got an eviction notice posted on her front door, stating that she is behind on her rent for three months. So, I questioned her about it, since I know I've given her my part of the rent because I neglected to pay my own car payments to do it. But, when it was time for her to plug me in about what was going on, she tried to downplay everything I threw at her.

"Girl, don't even let that eviction notice stress you out," she replied in a nonchalant manner, as she tossed and turned in her bed for a more comfortable position.

But, her response wasn't good enough for me, so I stood there next to her bed, with the notice in my hand, and said, "What the hell you mean, don't let it stress me out! Do you have any idea that your landlord wants your ass out of here in less than thirty days?"

"Oh, he ain't gon' put me out," she said, her voice barely audible from it being muffled by the pillow. "He's just trying to put some fire under my ass, so I'll pay him."

"Teresa, that man doesn't want your money." I shouted, as I waved the notice over her head. "He wants to take back possession of his fucking apartment."

"Well look, if it'll make you feel any better, I'll make a phone call to him as soon as I get up, and straighten this whole thing out."

"And what could you possibly tell him?" I said in an agitated manner. "Because, I know he's not trying to talk to you, for real. Especially, since you haven't lived up to your obligation. But, the fucked-up part about all of this is that I gave you my car payment money to pay the rent, and you didn't even do it. So, now we're going to be two dumb-looking homeless motherfuckers."

"Oh, stop acting like a drama queen!" she commented immediately after she turned her body around to face me. "Because the man ain't gon' put us out. Now, just chill out, 'cause you're fucking up my high right now with all this yelling."

"Your what? That's your damn problem. And you're too fucking stupid to see it."

"Please don't start that preaching shit to me, like your life is so much better."

"You know what, Teresa? My life may not be better than yours, but at least I am not laying around here, fucking different niggas for just a couple of pills of dope, while you're carrying another nigga's baby and ain't got a stitch of food or toilet paper in the damn house."

"Oh, so now you got a problem with me fucking niggas for dope I got you high with? 'Cause, if my memory serves me right, you ain't had a dime to put in on the re-ups in a good little while. So, if it wasn't for me tricking, then tell me, how was you gon' get your shit off?"

"Wait a minute, you must've forgot that I supplied your ass with tons of money in the fucking beginning. Remember, when I maxed out my whole bank account and all my credit cards to get you high? So, don't act like you're the only one who has made sacrifices around here. Because if anybody has done that, then it's me."

"I didn't say you didn't. But, I just don't need you standing over top of me, pointing fingers, like you're better than me."

"I never acted like I was," I began to explain. "I'm just going through the motions right now because I miss my daughter, who I ain't seen or talked to in months. And then on top of that, I'm broke and I'm running from the fucking repo man."

"Girl, don't beat yourself up. Shit is gon' get better. Just watch and see," Teresa commented as her tone changed.

"Yeah, I hope so. 'Cause the way my life is spiraling downhill, I could sure use a break."

"Don't worry, it'll happen. Now, calm your ass down and stop getting uptight about everything."

"Somebody's gotta do it," I told her and slowly found myself backing out of her bedroom.

Now don't get me wrong, I was still kind of leery about how she was downplaying this whole situation, but what could I do? It was her place, so I had no other choice but to wait and see what happened next.

A half a day nearly went by before Teresa got out of bed to join me in the living room. I was watching the local news when she walked in, looking like a skinny crackhead. I mean, I didn't notice it before but homegirl was in bad shape. Now, she was already a small-figured woman, so to see her and notice that she had dropped at least twenty pounds was not pleasing to the eye. But, the worse part about it was that she had lost most of that weight in her face. So, she definitely didn't look like Toni Braxton anymore with that stringy-looking ponytail and sunken-in cheeks.

"Why you didn't tell me the water was turned off?" she asked me, holding a toothbrush in her hand.

"I did tell you."

"When?"

"About an hour after I came in your bedroom, talking about the eviction notice."

"So, when exactly did they turn it off?"

"I don't know. But, when I tried to wash the dishes around nine-something this morning, that's when I realized it was turned off."

"Motherfuckers!" she yelled as she threw her hands into the air. "They ain't got nothing else better to do than to fuck with my shit!"

"You should've just paid 'em," I said in a nonchalant way, not once turning my head from the television.

"Paid them with what?"

"With some of that rent money I gave you," I replied sarcastically.

"Oh Lord, there you go on that trip again!" she said, and stormed back out of the living room.

I heard her march down the hallway and slam the door to her bedroom, but she came strutting her dumb ass right back into the living room about ten minutes later. So, I'm guessing she found some kind of outlet in her room to calm her ass down because when she reappeared before me, she acted as if nothing had happened. "Wanna take a ride?" she asked in a giddy way.

"Where are you trying to go?" I wanted to know. Because in all actuality, I really don't feel like being in her company right now.

"I'm gonna take a ride out to Grandy Park," she continued, as her smile got even cheesier.

"And do what?"

"Whatcha' think I'm gon' do? I'm gon' get us some good shit to get high off of."

"With what? 'Cause you don't have any money."

"Yeah, you're right. But, I got these," she said as she held out her left hand.

I shook my head and said, "Don't tell me you're getting ready to trick somebody else up with those fake-ass pills of baking soda you just put together."

She smiled, slid all three dummies into her top shorts pocket and said, "It ain't just baking soda. I got some Benita mixed in with it too, just in case one of them slick niggas wanna go behind me and test it."

"Girl, you play some dangerous-ass games!"

"Wait, don't start that judging shit again."

"I'm not. But, you really scare me with the shit you take yourself through to cop that next pill of dope."

"You know what's that called?"

"What?"

"It's called survival. 'Cause, if you noticed, if I don't

go out and take a few chances, then I'm gon' sit around here, ill. And going through that phase of getting diarrhea and stomach cramps ain't no fucking joke. So, that means I gotta constantly stay on the grind.

"Well Teresa, I can't knock what you do. But, you do need to be careful."

"Oh, don't worry. I will." she assured me and then she said, "So, are you gonna roll with me or not?"

"You go ahead. But, make sure you bring a couple gallons of water when you come back."

"All right, I can do that. But, whatcha' gon' do while while I'm gone?"

"Well, first of all, I'm gonna go in that kitchen and see what I can scrap up together and eat. And then I'm gonna bring my ass right back in here and finish watching the news."

"All right. Well, I'm gon' see if I can pick up a few grocery items too, like some of them ninety-nine–cent Banquet meals."

"Oh yeah, they're good. But, make sure you get the meat loaf and the Salisbury steak kind, with the mashed potatoes and corn. And if you got enough for a soda, get a strawberry one."

"Well, I'll see because you know I gotta put a few dollars in the gas tank."

"Oh yeah, your shit is on 'E'," I commented with laughter.

"Your shit is too!"

"You're right. And that's why it's parked."

"Well, as soon as I make this move, my baby is gon' be all right."

"Well, go head and take care of your business. But, don't be gone long."

"I won't," she said and then she left.

Chapter 20

Reality Check

Could you believe it? I'd been sitting in the fucking house since yesterday with no food and no running water, waiting for Teresa to bring her ass back from Grandy Park, and the bitch hasn't walked through the door yet.

Knowing her luck, she was probably laid out somewhere in a back alley, from somebody whipping her ass behind selling them those dummies she concocted in her bedroom yesterday. But then again, her ass could've gotten pulled over and arrested for driving under a suspended license. So for her, the ball could roll any way since her moves were always unpredictable, which is why I have to make some moves on my own. Because if I continue to sit here and wait for her to come home, then I'd probably end up starving to death.

And I can't have that, so the only thing I can do

that'll work in my favor would be to pay my in-laws a visit and pray all the way there that I don't run into Eric. Because there is no telling how he'll react, especially when he sees that I look worse off than I did the day I found out he put my things into the garage and changed the locks. Knowing him, he would have a field day, pointing fingers and insulting me. Pegging my downfall would be very gratifying for him. So, my best bet would be to get in and get out without hassles. And that's exactly what I plan to do.

When I told Teresa my car was on "E", I truly meant it. So, I counted my blessings right then for the miracle I received that enabled me to drive all the way to Sand Bridge from Teresa's apartment, without running out of gas. It was approximately four-thirty in the evening and it was rush hour, so the fact that it only took me fifteen minutes to get there definitely weighed in my favor as well. And when I pulled up to their house and noticed that my husband's car wasn't parked out front, I instantly felt a huge burden being lifted off my shoulders. But not only that, the acceptance I felt when I was greeted at the door was indescribable. I mean, I couldn't even put it into words the joy I felt when my mother-in-law hugged me. She even let out a few tears.

"Faith, sweetheart, where have you been?" she asked me the moment she embraced me and led me into the house.

"I've been staying at a friend's house." I replied as we walked in the direction of the kitchen.

And as soon as we turned that corner, I saw my father-in-law sitting at the table with his face buried in his dinner plate. But, when he looked up to see that it was me, he leapt up from the chair and rushed over to hug me.

"Girl, where you been?" he asked with much delight in his voice.

I could truly sense that they were both being genuinely concerned about my well being, so I took a seat at the table and reiterated to him the exact same answer I just gave her when I walked through the front door. "I've been staying at a friend's."

"Well, how have you been?" his questions continued.

"Not too good, since Eric and I separated."

Mrs. Simmons stood directly behind me and began to rub my back and said, "Well, we kind of figured that when we hadn't heard from you. But, we have been praying for you and God has shown us that you're going to be all right."

"Did God show you that I was going to get my family back?" I asked her as my eyes became glassy.

"Just put your life back together and we'll help you work on that," she told me.

Hearing her response sent a clear message to me that my marriage was doomed. So, I placed my hands over my face and began to cry uncontrollably.

"Y'all just don't know, but I do want to get myself together. It's so hard, though," I told them.

Mrs. Simmons embraced me with a huge bear hug and said, "But, it doesn't have to be baby. And if you're ready to make a change, we will help you."

"We sure will." My father-in-law agreed as he took my hand in his. "Now, stop that crying, 'cause you gon' be all right, darling."

"She sure will," Mrs. Simmons commented and

then she grabbed a paper towel from the countertop and handed it to me.

"Want something to eat?" Mr. Simmons asked as he took another bite of food from his plate.

"Sure, I would love some," I didn't hesitate to say after I took inventory of his plate.

"It looks good, huh?" his questions continued.

After seeing how packed his plate was with the crispy fried chicken, macaroni and cheese and corn on the cob, my reply to him was, "Yep, it sure does."

"Well, go on in the bathroom and wash your hands while I make you a plate," Mrs. Simmons instructed me.

"Okay," I said and left the kitchen. When I returned, Mrs. Simmons had a placemat set up for me with a plate of piping hot food sitting on top of it. And there standing next to it was a tall glass of sweet iced tea. Boy, did I think I was in heaven.

"Go 'head and enjoy," she insisted as she took a seat next to mine and proceeded to dig into a plate of her own.

Now during dinner, we chatted a little bit about where I was living, the issues with my car and the deal about why I hadn't been looking for employment. And through it all, I was blatantly honest with them and they appreciated it. So, after dinner was over, I took a long, hot shower and slipped in a pair of fitted BeBe jeans I had left here some time ago, since all my other clothes were dirty. Speaking of which, Mrs. Simmons also allowed me to wash all the clothes I had in my car. Too bad, I left the bulk of them back at Teresa's apartment. But, it was okay. I'll get around to getting them later.

Meanwhile, we all sat around in the den area and

talked a little more. But if I would've known that they were going to be giving me jaw-dropping expressions, then I would've kept everything to myself. I mean, it was evident that they couldn't handle what I was saying. But hey, it was too late! The cat had already been let out of the bag.

"So, you mean to tell me you've been using anywhere from five to ten capsules of heroin a day?" Mrs. Simmons asked me as if she wanted some kind of clarification.

"Yep," I said as I nodded my head.

"But, you're not shooting it up, right?" Mr. Simmons interjected.

"No, way! I'm too scared to push a needle in my arm."

"So, you say the lady you're living with is on heroin really bad as well?" Mrs. Simmons continued.

"Yeah, but she's worse off than I am."

"How so?" she wanted to know.

I sighed heavily and said, "Mrs. Simmons, I have seen that girl go through a period of depression because of the loss of her brother. Then I've witnessed her get her butt kicked by different drug dealers, because she either stole something from them or owed them money; and then not even a hour goes by and she's right back on her feet, with black eyes and busted lips, trying to mastermind another scheme to get her next high."

"Oh, my God! This girl is a walking time bomb," she expressed.

"You got that right," Mr. Simmons interjected once again. "So, we gotta' get you out of that environment and get you back to the status you used to be at."

"That's right!" Mrs. Simmons declared as she

began to massage my knee. "And if you're ready, we can make a few phones calls today and get you on your way."

"We sure can. But, you've got to be ready," he added.

"Well, if this is the path I've gotta take to be reunited with my family, then I'm ready," I assured them. "But, I'm gonna need to go back to my girlfriend's apartment to get the rest of my things."

"How long will that take you to do that?" Mrs. Simmons wanted to know.

"What time is it now?" I asked.

Mr. Simmons looked down at his wristwatch and said, "It's seven o'clock."

"Well, it shouldn't take me no longer than an hour or two to pack up the rest of my things and tidy up a bit."

"Well, what are you waiting for? Go 'head and take care of it," he continued.

"Yes, baby, hurry up and go on over there so you can get back here before it gets too late," Mrs. Simmons added.

"Okay, I will. But, I'm gonna need a small favor from you guys," I said, with a little hesitation.

"What's that, sweetie?" Mrs. Simmons asked first.

"Well, to be honest with you two, I rode over here on mere fumes. So, I was wondering if I could get a few dollars to put some gas in my tank?"

"Oh sure, darling." Mrs. Simmons replied. And then she looked at her husband and asked him if he had some cash on him.

"Yeah, how much you need?" He asked her as he went into his wallet.

"Just give me thirty dollars," she instructed him. "That should be enough to fill up her gas tank."

So, immediately after he counted out thirty dollars exactly, he handed it straight to Mrs. Simmons who, in turn, handed it to me. And before it reached my hand, I told them both how much I appreciated their help.

"You don't have to thank us," she told me. "Just show us your appreciation by taking that first step to getting yourself together."

"I will," I promised them and then we all hugged as I was about to leave.

"Hurry up and come back, now!" Mrs. Simmons said as she waved me off from her front door.

"I will," I assured her as I began to drive off.

Now I was not lying when I told you how much relief I felt after airing out my dirty laundry to my in-laws. But, what really felt good was the fact that they did not judge me. All they required of me was for me to get my life back in order, and that's just what I intended to do.

Chapter 21

Fucking with a Head Banger

I only used fifteen of the thirty dollars to put some gas in my car, which wasn't too bad, considering it gave me almost a half a tank. I kept the other fifteen in my pocket because I didn't want to feel like I was broke all over again. Believe me, that was an awful feeling and I didn't want to ever experience that again.

Now, when I arrived back at Teresa's apartment I noticed from the way I left the place that she still had not made it back in, so instead of me coming there to do what I was supposed to do, I found myself walking back out the front door and taking a drive out to Grandy Park. I realized that I wouldn't rest tonight unless I knew she was all right. So, when I got out there, the first person who rushed up to my car was Papoose. Now, the last time I saw this crazy motherfucker was when he brought my car back to me later than he was supposed to. And then, when I tried to straighten him out about it, he got in my face and threatened to fuck me up.

So, after that incident happened, I made it my business to stay away from him. "I got that Predator," he told me as he leaned into my car window.

"I'm not trying to score right now. I came out here to see if I can find my girlfriend, Teresa."

"Who, that little, skinny, light-skinned chick with the long hair?"

"Yeah, so have you seen her?"

"Nah, I ain't seen her today. But, she came through last night, a couple times."

"Who was she with?" My questions continued.

"I saw her with that ugly chick Zena, the first time she came through. But, she was by herself the second time I saw her."

"Well, how long you been out here today?"

"Damn, you sho' asking a nigga a whole lot of mu'fucking questions not to be spending no money!" he replied in a sarcastic manner.

"Look Papoose, I ain't trying to clock you, for real. I'm just trying to find out if somebody seen her today, so I can stop worrying about her."

Papoose laughed and said, "Come on now, your peoples is a dope fiend. A fucking gutter rat. So, you ain't suppose to be worried about her, 'cause she's gon' be a'ight!"

"You know what, Papoose, she may be all those things, but she's still my friend."

"What's that, some kind of speech to form an allegiance for all the dope fiends?" he continued with more laughter.

But, I didn't find his comment funny, so I shook my head with disgust and said, "That's really cute."

"Nah, what's cute is you," he said as he rubbed his hand across my shoulder. "I ain't never seen you look like this. And your pussy looks real phat in dem jeans too," he continued as he looked down at the crotch of my pants.

Hearing this lame-ass nigga comment on how phat my pussy looked in my pants was not what I deemed a hot pick-up line, so I placed my right hand over my crotch and said, "Well, the reason why I look like this is because I'm trying to clean up my act."

"When did you decide to do that? 'Cause I just saw you out here day before yesterday."

"I know. But now, I'm tired of running these streets and then waking up in the morning with no money and no food to eat. So, I figured if I want a better life for myself, then I've got to go and check into a rehab center."

"So, when you gon' do that?"

"In the morning."

"Damn, that's good," he said, as he opened up his right hand. "But, before you go, let me give you a sample of this bomb-ass shit I got, as a going-away present."

"Nah, that's all right." I replied in a hesitant manner.

"Girl, you better take this shit! 'Cause, it ain't often that I give out freebies like this," he insisted as he threw two pills onto my lap. "And just in case you decide that you ain't trying to go to that rehab joint, come holler at me. I'll put you up in a nice spot and you ain't gotta ever worry about waking up with out some dough in your pocket or food to eat, 'cause I'll look out for you decent," he continued, as he stood up and backed away from my car.

I chuckled and said, "Yeah, right!"

"Oh, so you think I'm joking?"

"I don't think you are. I know you are," I replied with certainty.

"Well, what am I gon' have to do to show you that I'm serious as a mu'fucka?"

"How old are you?"

"I'm twenty-three, why?"

"Well, I'm thirty-five and I'm married. So, it'll never work."

"A'ight! If you say so. But, if you decide to change your mind, come look me up, 'cause I can use a new girlfriend."

"Yeah, okay," I said with little or no enthusiasm at all. And then I pressed down on my accelerator and waved him off as I began to drive away. "Thanks," I told him and kept right on going.

Now, don't get me wrong, the guy was a cutie himself. And he reminded me of that R&B singer Tyrese. I'm talking about the height, the blackness of his skin complexion, not to mention his body. And not only that, homeboy was wearing the hell out of a fucking white tank top. He's even got a nice build. But, the motherfucker crazy! So, all that shit he was talking, he could save it for one of those little hood rat chicks out here, because I wasn't going for it. Not today, or tomorrow. And that was some real shit!

So, as I continued to cruise down the main strip, I looked down and grabbed both caps of dope from my lap and slid them in the top right side pocket of my jeans. And the moment I looked up, there standing at the corner, looking like she was about to cross the street, was Zena, so I immediately pulled my car over to the curb and called out her name.

"What's up?" she said as she approached the car, looking half dead with a ton of open sores all over her arms, legs and neck.

"You seen Teresa today?" I didn't hesitate to ask.

"Yeah, she just came through here about two hours ago."

"Did she say whether or not she was going back home?"

"Nah, she didn't say. But, she was wit' that nigga Walt, so they probably went back to his spot."

"Who is he? And where does he be at?" My questions continued as I tried to jog my memory as to who he was.

"You don't know Walt?" she asked me.

"Not to my knowledge," I assured her.

"I'm surprised, 'cause everybody knows that crafty-ass nigga."

"How does he look?"

"Shit, he looks like us!" She began to explain. "He ain't nothing but a fucking junkie, like the rest of us."

"I kind of figured that much out. But, is he tall, short, what?"

"Oh he's a tall, old-school nigga with a whole bunch of hair on his face. And he always wearing this red baseball cap."

"Where is his spot?"

"He lives out Huntersville, on 'A' Avenue. Mu'- fucka's who ain't got nowhere to go be camping out over there. But, in order for you to get through the door, you gon' either have to pay the house man two dollars or share your dope wit' 'em."

"So, I'm assuming that Walt is the house man."

"That's right," she replied and then, out of nowhere, she starts digging in several of the open sores on her arm.

"Girl, you need to take your ass to the hospital and have them look at that before it gets infected," I warned her.

"It's already infected," she responded nonchalantly.

"Well, why don't you go and get it treated?"

"Because I ain't got time. Dem doctors and nurses at dem muthafucking hospitals be having you sitting 'round that joint, waiting all day long like you ain't got shit to do. So, I just said fuck it! But, I have been taking a few of dem antibiotics whenever I run across somebody with 'em."

"Well, are the antibiotics working?"

"They might. They might not be. Who knows?" she continued as she began to scratch a couple of the open sores around her neck, which eventually started leaking pus. The shit scared the hell out of me and I was ready to go. So, I told her I'd see her some other time and drove the hell off before some of that shit she had coming out of her skin, dropped into my car. And you know I couldn't have that.

As I drove off, I looked into my rearview mirror and watched her as she continued to stand there, with no regard for her health. She honestly had no remote interest to go and get herself treated for those abscesses because in other words, she wasn't trying to miss out on the next big thing out here on these streets. Poor thang! She was really far gone and too blind to even see it.

* * *

Well, since I know Teresa was hanging out in Huntersville at Walt's house, I didn't have to worry about her silly ass anymore. Too bad, I wasn't gonna be able to tell her goodbye. But hey, she was the one who left me in the house stranded. So, I couldn't really feel bad. And now I could carry my ass back to her place and pack up my things. But while I was there, I would take the time out and leave her a letter where she could find it.

I didn't take me long at all to pack up the rest of my things and put everything in my car. And right when I was about to leave, I realized that I had forgotten to do something. So, when I returned into the house, I then realized that I had forgotten to write Teresa a goodbye letter.

Now as I was about to sit down at the kitchen table and lay out a few words on this sheet paper I dug out of an old note pad, Teresa came walking through the front door, looking like she was spaced the fuck out.

"Oh, so now you decide to come back home," I commented sarcastically.

"Whatcha' mean by that?" she asked me, as if she hadn't the slightest clue of what I was talking about.

"Come on now, Teresa. You been gon' ever since yesterday afternoon. And before you left, you told me you were gonna come right back after you made a few moves and went to the damn grocery store. But instead of doing that, you left me in this motherfucker stranded, with nothing to eat and no fucking running water. So, you're gonna stand here and ask me what the hell I mean?" I replied with a bitter expression.

Teresa sat down to the table and said, "Girl, I forgot all about that," she told me as her words slurred.

"No shit!"

"No, I'm serious," she began to explain. "I got out there yesterday and tried to push them three dummies off of a couple of people, but wasn't nobody trying to score from me. Everybody was running to them niggas with that new dope called Helter Skelter. So, I ended up holding on to them damn things and then I fucked around and had to throw 'em down on the ground when the narcs came rolling through there."

"Well, why didn't you just come back here?"

"Come back here for what? I ain't have shit to bring here with me," she replied in an animated way, making gestures with her hands. "And not only that, I started feeling really ill, so I just stayed my ass out there until I was able to trick some shit up."

"Well, did you get what you needed?" My questions kept coming in a sarcastic manner.

"Not really. But, a few muthafuckas looked out for me," she told me and then she said, "Oh yeah, Zena told me you came out there looking for me."

"Yes, I did. You had me worried to death, sitting around here waiting for you. Shit, I didn't know what to think."

Teresa gave me another one of her cheesy smiles and said, "Ahhh, that's so sweet!"

"Sweet, my ass! I am not going to keep going through this dumb shit with you. That's why I packed up my shit."

"Where you going?" she asked as her facial expression changed.

"I'm gonna check into a rehab center in the morning."

"But, why?"

"Because I'm tired of living like this. I mean, look at this place. It's a fucking mess. We don't have a damn thing in here to eat. The water is cut off. The lights are going to be next. And then, on top of that, you're about to be put out on the streets for not paying the rent. So, do you think I wanna sit around here and wait for all that to happen, when I can leave now?"

"Oh, so you're trying to shit on me, now?" she struck back, but this time her words came out a little more clear.

"And why would I do that?" I asked her. "I'm in no better position than you right now. I'm only trying to get you to see what's really going on around here."

"I don't need you to point shit out to me. I'm not blind!"

"Well, if you ain't blind, then do something about it."

"I will. You'll see." She told me as if she was trying desperately to convince me.

"Okay. I believe you," I replied and stood up from the chair.

"So, you're getting ready to leave now?"

I sighed and said, "Yeah. It's time for me to go."

"Well, can you at least stay here for one more night?"

"I can't."

"Why not?" She pressed the issue.

"Because I promised my mother-in-law that I would come right back, after I gathered up my things."

"Oh, so that's whose putting you in a rehab?"

"Yep," I said and I slid the chair underneath the table.

"What is your husband saying about it?"

"He doesn't know. Me and his parents are going to keep it a secret until after I get out."

"Do you know where you're going?"

"Nah, not yet. They said they were going to make a few phone calls while I was gone. But, it really doesn't matter. I just want to get it over with, so I can get my family back."

"Well, I can't blame you for that," Teresa said, as she stood up next to me. "I would be trying to do the same thing if I was in your shoes. So, before I let you out of my sight, we are gonna have to celebrate one last time."

"Nah, that's okay."

"Come on, Faith, one last time ain't gonna hurt you."

"I know. But, Mr. and Mrs. Simmons are waiting on me."

"Okay, I understand all that. But, this is your last night of freedom. So, enjoy it!" she pressed on.

So, here I was, once again standing before my best friend, hesitating to make a judgment call. And it seemed like every time she forced my back up against the wall, I always gave in. I mean, it was like she had this effect on me, whereas I couldn't tell her no. But, I told myself I couldn't let her have her way this time, which meant I needed to stand my ground. So, I looked at her and said, "Sorry! But, I got to go."

"So, you gon' run out on me like that?" she sounded disappointed.

"Teresa, I am not trying to fuck around with that anymore."

"I understand all that. But, you act like the shit is gon' kill you. And besides, a whole lot of muthafuckers who be getting ready to go off into detox, always get fucked up the night before they leave. It's like a fucking ritual."

Now instead of commenting, I just stood there. So, she grabbed me by my arm and pulled me in the direction of the living room. And like a dummy with no brains, I followed. "Now, all I got is a little bit of this shit left but since this is your last night, I'm gon' show you some love," she continued as she laid everything out on the coffee table. And as she was doing that, it dawned on me that Papoose had given me two pills of his dope earlier. So, I pulled them out of my pocket and laid them out on the table with the rest of the stuff. And that's when Teresa's eyes lit up.

"Wait a minute, that looks like two caps of that Predator," she didn't hesitate to say.

"It is."

"And how the hell did you get that?"

"When I came out there looking for you today, Papoose ran up to my car and just gave 'em to me."

"Whatcha', mean, he just gave 'em to you?"

"Well, first of all, he flagged me down to see if I wanted to cop. But when I told him that I wasn't trying to fuck around like that anymore because I was going in a rehab, he threw both of the caps at me and told me to take it as a going-away present. And then before I pulled off, he commented on how phat my pussy looked in these jeans, and then he had the nerve to tell me that if I changed my mind about going in, then to come look him up 'cause he's looking for a new girlfriend."

"Oh yeah, if that nigga said that, then he's trying to get with you, for real."

"Girl, please, I am not thinking about none of that shit he was talking about."

"Well, did you tell him that?"

"No. I just laughed at him and pulled away."

"Well, you should've gotten his cell phone number."

"For what?"

"Because, if a nigga will give you free dope one time, then trust me, you'll be able to get it again."

"Girl, I am not fucking with that young-ass boy."

"Shit! Don't sleep on him. 'Cause, that young boy got plenty of money. And if you played your cards right, he'll damn sho' give you some of it."

"Well, that's flattering. But, I'm trying to get my husband back. So, fuck that young boy!"

"Well, suit yourself." Teresa said as she injected the needle in the side of her stomach, which of course freaked me the hell out. So, I said, "What the fuck are you doing?"

"Girl, calm down! I got this."

"Whatcha' trying to do, kill your baby?"

"Now, how am I trying to kill her when all I'm doing is skin popping?"

"Why aren't you shooting it up in your arms?"

"Because I've used up all the veins in 'em."

"Well, I know you still got some good veins in your legs."

"Yeah, I do. But, I'm just not trying to go there right now."

I shook my head in disbelief, closed my mouth and didn't utter another word. I could sense she was getting irritated because I was fucking up her high, so I chilled out and let her do her thing. Now, once I got my nerves back intact, I pushed the tip of the straw in both of my nostrils and waited for the drug to take effect. And as expected, the shit started working instantly. So, once again I was traveling down the yellow brick road. And I was loving every minute of it.

Chapter 22

Forced to
Hit the Streets

After Teresa and I put a hurting on both caps of that Predator, we went out right back out Grandy Park around four o'clock in the morning and scored two more caps. Too bad we couldn't get some of that Predator, because our minds was dead set on copping some. So instead, we ended up scoring from some rookie-ass nigga out there named Spanky. He was holding the red bags, which was some okay dope, so he let us get them both with the last fifteen dollars I had in my pocket. And of course that meant that I was broke all over again.

Now, when we returned back to the apartment, we divided up our purchase. I took one pill, she took the other one and we both wasted little or no time going right through it, so our high was an instant hit, but it didn't last very long. And trust me, it made us livid too. So by six in the morning, we were right back to square one, sitting around in her living room, trying to think of a way we can come up with ten more dollars so we can score another pill of dope. And from the way things were looking, our options were very limited.

"You don't have anything to sell?" Teresa asked me while she paced back and forth through the apartment.

"Nah. You know I've already sold every piece of jewelry I had, except for my wedding band. And you know I can't get rid of that."

"What about your car?"

"What about it?" I asked with uncertainty.

"You can lend it out again for about $200 worth of dope. Just like last time," she replied, as if she had come up with a brilliant idea.

So I threw the same exact idea back into her lap, but she wasn't so receptive. "Girl please, ain't nobody gonna want to rent my beat-up ass car. But trust me, they'll love to have yours."

Now instead of responding immediately, I began to weigh the pros and the cons of this so-called brilliant idea of hers. Because, remember, I'd been burned before by letting irresponsible-ass niggas drive my shit around town with no consideration for timing or for the wear and tear of it. So, as I began to even entertain the thought of allowing it to happen again, Teresa came out of nowhere with another one of her suggestions.

"Listen, I know you don't want to do it, but look at it this way," she began to say, "at the end of the day, we are going to be high as a motherfucking kite. And you are going to have your car back, even if means that you gotta get the police involved to get it. So, it's a win-win situation."

"But, who wants to go through all that?"

"Nobody. I just threw that out there, so you'll feel a little better about going through with the whole thing."

"Well, I'll tell you what, whoever I decide to let drive my car has to have a license this time, or I just say fuck it!"

"All right. I think we can manage that," Teresa replied in a giddy manner, because she knew she was about to get her hands on some more of that good dope.

It was six-thirty in the morning and I was right back out in Grandy Park again, cruising through the main strip, looking for a semi-responsible young boy to lend my car to. And when Teresa finally spotted one, she told me to pull over. So, I did. And that's when she said, "You see that light-skinned nigga right there, with the white tee and blue jean shorts?"

"Yeah. What about him?" I replied.

"Well, his name is K-Rock. And he's down with dem niggas who got that new dope called Helter Skelter. So, if we can get him to give us a little bit of cash to put in our pockets and some of that good shit he be having, then we gon' be straight."

"All right. Well, go and see what he's talking about, but make sure he's got a license."

"A'ight," Teresa said, as she stepped out of the car.

"Oh and I want to see it too." I told her as she walked away.

Meanwhile, I was sitting back in my car, watching Teresa while she waited in line behind a crowd of fiends, whom this guy was serving. Suddenly, I got a tap on my window. Now I will not lie, the shit scared the hell out of me because it was so unexpected. And when I looked around and saw that it was Papoose, I nearly wanted to pass out because I had just told him the day before I wasn't fucking around with dope anymore, because I was trying to get myself together. And here I was, posted up in a drug spot, waiting for my home girl to make some arrangements so we could make a trade-off with a nigga named K-Rock. Now, could you imagine how humiliated I was feeling?

So, as I began to roll down the driver's side window, I braced myself for the inevitable. Niggas like him will disrespect and clown a person on drugs real quick. They look at us like we're less than them, because of our substance abuse. And they categorize us as being weak too. That's why you would find a whole lot of old-school dope fiends getting their asses kicked out here by these young-ass dealers. But quiet as it is kept, on a good day these old-school cats will stomp a mud hole in these young-ass boys if they didn't fear that there will be some kind retaliation from the other crew members. So, when shit gets really hectic, a fiend will just lay there and take an ass whipping real quick, versus fighting back and getting their asses shot later. And I can't blame them one bit.

"What's up, beautiful?" Papoose didn't hesitate to say.

"You can sure spot me anywhere, huh?"

"I recognized your car."

"Yeah, it does kind of stand out," I said.

"So, whatcha doing back out here?" He jumped straight to the punch. "I thought you was going in that rehab joint this morning."

"Yeah, I was." I began to say, as I was preparing a lie in my head. "But, the center I was scheduled to go to didn't have my paperwork right, so I've got to wait a couple of days until they can straighten everything out."

"So, who are you out here with?" His questions continued.

"My girlfriend, Teresa."

"Where she at?"

"Right there." I replied, pointing in the direction where Teresa was standing.

"Oh, she's trying to score from K-Rock?"

"I don't know what she's trying to do. All I know is that she asked me to bring her out here because he owed her a favor."

"Yeah, a'ight! Whatever!" he commented as if he didn't believe one word I just said. "So, what's up?" he continued.

"Whatcha' mean?" I asked.

And before I knew it, he stuck his head through my car window and tried to kiss my neck. So, I jerked my head a little and asked him why was he trying to kiss me.

"Because I'm trying to be wit' you. But, you're playing games." He replied as he pulled his head back out of the window.

"But, why?" I asked, hoping to get a logical explanation.

"Come on now, look at you!" He began to say, "You're cute as hell. You got a banging-ass body. And I can tell you're intelligent by the way you be talking sometimes. So, all I'm saying to you is that you don't need to be going to a rehab center to get your shit together. 'Cause if you really ain't trying to fuck with that dope no more, then I can help you."

I laughed and said, "Now, how can you help me?"

"Trust me, sweetheart I know plenty of mu'fuckas

who can getcha' some of them meth pills. And when you get a couple of them joints in your system, you ain't gon' have no choice but to kick that habit."

"Well, what is it going to take for you to get me some?"

"All you got to do is say the word and I'll put you up in a nice-ass hotel and we can get the ball rolling."

"Well, let me ask you this."

"What's up?"

"What are you going to get out of all this?"

"I'm just trying to be with you. That's it and that's all."

"Do you have any idea how old I am?"

"I think you already told me. But, it really doesn't matter, if you wanna know the truth," he replied with such sincerity. And from his tone alone, I couldn't do nothing but take him up on his offer. So right when I was getting ready to give him the green light, Teresa came running up to the car saying, "Hey Faith, he said he'll do it, but he'll only give us fifty dollars in cash and the rest in dope."

Papoose looked at me and said, "What the fuck is she talking about?"

"Well, um . . ." I said as I began to stutter. So, he cut me off in an instant and said, "I hope you ain't about to do nothing stupid with that nigga K-Rock."

"Nah," I replied as I shook my head.

"So, what is your girlfriend over here talking about? He pressed the issue. "Because if you don't tell me, I can go over there and find out on my own."

Feeling my back against the wall, I saw no other option but to be honest with him, since he had an interest in helping me. So, I gave in and told him what me and Teresa's intentions were. And of course, he made his objection towards it. And while he was going off at the mouth about why I didn't need to lend out my car, Teresa just stood there and listened.

"So, whatcha' want me to tell 'em?" She finally got a word in.

"Tell 'em she ain't interested."

But, Teresa wasn't trying to hear that bullshit Papoose was talking so she looked at me for the final say. And that's when I said, "Yeah, tell 'em that's all right."

Pissed off by my response, she said, "Why the hell you changing your mind today, out of all days? Shit, you know I need my fix."

"Well, that's too bad, because she's got other plans!" Papoose interjected.

"What kind of plans?" she asked looking directly at me.

"He's going to put me up in a hotel and help me kick this dope habit," I told her.

"Girl, please, what hustler you know gon' take a dope fiend off the street and clean her up? When he can go out here and pick up any woman he wants, that's already clean."

"You looking at 'em," Papoose blurted out.

"Yeah, whatever," Teresa replied and threw her hands in the air.

"Sweetheart, don't be mad 'cause ain't nobody trying to get you off the streets!"

"I'm not mad, because I'm not ready to get off these streets."

"It's hard to tell 'cause as big as your stomach looks, you need to be at home," he said laughing.

"Don't worry about me. I'm fine."

"Yeah, that's what they all say. But, I ain't gon' get

on you too hard, 'cause you're Faith's peoples. So, to show you I ain't no bad individual, I'm gon' look out for you since I'm getting ready to snatch up your peoples right here. Now, all you gotta do is hold tight and I'll be right back. A'ight?"

"A'ight," Teresa said and then we both witnessed him as he dashed to the apartment building sitting directly across the street from where we were parked.

And almost immediately after he disappeared by the black iron door, Teresa rushed over to the driver's side door and began to throw a whole bunch of questions at me.

"What the hell has gotten into you, just that fast?"

"Nothing."

"Shit! I can't tell, when you got that motherfucker answering all your questions for you."

"Look, all I wanna do is get my shit straight. And he said he's gon' help me. So, why would I turn that down?"

"Faith, that nigga is a fucking heroin dealer. So, how in the hell is he going to wean you off some shit he's out here selling, all day long?"

"He told me he was going to get me some of those meth pills."

"Girl, please, that shit ain't nothing but a fucking Band-Aid. 'Cause if the shit really worked, don't you think there wouldn't be a soul out here getting high?"

"I don't know."

"Well, you better find out. 'Cause, this game out here is for real. And trust me when I tell you that Papoose got some other shit up his sleeve for your ass. So, you better keep your eyes open and watch every move that motherfucker takes."

"Oh trust me, I will."

"You better, because I've seen him fuck up plenty of these bitches asses out here behind dumb shit. And the nigga didn't blink his eyes not one time."

"Well, I'm not gonna have to worry about that, because I'm gonna tell him from the door that I don't tolerate men hitting on women."

"And you think that's gon' work?"

"Yeah."

"Well, think again. 'Cause that nigga doesn't have one ounce of respect for no one but himself."

"Yeah, okay. We'll see," I replied in a casual way, only to let Teresa know that all that stuff she's talking about doesn't apply to me. So, I am letting it go right over my head.

Soon after our discussion had ended, Papoose came running back toward us with a blue logo-type T-shirt in his left hand. His other hand was balled up in a fist, so he could have anything hidden in there.

Sounding out of breath, he walked up to Teresa and handed her a couple pills of his dope. And like clockwork, her face lit up like a corner street light. "Good looking out!" she said with one of her most famous cheesy expressions.

"Don't mention it," he told her. "Just take your ass on home and get off these streets."

"But, how am I gon' get there? Faith was my ride."

"Here take this twenty dollars and call a cab." he continued as he handed her a twenty-dollar bill.

"A'ight. No problem," she said, as she eagerly took the money out of his hands.

"Are you gon' be all right?" I asked her while she was trying to get herself situated.

"Oh yeah, I'm straight," she replied acting all giddy.

"Well, take care. And I'll see you later."

"A'ight." she walked away from the car.

"I wonder if she's going to be all right," I commented to Papoose the moment he sat down in the passenger seat.

"Hell yeah! Home girl is a veteran out here. So, trust me, she's gon' be a'ight!"

"If you say so," I replied, sighing heavily; and then I started up the ignition and drove off.

Chapter 23

Using My
Money Maker

We drove approximately thirty-five minutes and ended up in the Great Bridge section of Chesapeake. And when we came upon the Marriott Hotel he instructed me to pull over, so I did.

"You got your license on you?" he asked me.

"Yes, why? You need me to get a room in my name?"

"Yeah," he replied and handed me three fifty-dollar bills.

I took the money out of his hand, got out of the car and walked into the hotel. It only took me about five minutes to book the room and pay for it, and when I returned to the car with the room key in hand, he had a smile on his face.

"What are you smiling for?" I asked him as I handed him the key.

"I'm just looking at how cute you are," he responded as he exited the car.

"Now, how many times are you going to tell me that?" I asked, desperately trying not to smile.

"Whatcha' don't appreciate compliments, or something?"

"It's not that."

"Then what is it?" he asked as we entered into the lobby of the hotel.

"It's nothing really. I just don't feel like I deserve a compliment right now. I mean, look at me. I got on the same clothes as I did yesterday."

"Shit, that ain't nothing a shower can't handle."

I laughed at Papoose's sense of humor and we both continued carrying on our conversation all the way to the room. Now, once we entered into the room, shit got a little more formal and it was evident that he couldn't wait to show off his manhood, too. But, I felt it was necessary to slow things down a bit because for one, my stomach was beginning to growl and two, I was also getting ill with the stomach cramps. So, right then and there, I knew that if I was going to do anything with this man, he was gonna have to pump me up with a couple of those meth pills and get me something to eat.

"I'm not feeling too good," I warned him as I sat down at the foot of the bed.

"What's wrong?" he asked me from the other side of the bed.

"I'm hungry, for one. And I'm starting to feel a little ill," I replied.

"Well, I guess you can order some room service. But, I'm gon' have to make a phone call to get you dem meth pills."

"Okay, I'll call and order room service. But, will

you make that phone call for me, before I get too sick to do anything?"

"Oh, don't worry, I'm gon' get on top of that now," he told me and pulled out his cellular phone.

Now by the time he made the phone call to his methadone connection, I had also called in a breakfast order for guest services to deliver it to the room, and it came in no time. Papoose and I both sat down at the table and enjoyed every bite of the buttermilk pancakes, scrambled eggs with cheese and the plentiful amount of turkey bacon they stacked on the plate. We each had a tall glass of ice cold orange juice that set the entire breakfast off. And before long, we were both laid out on the bed with our stomachs filled to capacity. He was stretched out on one side of the bed and I was on the other side, laying back with my eyes closed, praying that this friend will knock on the door in the next twenty minutes or so. And to my surprise, he did. So, Papoose greeted him at the door.

"Come on in, nigga!" he said and gave the guy a handshake to shoulder hug.

And when the guy stepped around the door, he and I recognized each other immediately. But, he was the first to say something. "Yo' don't I know you?" he asked me as he walked closer to the bed.

I nodded my head.

"From where, though?" he pressed on while Papoose stood alongside him and waited for me to answer.

"I'm Tee's friend," I finally responded.

"Tee?" he said with uncertainty.

"Yeah, Tee," I said as I turned completely around toward him. "The one whose brother got killed in Grandy Park, not too long ago."

"Oh yeah!" he said, as he placed one hand over his

mouth and laughed. "I remember you. You're the chick who came over there and saved Teresa and her brother Eugene from getting their ass fucked up real good, because they owed me some dough."

"Yo', how she do that?" Papoose interjected.

"Yo', Papoose man, Shorty right there is a lifesaver, son! I mean, when dem two fucking junkies couldn't come up with my dough, Shorty came through for them and paid me herself."

Papoose smiled and said, "Word!"

Lamont nodded his head and said, "Yep. She saved their ass!"

"Damn, Faith, you're all right!" Papoose said to me.

"Yeah, she's cool!" Lamont blurted out. "But, a few weeks later, I had to slap her ass on the floor for trying to stop me from fucking her friend up."

"Oh shit! She's a trooper too!" Papoose said with excitement.

"Yeah, she's got plenty of balls! But, I had to strip dem joints from her after she ran up on me," Lamont replied as he continued to chuckle. But then his laughter stopped when his cellular phone started chirping, so he said, "Wait, let me see who just sent me a text message."

So, Papoose walked away from him to give him enough space and privacy to read his message. But, it seemed like whatever message he had just received was very short, because he closed his Sidekick back up and placed it right back on his hip. And from there, he went into business mode. "So, whatcha' trying to get?" he asked Papoose, who by this time was sitting at the table, counting a small stack of cash he pulled from his pocket.

"How much are they going for?" Papoose wanted to know.

"Five joints a piece," Lamont replied, as he pulled a clear ziplock bag from his left pocket.

"Well, ummm . . ." he began to say, as he ran a few numbers in his head. "Give me twenty of dem things."

"A'ight," Lamont said as he counted out twenty white tablets and handed them all to Papoose.

In exchange, Papoose handed him one hundred dollars. And after the transaction was completed, Papoose escorted him outside the room. But before Lamont made his exit, he looked back at me and said, "Have fun!"

And of course I didn't respond, I just waved the clown off and said to myself, "Good riddance."

Now while they were both standing outside in the hallway, I could hear them laughing and joking. But for the life of me, I couldn't make out what they were saying. So, I laid back on the bed and turned onto my stomach for a little comfort and here came Papoose walking through the door, smiling like he had just won the fucking lottery or something. And that's when I asked him, "Whatcha' smiling for?"

"Because I'm happy."

"What are you happy about?"

"About a whole lot of things."

"Like what?" I pressed on.

"If I told you, you wouldn't understand."

"Well, try me."

"Nah," he said, as he climbed onto the bed, "maybe I'll tell you later."

"Okay, that's fine." I said.

So, he slid a little closer to me and asked me how badly did I want those pills? And my answer to him was, "What do you think?"

"Well, I can't answer that. Because I would be

putting words in your mouth. So, I want to hear it from you."

I hesitated for a moment, trying to gather up the right words in my mind that would best describe how I was feeling at this very moment, but for some reason all I could say was, "Because I'm hurting."

"A'ight," Papoose said as he stripped off his white tank top and placed two of the methadone pills right on top of his stomach, revealing his awesome-looking six-pack. "Now, show me how bad you want these two pills right here," he continued as he looked me directly into my eyes.

Now, I knew exactly what that meant. And for him to come off on me like that, humiliated the hell out of me. But, what other option did I have? I mean, this nigga had me exactly where he wanted me and there was absolutely nothing I could do about it but go with the flow. So, I got up on my knees and crawled over towards him.

"Take off your shirt and your bra," he instructed me.

So, I stopped in my tracks, knelt on my knees and pulled off both my shirt and bra. And after he got his first glimpse of my breasts, he said, "Damn, Shorty, you got some pretty-ass titties!"

I didn't comment, but I did smile.

"Are dem' joints real?" he asked me with a puzzled expression.

"Yes, they are," I assured him and then I got back down on my hands and started crawling towards him. And as soon as I got in the position he wanted me, he had me unzip his jeans and pull his already-hard dick through the open slit of his boxers.

"Lick the head," he told me as he started massaging and squeezing my left breast in his hand.

So, I did. But then he said, "Let me see if you can put my whole joint in your mouth."

Now before I did just that, I measured his entire dick with my eyes and played around with it with my tongue. And once I was sure that I wouldn't humiliate myself and gag on it, I pushed the whole thing into my mouth like it was nothing. And he went crazy. "Ahh, shit!" he said as I tightened my mouth around the base of it. "You got some mu'fucking skills, girl!"

I didn't comment because my mouth was too full. But, I was able to look him into his eyes and wink. And that drove him crazy too. So, I had to admit that I was starting to enjoy myself.

Meanwhile I was serving homeboy up, unbelievably my pussy started getting all moist and wet. I mean, it was a total shock to me because I was getting turned on by a man who wasn't even my husband, and it was beginning to feel really strange. But, then I figured that your heart wasn't going to lie to you. So, I said fuck it, and kept on doing what I was doing.

"Damn right, Faith, suck this dick, girl!" he kept saying as he moaned uncontrollably.

And it's crazy because when you hear a man moan with passion the shit will turn a woman on and make her go that extra mile to get him to climax. So, that's what I did as I started stroking the shaft with one hand and sucking the tip of the head with my mouth. "Ahh shit!" he said immediately after I engulfed his whole dick into my mouth once again.

"You like this, don't cha'?" I asked in a cocky manner between licks.

"You mutha'fucking right!" Papoose screamed out to the top of his voice.

And for a minute there, I thought this nigga was turning into a little bitch from that scream he hurdled out of his mouth. But, I chalked it up and laughed and knew from that point that I was doing my thing.

"Oh yeah . . . Shorty, I'm about to cum," he warned me and closed his eyes.

So, I tightened my mouth around the head some more and continued to pump his dick like I was trying to get water from a well. And after thirty more seconds of this, homeboy's body started trembling like he was about to go into cardiac arrest. "I'm cumming! I'm cumming!" he warned me once more. And then out of nowhere, this nigga shot about two ounces of this warm, milk-like texture into my mouth, but I refused to swallow it. So, I played it off and opened my mouth just enough around the head and released every drop of it down the sides of this dick while I was still sucking on it.

"Oh yeah," he said as he opened up his eyes and slapped the back of my ass. "You got some good mutha'fucking head!"

"Yeah, my husband tells me the same thing," I told him as I began to search for the two methadone pills that fell somewhere on the bed, near where we were.

"Well, your husband sho' knows what he's talking about," he commented as he got up from the bed and headed into the bathroom.

But, I wasn't paying his ass no mind. My main concern right now was locating those two pills. So, I continued my search and finally found them both. And when I got them in my hands, I rushed to the table and grabbed my half-filled glass of orange juice, threw my head back, tossed both of them down my throat and sent the orange juice down behind it.

Now, it took about ten minutes or so for the pills to work. And when these bad boys started taking effect, I felt like I was high all over again.

I mean, the shit was good! And Papoose was right, it definitely killed the cravings of that heroin, too. So, I figured with the rest of that supply he had for me, I was going to be all right.

Chapter 24

The Devil in Sheep's Clothing

Papoose and I have been staying in this hotel room for about three weeks now and I must admit that I have truly become accustomed to how he's been taking care of me. And can you believe it, he calls me his girl-friend, which I think is kind of cute. All we do every-day is eat, sleep, fuck each other's brains out and, at the end of the day, I get my meth pills, so I am cool with this setup! The only thing I don't like is when he leaves me in the room all day so he can run the streets in my car. Now, I know he's out there taking care of business most of the time, but I get tired of sitting in this room and not being able to go anywhere. He tells me he only keeps me there as a part of my recovery. But, I think that's bullshit, because I believe the real reason he keeps me locked up in this room is because

he is out there running around with a whole bunch of
hos and niggas in my car, and just don't want me to
know about it. So, to feed my curiosity, I tried to call
Teresa's home telephone number to see if she could
school me as to what was really going on, but her
phone service was disconnected and that sent me right
back to the drawing board. But, then again, I figure
something will surface and I will have all the answers
I need.

Now after all this time I've been spending at this
hotel with Papoose, just tonight I've been yearning to
be back at home with Eric again. But, I know that
will be a long shot since I've admitted to his parents
that I have a dope habit, and blew smoke up their
asses when I told them I was going to let them put me
in a drug rehab center. But then again, I figured if I
went over to the house and showed him how I've
been keeping my weight up and tell him how I've
managed to stay clean from heroin for over three
weeks now, maybe he'll let me come back in the
house. And if not, then I just hope and pray he'll let
me spend sometime with my baby. But, I guess I'll
never know the answers to those questions until he
and I come face to face with one another.

Later that night, Papoose came walking in the
room shy of three a.m., and he was not the same
person he was earlier. He was cursing like his mind
was going bad. As a matter of fact, he was showing
me the other side of him and that other side is very
volatile. So after he slammed the door and turned
on the light, I knew I was going to be up for the rest
of the night.

"Ay yo', Faith," he called out my name as he threw my car keys down on the table.

"Yeah," I replied, barely audible.

"You up?"

"I am now," I told him as I turned over, barely able to focus my eyes to the lighting. But after I batted my eyelids a few times, my vision came in clearly. And what do I see standing before me, is this nigga with a whole bunch of scratches all over his neck and face. So, I sat up in the bed and asked him what in the hell happened.

"Yo', I almost killed your bitch-ass friend tonight!" he said in a belligerent manner.

"Who, Teresa?" I asked as my mind began to run rapidly.

"Yeah," he said nodding his head as if he was replaying their confrontation in his mind.

So, when I asked him what happened, he went into this whole spiel, saying, "Ay yo', Shorty, you have no idea how much I had been looking out for your fucking friend. And it seemed like every time she came to score some dope from me, she was always either coming up short or wanted me to give my shit up for free. So, I let her ass slide a few times 'cause that's your peoples. But, when she came to me tonight, talking about she copped some bad dope from me earlier, I told her to get the fuck outta my face. So, she tried to stand there and get loud with me, and tell me that if I didn't give her another pill, she was gon' call the narcs on me. And when she told me that, I punched that bitch right in her face!"

"Are you serious!" I asked him as my mouth popped wide open.

"You muthafucking right, I'm serious! That bitch

disrespected me, so I knocked her ass out!" he continued as he became a little animated with the constant movement of his hands and his body.

"And what did she do?"

"Oh, she tried to fight me back, that's why I got all these scratches on me. But trust me, me and my boys laid that bitch out after she ran up on me like she was fucking wild woman or something."

"Damn!" I said as I began to get a sour taste in my mouth. "Y'all didn't hurt her real bad, did you?"

"She ain't dead! So, she's a'ight!" he commented in an unconcerned way. "But, one of my homeboys did call me and tell me that the ambulance and the police came out there after I left, and that they think she told them I was the one who beat her ass because the police started asking people where could they find Papoose."

"Nah, I don't believe that, because that's not Teresa's style," I said, running to her defense.

"I hope it ain't. 'Cause I tell you what, if she did, she better not ever show her face at Grandy Park again!"

"Well, don't worry about it. I'll talk to her," I assured him.

"Nah, you ain't gotta' talk to that bitch! As a matter of fact, I don't want you fucking with her, period, 'cause she's a rat and rats ain't to be trusted!"

"So, you're telling me that I can't even call her?"

"Hell nah! You can't call that bitch!" he told me in an aggressive manner. "I don't even wanna hear you say her muthafucking name 'round me no more. 'Cause if I do, I'ma go the fuck off."

I listened to his idle threats, but I took it with a grain of salt. And when he finished ranting and raving about how he'll kill somebody if they crossed him, he marched off to the bathroom. I heard him turn on the shower, so I knew then that he was about to bathe. And that's when I turned back over on my stomach to get me some more shut-eye. But of course, that was short-lived when he later climbed on top of me from behind and started spreading my ass cheeks, and sliding his fingers down inside my ass-hole.

"Shorty, don't go to sleep, 'cause I'm trying to get in this ass!" he insisted as he took his dick out and started using it as a whip to smack the back of my butt checks.

Whack! Whack! Whack! was the only sound bouncing off the walls in our room. And as my ass started jiggling back and forth from the effects of the blows from his dick, he started getting more and more excited. And when that happened, he instructed me to get on my knees. So, I did. But, something wasn't quite right for him, so he said, "Wait a minute, I want you to lean forward and lay your head down on the pillow like you're a mu'fucking sliding board, but keep your ass cocked up in the air so I can ride dis dick inside you real good!"

"Do you want me to spread my thighs open too?" I asked him as I prepared myself to be pounded with his nine-inch rod. I mean, this young boy had it going on, for real! And if I didn't watch it, he was gonna have my ass 'round here dick whipped.

"Yeah, spread 'em just a li'l bit," he said.

So, I did. And then all of a sudden, I felt this rock-hard dick creeping between my thighs and landing smack-dab in the wet pool of my pussy. So, I imme-diately started grinding on it, using both my hips and my clit to navigate the ride. And before I knew it, I had his whole dick soaked and wet. So, of course I was loving every minute of it. He was too, because he couldn't keep his mouth closed for nothing.

"Ahhh . . . yeah, work that pussy!" he said as he smacked my ass a couple times.

"You like the way I'm riding this dick, huh?" I asked him as I continued to rock my ass back and forth.

"You muthafucking right!" he replied with excitement. "That's why if I don't go in your ass now, you gon' make me cum!"

"Well, go 'head and put it in." I instructed him and completely stopped moving. And within seconds he had every inch of his hard meat buried in my ass. He used all the juices from my pussy as a lubricant to push his way inside me, to prevent him from ripping the lining of my anus apart. And believe me, it worked like a charm.

Now, as he began to pump his dick deep inside me, I started feeling tons of pressure because quiet as it was kept, this nigga was fucking the shit out of me. So, I figured the only way to get this nigga off me was to hurry along the process by making him cum quicker. And that's exactly what I did.

"Oooooh . . . yeah, ride this ass, baby!" I instructed him and then I bit down into the pillow for solace as I tried to endure the pain.

"Yeah, you like the way I be fucking this phat ass, don't cha'?" he asked me, as he spread my cheeks open a little bit more for leverage.

"Yeah baby, your dick feels real good in my ass! That's why I want you to bust off in me right now." I continued egging his ass on, hoping he was about to cum. And sure enough, he was.

"Ahhhhh . . . baby, I'm about to cum!" he warned me and started pumping himself in me faster.

"Damn right, baby! Cum in this ass!" I demanded.

And then *bomb*! Like a rocket, this young boy shot his shit off clean inside of me. And by the time he was done jacking off in me, I had already counted from one to twenty. So, that let me know that homeboy was filled up. Shit, he could've given me a set of twins with all that cum he had draining out of my ass. It felt like my asshole was a running faucet, because it kept coming and coming. And when he realized this, thankfully he handed me a towel and it worked. But after a while, I ended up going to the bathroom anyway to freshen up. My days of not washing my ass were over. And you can betcha' last dollar on that, too!

After Papoose bust his nut off in me, he ordered a movie from the In-Demand channel, so we laid back in the bed and stayed up for another two hours until he drifted off to sleep. By this time, the sun was about to come up and when I looked at the clock on the night-stand and saw that it was almost six a.m., I suddenly got a burst of energy and began to make plans to leave the room for a few hours. But before I left, I knew I was gonna have to make sure he was in a deep sleep because if I didn't, then he was gonna take the car keys from me and cuss my ass out. So, I waited another whole hour and when I heard him snoring, I slipped on a blue jean skirt, a cute little top and a pair of sandals, grabbed the hotel key and crept out the door.

When I got in my car and started driving away, I began to feel a sense of freedom. It felt good too. But what was going to feel even better was when I finally get a chance to see my best friend after all this time.

I was shocked to find her at home when I knocked on the door. I thought I was gonna have to ride up and down the street, looking for her busy body. So, when she opened up the door and I saw the condition she was in, I immediately got filled up with emotions. "Oh my, God! Look at you," I said as I embraced her.

While I was hugging her, she said, "You know that son of a bitch did this to me!"

I released her from my embrace and asked her who was she talking about, even though I had already heard the story.

"I'm talking about that punk-ass nigga, Papoose."

"Papoose did this to you?" I asked her, trying to act surprised as I examined the black eyes and busted lip.

"I'm surprised that woman beater didn't tell you," she continued as she closed the front door behind us.

"Nah, he didn't tell me anything."

"Well, I thought he did. That's why you came 'round here."

"Nah, I came around here because I had been trying to call you, but your phone is off," I began to explain as we took a seat at the kitchen table.

"Yeah, it's been off for a while now."

"So, what have you been doing while I've been gone?"

"You know, the same ole shit!"

"How far along are you?" I asked her, looking down at her round tummy.

"I'm almost six months."

"Have you found out what you're having?"

"Nah," she replied uninterested.

"Why not?" I pressed the issue.

"Well, because for one, I ain't been to the doctor yet."

"Oh shit, Teresa, you mean to tell me you haven't had any prenatal care yet?"

"How am I gon' be able to see somebody when I ain't even got a lick of health insurance?"

"You can go to the free clinic. And if you want me to, I can take you down there this morning."

"Nah, that's all right," she said as she peered over at her kitchen wall. "I'll get down there sometime later on this week."

"You promise?"

"Yeah, I promise," she replied, but not in a convincing way.

So, I perceived it as if she wanted me to leave well enough alone, and that's what I did. But, before I could jump into another subject, she beat me to the punch and made the comment, "I see that nigga is taking care of you."

"Yeah, he's doing okay," I replied trying desperately not to sound boastful.

"Well, just take one long look at my face, because he's gon' do the same shit to you as soon as you piss him off!"

"No he's not. Because I'm not gonna have it."

"And whatcha' gon' do, stop him?"

"Listen, Teresa, men know who they can put their hands on from the very beginning. So, when you lay the laws down up front, you won't have any problems."

"Yeah, okay. Don't fool yourself."

"Trust me, I'm not," I assured her and gradually turned my head to look around the kitchen.

"Well, for your sake, I hope you're right!" Teresa continued.

"Look, Tee, please stop dwelling on that. Because I wouldn't dare let a man put their hands on me like they do you. And just in case it did happen, that motherfucker will be put behind bars."

"Oh, you ain't gotta' worry about that," she began to say, "because just this morning, I took my ass downtown and took out warrants on that sorry motherfucker you laying up with, and his stupid ass friends."

Hearing Teresa tell me she has just come back from taken out warrants on Papoose and his friends instantly gave me the chills, because I knew she had just signed her death certificate. So, I wanted to warn her but I knew if I did that, then I would be endangering my own life. And I have too much to live for, so I elected to give her a small piece of advice instead.

"I hope you haven't told anybody else you did that."

"Nah, you're the only person who knows," she assured me.

"Well, do yourself a favor and don't tell nobody else."

"I'm not. I'm just gon' let the police run up on that bastard, like they did that nigga who killed my brother."

"Oh shit! They caught him?"

"Yeah. The detective came by here last week and told me they caught him coming out of his girlfriend's house the night before they came here."

"Ahh man, I know you and your family was happy to get that news."

"Well, yes and no. Because if the police don't

hurry up and find the lady who promised to testify against Bing Bing, then that asshole could go free."

"You've got to be kidding me!" I said with disappointment.

"No, I'm not. That's why I am not taking no more shit off these niggas 'round here. And I mean it."

"Well, you know you're gonna need to stay out of Grandy Park, now that the police is looking for Papoose?"

"Yeah, I know that."

"Well, where are you going to go when you wanna score?"

"I got other spots I go to."

"Well, good. Because I don't need to be hearing about you getting beat up again."

"Oh, that ain't gon' ever happen again!" she replied sarcastically.

She and I chatted for a few more minutes and then I told her that I had to be going, because I wanted to make another stop before I went back to the hotel room.

"What hotel y'all in?" she asked me in a very cunning way.

But, I caught on to her tactics and brushed her off with a lie by telling her we were way out at a Holiday Inn in Newport News. I did this because I wasn't going to allow her to use me to get Papoose locked up.

And besides, I wasn't ready to give him up that easily. His dick is too good, he looks out for me with his meth connection, and I have somewhere to lay my head and don't have to worry about the water and lights being cut off.

Now, what more could I ask for at this point?

Unless it was to go back to the house me and my husband built. Other than that, I'm fine right where I am. But, she will never know that. So, as I was about to leave out of her domain, she asked me for a few dollars. And when I told that I didn't have a dime on me, she acted like she refused to believe it.

"You mean to tell me that you're laying up in the fucking Holiday Inn, with a nigga who sells plenty of dope, and you ain't got one red cent in your pocket?"

"I just told you I snuck out of the room and forgot to bring my handbag."

"So, whatcha' saying is that you can bring me some money back?"

"No, I'm not saying that. Because when I leave here, I'm going to my house to see if Eric will let me see Kimora and then after that, I'm going straight back to the room."

"So, you ain't coming back out no time soon?"

"No, I'm not."

"So, when am I gonna see you again?"

"I don't know. But, hopefully it'll be soon." I told her and then I kissed her on the cheek and left.

Chapter 25

What Da' Fuck
Was I Thinking?

Timing couldn't be better for me to drive up and see Eric and Kimora walk out the front door. And believe me when I tell you that my face lit up. But, what was more enjoyable was the fact that he was so busy trying to strap her down in her car seat, that he didn't even hear me until after I got out of my car and closed the door. "Good morning!" I said in a cheerful voice, as I began to walk towards his vehicle.

"Mommy! Mommy!" Kimora yelled after she turned around to see who had spoken.

"Hi, baby!" I replied as I rushed over towards them both.

But, Eric had a different plan in mind because when he saw me moving toward them, he left Kimora sitting alone in the backseat and met me before I even got within five feet of her. "What are you doing?" he didn't hesitate to ask me.

"I came to see my baby," I told him as I peered over his shoulders to get a better look at Kimora.

"But, didn't I tell you that you couldn't come around here anymore?" he tried to whisper.

"Yeah, but it was under the condition that I get myself together, and I have."

"When, Faith?"

"Eric, I've been clean for over three weeks now. I mean, can't you see a difference?"

"How did you get clean?" his questions continued, without even answering mine.

"I checked myself into this hospital," I lied and said. "And what they've done is put me on methadone to kick my heroin addiction, and it's been working."

"Well, that's great," he commented with little enthusiasm.

But before I could make a comment with regards to his applause for my early achievements, a tall, dark-skinned woman who looked like she could be the model type, stood at the front door with her hair flowing over her shoulders, dressed in a black fitted business skirt and a white silk blouse. She made her presence known by calling his name. So, he looked back at her and said, "Yes?"

And she replied to him by saying, "Do you have everything you need before I lock the door?"

"Yeah," he told her and then he turned his attention back to me.

And right about now, I am fucking pissed. So, I didn't hesitate to ask him who she was? And he didn't hesitate to respond.

"That's none of your business." he replied cold-heartedly.

"You're a fucking liar! It is my business, especially when she's standing in the foyer of my house."

"Look, I'm not gonna argue with you!" he replied abruptly and turned to walk away from me.

But, I followed down behind him because I was determined to find out who this woman was, one way or another. "Eric, who is she?" I pressed on.

So, he stopped in his tracks shy of two feet from Kimora and turned back around to face me. "She's a friend," he told me in a perturbed manner.

"What kind of friend?" My questions continued. "And what is her name?"

"Why? I mean, does it matter?"

"You damn right it matters!" I expressed. "Especially, since you got her around my damn daughter!"

"Well, where were you when my lawyer and I stood before the judge a week ago to have the separation hearing?"

"Wait a minute, no one told me about no hearing."

"Well, the subpoena was mailed to Teresa's house a couple days after you took your things out of the garage."

"I'm sorry, but I didn't get it."

"Well, I'm sorry too." he said and tried to walk off again.

"Wait a minute, you still haven't told me who she is."

Eric took a death breath and exhaled. "She's my attorney, okay!"

"Oh, so you're fucking your attorney now?" I blurted out with frustration because by now I was more than pissed, I was insulted.

"Please don't do this right now!" he begged me in a low whisper as this woman started walking towards his vehicle with briefcase in hand.

"You know what, I am so tired of doing things when it's fucking convenient for you!" I yelled. "You never give me the benefit of the doubt. It's always your fucking way or no way at all, and I'm sick of it."

"Eric, is everything all right?" I heard her ask him in a low but noticeable tone.

So, I peered over his shoulder with the evilest expression I could muster up and said, "What are you, his fucking bodyguard?"

"No, but I'm his attorney," she continued in her firm but soft-spoken voice.

"Okay, Ms. Attorney, what might your name be?" I struck back in a cocky manner.

"I'm Kimberlie Latimer," she told me as she opened up the car door.

"Oh yeah, well I'm his wife, Faith," I told her.

So, she smiled and said, "I know who you are."

"Oh really," I said as my mind started racing, "now that seems kind of odd, knowing that I know nothing about you."

"Well, it's simple," she began to explain, as she stuck her briefcase on the front seat and started walking in my direction.

Now, by this time, Eric had excused himself to go and check on Kimora, who by this time was calling my name. And as bad as I wanted to attend to her, I just couldn't shake the opportunity of digging deep into this high-class dick sucker. So, I met her halfway and when we came face to face with one another, she continued by saying, "First of all, he's my client, so that means we work very closely together. And second, he's a very emotionally caught up type of guy, so I'm also here to counsel him, if you will."

"Ahhh, that's so touching!" I replied sarcastically, "But, what I need to know is, are you two fucking each other?"

"I'm sorry, but I will not answer that," she told me flat out.

"Whatcha' got something to hide?" I pressed the issue.

"No. But, that's just not my place to say. You need to ask him," she insisted.

No, this bitch didn't just tell me it wasn't her place to tell me whether or not she's fucking my husband. What the hell is she doing, taking the attorney-client privilege clause to heart? Or is this bitch afraid I will railroad the both of their asses, when everything is all said and done?

Well, I'm not sure which one it is, but I see I 'm not getting anywhere with this ho, so I'm gonna step over here because this nigga is gonna tell me something. "Eric," I said, as I watched him climb into the driver side, "Ms. Kimberlie told me to ask you whether or not y'all were fucking?"

Annoyed by my tone and my words, Eric lashed out at me and said, "Why are you carrying on like this in front of Kimora? Do you have any decency?"

"Just answer my question!" I demanded.

But, it was obvious that he wanted to avoid answering my question, as she wanted him to; because after she closed the passenger side door and buckled her seat belt, she interjected and said, "Come on Eric, we've gotta go."

So, he started up the ignition and put his car in reverse and I became enraged. "So, you're just gonna pull off with me standing right here?" I screamed at him.

"Faith, I'm sorry, but we've got to go," he said.

"You're gonna leave, just like that?" I continued, my voice screeching.

"Mommy, Mommy, please don't fuss!" Kimora yelled to get my attention, as she began to cry.

"Now, see what you did?" Eric roared.

"Ahhh . . . Mommy is so sorry, Kimora," I tried apologizing.

But Eric stopped me right in my tracks by saying, "Just stay away from us." And then he pressed down on the accelerator and backed all the way around my car.

So, I kicked the driver's side door and yelled, "When the fuck are you going to let me spend time with my baby?"

"I'll see you in court," he yelled back and then he proceeded down the street.

I stood there with so much resentment and anger in my heart that I could've shot them both if I had my hands on a gun. I mean, how dare he just gon' go on with his life, without even divorcing me?

And then on top of that, to keep me away from my only child is the most despicable thing he could do to me. But, I am gonna have my day. He'll see.

Chapter 26

Back at the Hotel

Papoose was awake watching television when I walked through the door. My heart sunk as low as it could go when I saw the expression on his face. But, I tried to play it off by rushing over to him and giving him a hug. "Miss me?" I asked in a cheerful mode.

"Get the fuck off me!" he demanded in a harsh way as he pushed me really hard.

To my surprise, I couldn't catch my balance, so I landed on the floor. And just when I was about to ask him why the hell he pushed me, he hopped off the bed and headed towards me.

"Where the fuck you been at?" he asked me as he stood directly over me.

"I went to see my daughter," I began to explain.

"Didn't I tell you I didn't want you to leave the room?" he continued as he slapped me dead in my face.

I grabbed the side of my face with both of my hands and looked at this bastard like he was fucking nuts. I was completely stunned by the way he was carrying on. He was acting like I betrayed him or something, which was not the case at all. So, I had to let him know how I was feeling.

"Look, I know you told me not to leave the room, but I've been missing my daughter and I needed to see her. But, not only that, I'm a grown woman and here you are, standing over top of me, trying to chastise me like I'm your child, which isn't right."

"Do you think I give a fuck about that?"

"I don't expect you to, but you need to keep your hands to yourself."

"Whatcha' say, bitch!" he uttered and grabbed a handful of my hair and snatched me off the floor.

Right now, I don't know if I'm coming or going. But, I will say that this fucking maniac is crazy! I mean, what is it with him not being able to keep his hands to himself? And why does he like making women suffer? Well, whatever it is, I've got to put a stop to it. So, as he lifted me to my feet by my hair, I felt large chunks of hair loosening from my scalp and I wasn't very happy at all by that. And from that point, I made it known.

"Papoose, you're pulling out my hair!" I yelled to the top of my voice as I tried to pry his fingers from around a chunk of my hair.

"Bitch, don't touch me!" he demanded, clutching my hair tighter.

And when he did that, he triggered my reflexes, so I lunged back and hit him in his face with my fist as hard as I could. "Let my motherfucking hair go!" I screamed.

Feeling the sting from my blow, Papoose reacted violently and threw me onto the bed and jumped straight on top of me and started punching me in my face. "You think you can beat me, huh?" he commented as the blows from his fists got more intense.

"Nah, I don't think I can beat you." I said in a convincing manner as I tried desperately to block half of the punches he was lunging at me.

"Oh, yes you do, bitch!" he replied as he continued beating me.

"No, I don't!" I screamed louder, still blocking his fists from causing more damage.

"Shut the fuck up!" he demanded as he tried to muffle my face with a pillow. "Whatcha' trying to do, let somebody hear you?"

Struggling to breath properly from Papoose's weight bearing down into the pillow, I couldn't do anything but act hysterically. A few times I was able to catch my breath. But, it wasn't long before I was being suffocated again.

"Papoose, I'm sorry!" I cried out, my voice barely audible.

And just as expected, he didn't hear me. Or was it more or less the fact that he was in control and his adrenaline was pumping very rapidly, so he wasn't able to stop his actions. I didn't know, but whatever it was, the taunting and the beating continued for another couple of minutes or so; but to me, it seemed like forever. So, when he finally let me come up for air, all I could do was lie there and cry. Replaying everything that happened to me this morning thus far was beginning to weigh me down. It wasn't enough that I had to see my husband with another woman, and have him humiliate me and to hear him tell me that it was basically over between us and that he'd see me in court. And then to come back to here and get the shit beat out of me because I wanted to leave for a while, was more than I could take. So, I began to ask myself, what did I do to deserve all of this? And when I tried to rationalize this whole situation, all I could think about was Teresa saying she told me so. And guess what? She was right.

But, what was so weird about it was that I didn't do anything out of the ordinary. This nigga I was fucking with was a possessive bastard. And to deal with him, you had to do everything he tells you or else. And see that's not the way I want to live my life, but then I thought about, what other options did I have? He's providing me with a place to stay, feeding me and making sure I stay off heroin. So, what am I suppose to do? I can't go back to Teresa's place, she could be getting evicted any day now. And who do you know that wants to live on the streets? Not me, so I guess what I'm gonna need to do is play my cards right and ride this boat as long as I can. I mean, all I have to do is stay in the room and do what he tells me and if I did that, I shouldn't have to go through one of these episodes again. And besides, now that I think about it, he does seem to care enough about me to want to keep me in check. I mean, why else would he get so mad and beat me up like he just did? He hadn't acted out like this before, so I guess he had all the reason in the world to do what he just did. Now, it's my duty to make sure I stay on my best behavior and do what he says until I come up with a better solution, since I'm not allowed to go back home.

* * *

After everything calmed down, Papoose made a few snide remarks to me about how he'll kill me the next time, but I brushed it off as if I didn't hear him.

Moments after he had gotten dressed, he snatched up my car keys from the dresser top and walked out of the room. He didn't say goodbye or anything. So, I figured he was going to use this time to calm down and that he would be all right when he returned. But little did I know, his trip on the outside was going to be short-lived. I was in the bathroom, nursing my scratches and bruises for about ten minutes, when he decided he wanted to damn near tear the door down. The shit scared the hell out of me.

"Yo', do you know I almost popped dis cracker in the head a few minutes ago!" he started off, breathing all out of control.

"What happened?" I asked him, holding a damp washcloth up to my mouth.

"Yo', don't act stupid! You know what's going on?"

"What are you talking about?" I continued as my heart started beating out of control once more. The signs of another ass whipping seemed like they were drawing near.

"Why didn't you tell me the repo man was looking for your shit?"

Somewhat relieved by the fact that he wasn't referring to the situation concerning the warrant Teresa had taken out on him, I exhaled and conjured up a lie, "Because my husband said he was going to take care of it."

"Well, he didn't. And now your shit is being towed away."

Not knowing what to say next, I just stood there and looked dumbfounded. But, that wasn't the reaction he was looking for, so he said, "Why you just standing there? You better do something."

"Do what?" I asked.

"You better get on that phone and call your husband and see if he can get your joint back."

"We got into an argument this morning, so he's not gonna want to talk to me."

Papoose sighed heavily as he walked over to the table to have a seat. And after he threw the keys down, he said, "So, whatcha' gon' do?"

I walked out of the bathroom to look him in his face and that's when I asked him what did he mean?

"I'm talking about how you gon' get your whip back?"

"I don't know."

"How much do you owe?"

"A little over fifteen hundred."

"Fifteen hundred!" Papoose screamed. "Shit! How much is your car payments?"

"Almost five hundred each. But, that's not including the late fees."

"Oh well, you're fucked up, Shorty!" he told me and pulled his cellular phone from his pocket.

Ten seconds later he was on the phone with one of his homeboys, telling them what had just happened and that he needed them to come and pick him up. He laughed a bit with whomever he was talking to and it seemed like as soon as he got off of the phone, his whole demeanor had changed again.

"I hope you got somewhere to go, 'cause when my peoples get here, I ain't coming back."

Shocked by his comment, I said, "Whatcha' mean, you ain't coming back?"

"Come on now, you ain't that stupid!" he replied

as he got up from the chair and started packing up his things.

"Oh, so now you have no more need for me because I don't have my car anymore?"

"Damn, you catch on quick," he told me and continued to gather up his things.

"That's kind of fucked up, don't cha' think?"

"Look Faith, you're a a'ight chick. But, this shit here I'm doing ain't personal. It's business."

"Whatcha' mean, it's business?"

"Come on now, you ain't slow. I mean, do you think I would've taken you off the street 'cause you got a phat ass and I wanted to fuck you?"

"No, but I thought you did it because you wanted to be with me."

"Nah, Shorty, I don't roll like that. I brought you to this room and put you up, 'cause you had some shit to bring to the table."

"Oh, so it was all about my car, huh?"

"You damn right. And quiet as it's kept, I didn't keep that safe locked 'cause I had my dough in there either. I kept it locked because my dope was in there, and that's why I ain't never want you to leave the room."

"So, you mean to tell me that if the police would've ran up in here while you were out in the streets, I could've caught a drug charge behind your shit?"

"What, you think I would've told dem the shit was mine?" he replied and laughed.

"Oh, so you would've just let them take me to jail, huh?"

"Yo', Shorty, don't take it personal. That's just how the game is played," he advised me and then he went back to packing up his stuff.

After he piled all his things into a bag, he stuck it

by the front door. And soon thereafter, one of his homeboys had arrived. So, as he was about to leave, I said, "Think I can get a ride to my girlfriend's house?"

Papoose looked back at me and said, "We ain't got enough room for you in the car."

"So, you're just gonna leave me here?" I asked him in a frustrated manner.

"Yeah," he responded and then he looked down at his watch and said, "It's ten o'clock now. So, you got about two more hours to call somebody to come and get you before checkout time."

"But, I don't know who I can call."

"Call a cab."

"Are you gonna give me the money to pay for it?"

"Hell nah! What, you think I'm some cornball-ass nigga?"

"No. But, I just thought you would do me that favor."

"Well, I don't do favors, Shorty!"

"I'll pay for your cab if you suck my dick!" the other guy interjected.

"Nah, cuz, you'll be better off fucking her in dat phat ass she's got! 'Cause boy, that joint will make your dick swell up like yeast when you start digging in it."

"Oh, that shit's good like dat?"

"Damn right! And it's tight, too."

"Ahhh . . . damn Shorty, you think I can hit dat joint real quick?" the other guy asked.

Instead of answering his friend's question, I looked over at Papoose, who was standing by the door, and said, "Oh so, you're just gonna trade me off, huh?"

"Shit! You ain't my bitch!" he blatantly replied.

"You know what? You are one foul-ass nigga!" I told him.

"Yeah, I know. Bitches tell me that shit all the time!" he said, laughing. "But, it ain't about me right now. 'Cause my homeboy right here is trying to holler at you. So, let 'em know whatcha' gon' do," he continued.

"I'll do it if he'll pay for me to stay here for the next couple of nights."

"Shit! Hell nah!" the guy said, "I ain't coming off wit' that much dough. The most you'll get from me is ten dollars."

Appalled by his comment, I said, "Ten dollars!"

"Damn right!" the guy continued. "And I usually don't give up that, since I got a whole bunch of freaks I can fuck for free."

"Well, I'm not about to suck his dick or let 'em fuck me in my ass for ten dollars. So, I guess the answer is no."

"A'ight, Shorty, well, you take care," the guy said and walked out the door.

"Yeah, we'll holler!" Papoose joined in and then he walked out of the room and didn't look back.

After Papoose left I sat in the hotel lobby for about an hour or so until I got this truck driver to give me a ride to Teresa's house. I told him that my husband was the one who beat me up and ran off with my car, so he kind of felt sorry for me. He was an absolute gentleman, if you wanted to know the truth. But, he was a cracker and I don't do crackers, so I let him go about his business after I got dropped off.

Chapter 27

Back Where I Started

Teresa was on her way out the front door when I returned with everything I owned in tow. So, the first thing she noticed was the bruises on my face. And without hesitating, she rushed down the sidewalk towards me.

"What the hell happened to you from the time you left me this morning?" she asked as she held my face in her hands.

"Me and Papoose got into it when I got back to the hotel room," I told her.

"Now see, you wouldn't listen to me," she began to say, "But, didn't I tell you that muthafucka was a woman beater?"

I dreaded the *"I told you so"* spiel but I couldn't deny the fact that she was right, so I nodded my head and said, "Yeah."

"Where the fuck is that punk motherfucker now?"

she continued as she became enraged. "'Cause I got the right mind to call the police and send their asses right over to where he is, so they can lock his bitch ass up!"

"Well, I don't know where he could've gone," I began to explain, "he left the hotel about an hour and half before I did."

"So, where is your car?"

"The fucking repo man got it while we were in the room."

"So, how did you get here?"

"By some white man I met in the hotel lobby."

"Well, come on in the house so you can put your stuff up," she insisted as she escorted me to her apartment.

Now when we entered into her place, I sat my things down and took a seat on the living room sofa. But, she had other plans. "Whatcha' doing? Get up and come ride with me. We can finish talking when we get in my car," she continued.

"Where are we going?" I wanted to know before I attempted to stand back up.

"I'm getting ready to ride out to Hunterville to my boy Walt's house," she told me.

"How long are you going to be there?"

"Not long. I just need to run in and out," she replied in a convincing way.

"Well, all right. Let's go." I said and got up to follow her.

Once we were in the car and were heading in the direction of Hunterville, it didn't take long for Teresa to get back on the subject about Papoose. She was so obsessed with him, it was pathetic.

"So, tell me, what made him put his hands on you?"

"Well, because he told me he didn't want me leaving the hotel, and I did it anyway."

"And who the hell does he think he is? Your fucking daddy?"

"He was sure acting like it when he was whipping my ass."

"Well, did you hit the bastard back?"

"I did in the beginning. But, you know how it is when you hit a man and he comes back and hits you even harder," I started off saying, "So, after I got stung a few times, I just gave up and begged him to stop hitting me."

"Well, I sho' wish I was there. 'Cause I would've jumped right on that bastard's back and helped you beat the hell outta' him."

I burst into laughter after hearing Teresa's remark. She did mean well, regardless of her many downfalls. And not only that, we are best friends, so I knew she'd always have my back. So of course, I felt the same way.

Now, we talked a little bit more about Papoose and then I went into the incident that transpired between Eric and me after I left her apartment.

Teresa couldn't believe it when I told her Eric was having an affair with his attorney. But, she did believe me when I told her how he humiliated the hell out of me in front of this woman, and sped off in his car when she told him it was time for them to leave. Now, on a normal day she would have had a lot to say concerning my marital problems with Eric, but the only thing I got her to say was, "Girl, fuck 'em! You don't need his selfish and immature-acting ass anyway. Always running to his family when y'all go through shit. Now tell me, what real man does that?"

Teresa was right, what real man does that? But, I didn't have a logical explanation for my husband's actions, so I left well enough alone because it would be senseless to dwell on it.

I sat in the car and waited for Teresa to run into this rundown-looking boarding house. The outside condition of the house was so wretched and sordid, I knew that city officials had to have come by and deemed it unlivable. And if that was the case, it was evident that Walt and his junkie friends thought otherwise.

Now after sitting in Teresa's car for nearly twenty minutes, I got a little perturbed that she would leave me outside for so long, after telling me that she would be right back. Plus, there was no doubt in my mind that she was up in that house getting high, and the thought of me having to wait out here for another twenty minutes gave me enough incentive to go in after her.

When I got to the front door and knocked, some old, tall, smelly guy with an awful set of bad teeth, wearing grubby-looking clothing and thick bifocals, answered it and asked me what did I need? So, I told him I had been waiting for Teresa outside for quite sometime and that I would like to speak with her.

"Well, I'm suppose to charge everybody who comes in here two dollars." he told me. "But, since you're just trying to talk to your friend, I'ma let you in. But you gotta make it quick."

"I will. And thank you," I told the man and walked right on by him.

Now as I began to walk through this long, dark hallway, there was this foul odor of urine that permeated the entire house. The shit was so unbearable that it made you wanna fucking gag. But, what was even more disturbing was that every room I looked in had at least seven or eight junkies in it, either smoking crack or shooting up dope. Watching these zombies stick each other with the same syringe, like that shit was okay, was unbelievable. I mean, that place was like a fucking freak show, if you asked me. So, the quicker I found Teresa, the faster I could get the hell out of here. And in order to do that, that meant that I had some more searching to do.

After going through every room on the first floor, I traveled up this old, squeaky-ass wooden staircase to the second floor and continued my search. I walked over and opened the first door to my right and got an eyeful of one fiend sucking another fiend's dick. Now, I'm not talking about a guy and a chick. I'm talking about one nigga sucking off another. Believe me, the shit was fucking disgusting and that was another time I wanted to gag. But instead, I said, "Y'all are some nasty-ass motherfuckers!" And then I slammed the door back shut.

Now, as I approached the next door I was kind of hesitant, especially after that last incident, so I took a deep breath and then I walked in and the first person I saw was Teresa. There were also two other people in the room with her, but they were off in the corner shooting each other in the neck with the same dirty-ass needle, like they were fucking doctors and nurses. I mean, to see them draw blood out of their veins and into the syringe, and then shoot it right back into their neck, was some horrific shit. But, they were enjoying it, so I got out of their way and proceeded over towards Teresa.

Now, as I took a couple steps towards her, I noticed she wasn't moving, which was a natural reaction for her after she spiked that shit into her veins. So, I was prepared to pick her up and haul her ass out of that room, if necessary.

"Hey Tee, let's go girl," I said, as I reached down and grabbed ahold of her arm. But to my surprise, she wasn't responsive at all. So, I let her arm go and grabbed her by her shoulders and started shaking her but she wouldn't respond to that either, which of course made me panic.

"Teresa, wake up!" I said in a hysterical manner. But, she still wouldn't move. So, I immediately used both my pointer finger and my middle finger to press against her neck to see if she had a pulse and when I didn't feel anything, I freaked out.

"What the fuck did y'all do to her?" I screamed, looking in the direction of the other two dope fiends.

"We ain't do nothing to her," the male junkie said.

"What's wrong, she ain't breathing?" The woman junkie asked as she tried to stand to her feet.

"No, she's not!" I screamed once again. "What the fuck did she have?" I continued as I opened up her eyelids and noticed that her entire eyeball area was white.

And when the other woman noticed it too, she said, "Oh, shit! Her ass is dead and stinking!"

"No, she's not!" I screamed not wanting to believe what this junkie was saying.

"Oh, yes she is, baby girl." the woman said once again as she looked Teresa all over.

"Damn right, she's gone," the other junkie agreed. "Check her pockets to see if she got some more of that shit, 'cause whatever she had gotta be a muthafucking missile if it took her ass out that fast."

"What the fuck you mean, check her pockets?" I became enraged. "My friend is dead! And all you're concerned about is checking her fucking pockets?"

"Hey listen," the man began to say in a calm voice, "I'm sorry you lost your friend. But if she got some more of that dope on her, then you might as well let us have it since she ain't got no more use for it."

Appalled by his words, I said, "Why the fuck would you want some dope that killed another person?"

"Listen, I'm a muthafucking veteran when it comes to that dope." He began to explain. "And the reason why your peoples OD'd off that shit is because her body didn't know how to handle it."

After listening to what this man had to say, I looked back at Teresa and started rubbing her hair back from her face. My tears started falling uncontrollably as I started thinking about how I could've prevented this whole thing from happening. If only I came in sooner. Or better yet, if only I would've tried to talk her out of coming here, then maybe she'll still be alive. And then I looked down at her stomach and thought to myself that her baby didn't even have a chance. What a fucking shame!

"Ay yo', baby girl." The guy spoke out, "I know you're fucked up behind losing your peoples, but you gon' have to cry somewhere else. 'Cause if the police finds you here hanging over her body, they gon' give your ass a murder charge, and that's some real shit!"

"Now, how can they give me a murder charge? I wasn't the one who shot the dope in her."

"They don't know that. And she ain't gon' be able to tell 'em whether you lying or not. So, you better do yourself some justice and get ghost."

"But, I just can't leave her like this," I protested.

"Well, suit yourself," the guy said and both him and the woman junkie raced out of there as fast as they could.

Now, after the fiends left I sat down on the floor next to Teresa and pulled her away from the wall and into my arms in a cradled position. And from that moment it seemed like everything I loved was being taken away from me. So, now I am feeling like my life means absolutely nothing. But not only that, what am I going to do with myself now? I'm not gonna have anywhere to go after Teresa's landlord put her things out in the street. My car is gone and I know I'm not gonna have Teresa's vehicle long, because her family is going to want to take it. So, it looks like I'm going to be up shit's creek without a paddle. And it ain't no one's fault but my own.

Meanwhile as I'm going through the motions, I heard loud footsteps running in my direction and then door to the room burst open, so immediately I became startled because I wasn't not sure what was gonna happen next. And then all of a sudden this tall, black guy with a red baseball cap appeared.

"Hey, what are you doing?" he asked me in a nervous way.

"What does it look like?" I replied sarcastically, because by this time it had become clear from a previous description given to me by Zena, that I was speaking to none other than the infamous Walt.

"Look, I know you're trying to have a moment to grieve over your friend," he began to say, "but I can't have you doing that here."

"What do you mean?" I asked, not understanding quite what it was he was trying to say.

"What I mean is that, I've got to get her out of here before the cops come."

"So, where are you going to take her?" I wanted to know.

"She's gotta go outside. I can't have her laying up in here dead. This is where I stay at. And if the police catches her here, they gon' put my ass in jail and close down my crib. And I can't have that."

Without saying anything else, he reached down and grabbed Teresa up off the floor, threw her over his shoulder and carried her downstairs and out the back door of this house.

Crying until my eyes were bloodshot red, I stood in the back door of Walt's house and watched him as he walked all the way down the back alley until he found a place to put her body, which was next to a tree.

Before he left her lying there, he reached down and started digging into her pockets. And after searching the second pocket was when I observed him pull a small item out. I couldn't see exactly what it was, but from the looks of his face, it had to have some kind of value to him, because he didn't hesitate to stick whatever it was in his pocket. So, after that was done, he covered her face with an old, grungy sheet. And when I witnessed that, I damn near lost it. I mean, I was feeling like complete shit for just allowing him to throw her body out like she was trash. But hey, what did I know? That type of shit was normal protocol for these people. And if he said that we could get a murder charge for being around her when the police found her body, then I couldn't do nothing but believe him.

"What's your name?" he asked me the minute he walked back into his house.

"Faith."

"Oh yeah, I remember Teresa telling me about you."

"I'm quite sure she did," I said, looking down the alley where her body was.

"Yeah, she talked real good about you," he said as he stepped out of the way to shut the back door closed.

"Do you think we should call the police and let them know she's back there, so her body won't rot?"

"Yeah, I'ma make the call from a pay phone, but in the meantime, you gon' have to leave. 'Cause, I'm getting ready to close this place down for a while."

"But why? She's not in your house anymore?"

"It doesn't matter. Because see, after they find her, they gon' knock on every door 'round here to see if anybody got some information for 'em. So, if you ain't trying to be one of those people, then it'll be wise for you to get out of here now," he insisted and walked away.

Seeing how serious this man was about this whole situation, I came to my senses and followed him right out the front door. And when we got outside, he locked the door and proceeded down the stairs. But, before he went about his way, he turned to me and said, "I wantcha' to take it easy, a'ight?"

I looked at him with a puzzled expression and said, "I will."

"And if you need anything, I want you to come by here and holler at me too."

"Okay, I will," I assured him.

"A'ight. Now, gon' get outta' here," he told me once more and started stepping in the opposite direction.

Chapter 28

Back at the Home Front

Just when I thought I was all cried out, I broke down like I a baby when I walked into Teresa's apartment. I couldn't tell you if I was coming or going. All I could do was lie back on her living room sofa and think about all the good times we had, and there were many. Especially the time when we went on a double date with two guys and we ended up skipping out on them after they paid for us to go out on an expensive dinner with them. I would've paid a ton of money to see their faces when the waiter told them we weren't coming back to the table to join them. Boy, those were the days!

Now after about four to five hours of crying and reminiscing, I pulled myself together enough to straighten up the place a little. I couldn't do much, like wash the dishes or clean up the bathroom, because the water was still turned off. However, I was able to clean up her bedroom, the living room and sweep the rugs, since the vacuum cleaner was broken. And after that was completed, I just sat there with my stomach growling out of control and wondered how in the hell was I going to get me something to eat? And then it came to me, that I could go to a pawn shop and pawn my fucking wedding band set. I mean, what use did I have for it? My marriage was on the verge of falling apart anyway. And since there was nothing for me to hold on to, I grabbed Teresa's car keys and headed back out into the world.

I went to three pawn shops before I decided to let my diamonds go. I mean, it was crazy how crooked the pawn shop owners operated. The first place I went to tried to offer me only two hundred dollars for my wedding set that cost my husband nearly seven grand. So, I told them to burn in hell and went off to the next place, who in turn tried to offer me fifty dollars more, so you know where I told them to go. But, the last place did me a little more justice by offering me four hundred. And even though it was more than what the other two gentlemen were trying to hand over, I was still somewhat hesitant. But, when this man explained to me that this was the best offer I was going to get from anywhere, that's when I decided to make the trade with him.

Immediately after I left this last pawn shop I stopped at a nearby gas station and filled Teresa's car up with gas. The next place I stopped was at this Chinese restaurant. I got me a take out order of shrimp egg foo young, two spring rolls and two cold orange sodas. I ate both spring rolls on the way back to the apartment and they hit my stomach in the right way. I was honestly feeling like I had some energy in my body. So, I was okay.

Now once I arrived back at the apartment, I grabbed my food and hopped out of the car. And when I turned around to walk in the direction of the apartment building, two black police officers came out of no-where and nearly scared the hell out of me.

"Excuse me," one officer said, "is this Teresa Daniel's car you're driving?"

My heart jumped straight out of my chest when this man approached me with that question. But, what was really scary was the fact that I knew he already knew the answer, even if I elected not to answer him. So, what was the point? And since I knew he had his reasons why he wanted to come at me with that particular question, I answered him by saying, "Yes, it is. Why?"

"And what is your name?" his questions continued.

"Faith Simmons. Why?" I replied, as I clutched my bag of food close to my chest.

Falling to answer my question, he continued by saying, "Are you related to her in anyway?"

"No. But, she's my best friend. Why?"

"Do you two reside together?"

"Yes, we do. And why are you asking me all of these questions? Is there something wrong?" I asked him.

"Calm down, Ms. Simmons," the other officer said.

"Well, I'm trying to. But, it's hard when someone is keeping you in the dark about something."

"I understand," the same officer said, "But, is there somewhere we can talk in private?"

"Yes, we can go in the house." I insisted and escorted them both into Teresa's apartment. And as soon as we walked inside I reached for the light switch on the wall and flipped it upwards to turn it on, but the damn thing wouldn't work. So, they stood at the front door while I tried the rest of the light switches and when I realized that they weren't working either, something told me that the electricity was shut off.

"I'm so sorry that we have to be in the dark. But, it seems as though the lights just got cut off while I was out," I began to explain as I walked back to where they were both standing.

"Oh, it's perfectly all right. We have flashlights," the first officer who approached me said. "Now, we came by here to tell a relative of Teresa's, that we found her dead in a back alley of a drug-infested area in Huntersville. And it appears that she died of an overdose of heroin."

"No, you must be mistaken." I said, as I backed away from them.

"No, I'm sorry. But, we're not mistaken. She had her driver's license on her when we found her body," the same officer concluded.

Even though I had already been through the hard part of seeing Teresa's stiff body laid up in Walt's house, having someone remind me that she was gone hit me harder this time around. I honestly bawled out of control and there was nothing these officers could do to calm me down.

"Can I ask you something?" the first officer wanted to know.

"Yeah, sure," I said, still sobbing.

"Does she have any relatives you can contact and let them know what we've just told you?"

"Yes, she has a mother. But, she lives out of state."

"Will you be able to contact her?"

"Yes, I will," I told him.

"Well, do that for us. And if her mother happens to have any questions, she can call either one of us," he continued while the both of them handed me their cards.

"Okay, I'll let her know," I told them and took both of their cards in hand.

They said a few more words before they left, but it all sounded scrabbled up to me. I guess, it was because I heard all I needed to hear.

Chapter 29

Blinded

It took me two days to finally get in contact with Teresa's mother and when I broke the news to her, I could feel her pain through her cry. She was really torn up when I told her where the police found Teresa's body and I couldn't blame her. But, what I didn't tell her was that I was in the vicinity and allowed one of Teresa's male friends to throw her body out on the street after we found her dead. I couldn't bear the thought of how she would take that information, much less how she would think of me, so I left it alone and prayed that Teresa will forgive me. Now since her mother lived out of town, she planned to have Teresa's body shipped back home with her and to bury her in a cemetery in her area. Of course I was opposed to that idea, but when Mrs. Daniels told me she would have a small memorial service done at a local funeral home, it made me feel really good that

I would be able to say goodbye. And as far as the things in her apartment went, when Mrs. Daniels took a mini-tour of the place and realized that there was nothing of value in the entire residence, she told me to only pack up the pictures and that I could keep everything else, including the car. So, I was ecstatic about that.

Teresa's memorial service was today and only a few people attended. Mrs. Daniels had her looking so pretty in that casket and no one could even tell she was pregnant. After the service, I kissed Mrs. Daniels on the cheek and bid her farewell. She encouraged me to keep in touch with her, so I told her I would. But, deep down inside, I knew I wouldn't.

All the drama and stress I had caused me to run right back to that dope. And just think that I was doing really good before all this shit fell into my lap. But, what was really bad was that my dope habit had doubled from three pills a day to six. People told me that them meth pills were going to increase my appetite for more dope, and they did. I couldn't stay out of Grandy Park for nothing in the world. I also have my share of running into Papoose on a daily basis and he makes it his business to dog me every chance he gets. I can't get no play from that motherfucker to save my life. And not only that, when he found out happened to Teresa, he tried to rag me out, saying, "You feel lonely with out your partner in crime, huh? Well, don't be sad, 'cause if she would not have died from that OD, then one of these niggas would've probably plugged her skull up with some lead, sooner or later."

Now hearing him say that really put a bad taste in my mouth, but I brushed it off because he's the most ignorant nigga I know. And besides, he'll get his one of these days.

Speaking of days, I've been living by candlelight for six days now and got a seventy-two hour eviction noticed posted on the front door two days ago. I've approximately twenty-four hours to pack up my shit and head out of here before I'm forced out by the local sheriff's deputy. And I am not looking forward to that. So, I've got to come up with a plan real quick. Meanwhile, I jumped in the car and decided to head out to Grandy Park for a re-up of those spider bags that were floating around. Now out of that four hundred dollars I got from the pawn shop, I only had forty dollars left to my name. So, I was gonna get two bags and save the other twenty dollars for tomorrow. But, little did I know I was going to find a ghost town when I made my entrance.

"Where the fuck is everybody at?" I asked this fiend, whom I'd seen roaming around every now and then.

"Everybody done closed down shop 'cause the narcs just came through here and did a sweep," he said.

"How long ago was that?"

"Probably about thirty minutes ago."

"So, there's nobody out here holding?"

"Nope. Your best bet is to go out to Huntersville to the Candy Shop. That nigga Walt, be having dem Huntersville boys up in their selling that good shit."

"You talking about Walt that wears the red base-ball cap?"

"Yeah, that's him," the fiend assured me.

"Well, all right, thanks," I told the guy and left.

On my way to Walt's place, which I had no idea that they called the Candy Shop, my mind started dredging up memories that surrounded Teresa's death. So, I was somewhat hesitant to step back into that house.

But, fear sure has it's way of taking the backseat when copping drugs are involved. Because as soon as I was about to turn this car around and find some-where else to buy me a couple of pills of dope, I thought about the huge chance that I could run into some garbage and I couldn't afford to do that right now. So, I immediately convinced myself that I was going to be all right.

When I pulled up, Walt was standing outside talk-ing to this young boy and from the looks of things, this young boy definitely looked like he was peddling something, so I hopped out of the car that instant.

"What's up, stranger?" I said with a cheesy smile.

Walt smiled back and said, "Hey, baby girl. Couldn't stay away for long, huh?"

With no remote interest to answer his question, I responded by saying, "I'm just trying to cop some good dope."

"Oh, well, you came to the right place."

"What's running around here?" I asked him as I got a little closer.

"Well, I got some people in the house holding that Helter Skelter. And this young'in right here got dem half of caps."

"Which one is better?"

"My shit is better!" The young boy spoke up.

"Is it for real?" I looked back at Walt for his approval.

"Yeah, it's real good. But, his joints go for fifteen dollars a pop."

"Oh nah, I ain't trying to buy a half of cap of dope for fifteen dollars, when I can get two for twenty," I told them both and started walking towards the house.

"Listen home girl, my shit is a missile. Ask anybody 'round here," the guy blurted out.

"I'm quite sure it is, but I'll take my chances with that Helter Skelter," I continued and proceeded into the house.

Walt walked behind me and pointed me in the direction of the house, where he let the other young boys set up shop. The house, of course was still smelly, but I guessed you'd get used to the smell after you've been in here for awhile. Now as we approached the side of the house where all the action was, I heard voices of men instructing others to form a line. So, I looked at Walt and said, "It sure is a lot of chaos going on around that corner."

He chuckled a bit and said, "It gets like this all the time."

"Is their dope really that good?" I asked him once again.

"Oh yeah, I wouldn't have dem in my spot if it wasn't."

"Well be honest, which dope you think is better, the shit your peoples got or the half of caps?"

"Personally, I would've coped one of dem' half of caps because the shit is mixed up with that Q & B and horse tranquilizer."

Shocked by his response, I said, "Horse tranquilizer!"

"Hell yeah, and that shit is on the money. too!"

"So, why ain't he got a long line of niggas trying to cop his shit?"

"He did a while ago. But, everybody ain't got the money he's asking for, so that's why I got a crowd of muthafuckers in here," he explained as we approached an old wooden door.

And before Walt had a chance to grab ahold to the knob and turn it, the door opened and out came three dope fiends. One by one, they all came strolling out of the room with their faces lit up. You can tell that their only concern was to get high because when they walked by us, they didn't look our way. It was as if they were programmed or something and believe it or not, good dope did that to you. So, I was truly looking forward to having that same expression on my face.

We walked into the room and it was filled up with a few more junkies trying to make a purchase, which meant that I had to wait in line. But, Walt walked ahead of me and whispered something in this fine, dark–skinned guy's ear. And when the guy looked into my direction, he waved me to come on over to where he was, so I did just that.

"You trying to make a trade?" He didn't hesitate to ask me, revealing a whole mouthful of platinum and diamond teeth.

I nodded my head.

"Where your dough at?" he wanted to know.

So, I handed him a folded twenty dollar bill and in exchange, he handed me the two caps of the lethal dope everybody called Helter Skelter.

"You ready?" Walt asked me.

"Yeah," I said and turned around to leave.

Back in the hallway, he asked me what was I about to do next. And that's when I told him I was going to head back to the apartment Teresa had before she passed.

"Ahhh man," he began to say, "please forgive my manners. How was her funeral?"

"Well, I wouldn't know because her mother had her body flown back to her home state. But, she did arrange for her to have a memorial service at the funeral home on 35th Street in Park Place."

"How did she look?"

"Oh my, God! Her mother had her looking good. And you couldn't even tell she was pregnant."

"That's good," he replied as we walked towards the front door. "So, who's at the house waiting on you?" He pressed the issue.

"Nobody."

"So, why you trying to go back there and be all by yourself?"

"I don't mind being by myself," I expressed to him.

"I don't either, but won'tcha' stay here for a while and take a load off?"

"Nah, I don't know about that. These people you keep up in here scare me."

"I ain't gon' have you 'round dem," he assured me. "I'ma put cha in my room and ain't nobody gon' bother you, either."

I was beginning to feel like he was backing me up in a corner with his offer, and so I figured it wouldn't hurt to chill out here. And besides, if the dope was good like he said it was, then I wouldn't have to get back in the car and drive all of this way to make another purchase; it was right here at my disposal. So, I followed him to his room and I had to admit that it didn't look like the rest of the house. He actually had a bed, a nightstand with lamp and a dresser with a mirror on top. It wasn't all that clean in there, but it beats hanging out in one of those other hollow rooms.

"Make yourself comfortable," he insisted.

"All right."

"Now, if you need anything, I'll be out in front of the house, making sure shit stays in order."

"Okay," I said.

"Lock the door after I leave too," he instructed me. "I would hate for somebody to come in here and disturb you."

"Oh, I'm fine. But, let me ask you something."

"What's up?"

"Who was that guy, the dark-skinned guy with the platinum and diamond teeth in his mouth?"

"Everybody calls him Black, why?"

"Just curious."

"Well, I guess you're entitled. But remember, if you need anything, just holler for me."

"I will," I assured him and then he left.

Chapter 30

The Ski Mask Way

A whole lot of shit has transpired since I stepped back into the Candy Shop. First off, Walt invited me to move in with him the very next morning after the sheriff set all of me and Teresa's things out on the street.

We didn't make it out there in time to get my things packed before they were actually set outside, but Walt and I were able to gather up all the things I needed. Speaking of which, we're together now. Yeah, I know that sounds strange and all, but he treats me with so much respect it's unbelievable. And not only that, when I needed somewhere to lay my head, he came to my rescue. He even showed me how to master this dope game.

People look for advice from him all the time. And what I like about him is that he keeps it real. Now, he may be a washed-up old man, but he's smart as shit and a lot of people trust him. And that's what I'm most attracted to.

Okay, now when he looks at me, he's always saying that he can't believe that he has a woman like me. He's always trying to make sure I'm all right and when we're in bed, he's always trying to go that extra mile. Now, his dick isn't all that big, but his tongue compensates for it all. Especially when he makes me ride his face. Boy, that forty-seven year old man lets me grind on his face like there is no tomorrow. And what really fucks me up is when he turns me over on my stomach and eats my pussy from the back. I guess seeing all this ass flapping in his face sends him off the deep end. So, if he likes it, I love it.

Today marked the ninth month that I'd been living here. And when I tell you I'd seen everything from niggas getting their asses kicked behind dumb shit, to the police running up in here and making arrests, to the stick-up kids walking out with shit that didn't belong to them. I even started shooting up dope, but the way that I spike myself is safe. Walt schooled me on how to work the needle properly.

And I have to admit that the shit really works. But what I've failed to mention was that two months ago I lent out Teresa's car to a young boy and the bastard wrecked the fucking car. So now, I am out of a vehicle and back to doing it the old-fashioned way. Other than that, everything is everything except for the fact that I know Walt is working for the police. Quiet as it is kept, I overheard Walt making a deal with one of the narc officers in private about setting up other people, just to keep this place running. And when I heard it, I was shocked like a motherfucker.

I mean, this was not the Walt I had grown to know.

This guy I overheard was somebody else. But, who am I to judge? I mean, if this was the only way for him to keep his spot open, then I guess I am gonna have to roll it with and keep my damn mouth shut. I figure he knows what he's doing, so I am gonna get out of the way and let him do it.

Walt got the young boys who peddled that Helter Skelter dope to leave him a few of their caps, just in case some people came through looking for it. Now, it wasn't unlikely for these guys to do this, because they'd done it before. And since Walt always had their money straight when they returned the following day, they handed him ten caps, closed down shop and left. So, once the coast was clear, he took his ass straight up to his room.

Now, I knew immediately what that meant, so I followed right behind him. Shit, I wasn't going to let him have all the fun by himself. I wanted to get high too. And that's exactly what I did. But, before we were able to cook our shit up and suck it up into the syringe, he had to make sure he only beat small quantities from each head of the caps.

If he took too much dope from each pill, then the fiends would notice it and they wouldn't cop it. And not only that, them niggas who gave him these caps to hold were going to notice it too. So, if you tried to hand them their dope back and it had been tampered with, they'd kill you for playing with their emotions. That's a no-no in this game. But, people like me and Walt will still tread that thin line. It's just in our nature. Now, I see why Eugene and Teresa used to get their asses kicked all of the time. They were fighting that temptation demon. And that mother-fucker is a hard one to battle.

"Hold up, Walt, you took too much off that one," I told him.

"No, I didn't," he protested.

"Yes, you did. Now, look at it," I insisted as I picked the cap up in my hand and held it out for him to take a look at it.

He took a closer look at it and said, "Yeah, you're right. That mu'fucka looks skimpy as hell."

"I told you," I said and set the capsule back down on the table in front of us.

"Look, it's a lot of dope in this one," I said as I pointed out one of the caps placed directly to the right side of the table. "You can take some of the heroin out of this one and put it back into that one."

"Well here, you do it," he instructed me and handed me the capsule with the least amount of heroin in it.

Using my eyes, I took both of the caps and weighed them both equally. You couldn't even tell that they had been tampered with. Walt assured me of that. So, once all the kinks were ironed out, we sat back and got high as a motherfucking kite. My man hooked our dope up to the point that I would've jumped out of the second floor window, if somebody told me I could fly. That's just how good I was feeling. And there was no other way I could describe it.

The following morning, around five a.m., those young boys came by and decided to open up shop early, since the word was out that there was a heroin drought going on, which meant they wanted to get in on the action. So, I opened up the door and let them both in, since Walt was nowhere to be found.

"Where he at?" Black asked me.

"I don't know. He left about two hours ago and said he'll be right back, but I haven't seen him," I told him.

"Did he leave you with the dough?" his questions continued.

"Nope. He took everything with him."

"A'ight. Well, me and my homeboy is gonna go in the back room and set up, so when he comes back, tell 'em to come holler at us."

"Okay," I said and then they walked off.

I went back up to the bedroom and waited for Walt to come back to the house but after waiting for another two hours, he still hadn't shown up. And this wasn't like him. So, I headed back downstairs and hung out by the front of the house, while the fiends ran in and out. I collected a few dollars while I was out there. Normally, he'd be out here doing it but hey, I didn't mind.

Meanwhile, as the time continued to roll by, this broke down-ass fiend we called Bootsey came walking towards me with his back hunched over, looking like he was carrying a set of fucking boxing gloves for hands. I instantly got an attitude, 'cause I knew he was about to beg me for something or another, so I turned my back on him and started walking towards the front door.

"Ay yo', Faith," he said between coughs, "I need to holler at you for a second."

I turned back around and said, "What is it, Bootsey?"

He walked closer to me and said, "I just wanna let you know that the police picked Walt up about thirty minutes ago, down by the corner store on Church Street."

Hearing what Bootsey had just said sent my heart flying out of my chest. And all I could think about was why in the world would he be hanging out down by the corner store? So, I looked at Bootsey and said, "Was he dirty?"

"Yeah, he sho' was. And I believe that junkie bitch Maxine was the one who called the police on him too, because when she ran up on him and asked him to let her get a cap for seven dollars, he told her nah, dat he needed straight money. So, she said a few words and tried to shine on him. But, he told her he wasn't trying to hear it. So, he walked away from her and that's when she told him that he's gon' wish he gave her what she asked for."

"That stinking bitch said that?" I said, my voice screeching.

"Yeah, she said it," Bootsey continued to say as he hurled out another cough.

"Do you know how much he had on him?"

"Nah, but it looked like he could've had about five of 'em on him."

"Did the police take any money from him?"

"Yeah, I seen 'em take some from his pockets."

"Could you see how much it was?"

"Nah, I was too far off."

"Ahh man, what am I going to do?" I said aloud as I threw both of my hands into the air.

"I don't know whatcha' gon' do. But, I do know that dem magistrates downtown Norfolk ain't gon' sho' him no mercy when it comes to that dope. They liable to give dat man a $25,000 bail for that little bit of shit he had."

"Are you serious?"

"Hell yeah, I'm serious. They're just nasty like that."

"Well, if they do that, then he ain't gonna ever be able to get out," I began to say. "And to be honest with you, it wouldn't matter if they gave him a low bail, because I'm still not gonna able to come up with a dime. I'm broke as hell and he knows it."

"Well, you better cut your losses now. And believe me, he'll understand," Bootsey expressed and then stepped off and walked back in the direction he came from.

I stood there, baffled, after receiving that awful news from Bootsey. I honestly did not know what I was going to do while Walt was in jail. I mean, how was I going to survive out here? Because as soon as people get the news that he is locked up they gon' wanna act like assholes and try to run all over me. But, hopefully after I talk to the Helter Skelter Boys and explain to them about Walt's situation, they'll want to step up and keep shit intact for me. I just hope they don't try to hold me responsible for the shit he got locked up with and count their losses. Because what happened to him was hardly my fault, and I trust that they would see it that way too. Speaking of which, I need to get high so I will be able to handle this shit better. 'Cause right now, I am about to fall apart out here and I can't let that happen. So, let me get my ass back in the house where I belong.

When I got back in the house, I ran everything down to Black and he didn't have a problem whatsoever when I told him that I was going to need him to kind of run things around there while Walt was away. So, I was very pleased to know that I was going to be all right. But, little did I know what I was going to be up against.

The whole time I've been living here, Walt had the electricity hooked up to the building next door through a heavy-duty extension cord and the people never had a problem about until now. So, I let Black handle it and he did.

But, what I later found out from one of the tenants next door was that, Black promised to give her boyfriend two pills of dope everyday for his lights, which was one pill more than he gave me for being selling his shit out of here. So, the guy was cool with that arrangement and the deal was made. Now, I never said anything to Black about what I had heard because I later found out that he wasn't as friendly as he appeared to be when Walt first let him and his homeboys in the house to sell their shit. But, I guess time and the change of events would alter anybody's tolerance level. It sure had an effect on mine.

Chapter 31

It's That Serious

Another junkie just died in one of the rooms upstairs from an overdose. And of course, it scared the hell out of Black and his crew, so they closed down shop early. But, come to find out, the chick who OD'd copped her dope from the nigga who sold the half of caps. I heard some people saying that it had rat poison in it and that's what killed her. So, luckily me and another guy was able to get her out of here before her body started stinking up the house. Couldn't have the police beating down this door trying to charge me with murder. No way!

Now, I was expecting Black and his boys to come back later that evening but they didn't show up. So, I played house sitter for the rest of the night and thank God, everything went smoothly.

* * *

The next day Black came through but he had a couple new guys with him. He also came with a set of new rules that I was not at all happy about.

"That shit that happened with the dope fiend O.D.'ing yesterday can't go down like that no more," he began saying, "So, from here on out, no one is allowed to come in here and get high. This spot is strictly for mu'fucka's to come in, cop their dope and carry their asses! Now, do you have a problem with it?"

"Well, the only way I would have a problem is if you told me I can't get high in here anymore."

"Nah, this doesn't apply to you. You can get high in this joint all you want. It's the other people that we don't want in here. It causes too many problems."

"Well, I'm fine with it. Just as long as I can still get a cap for every five sales I bring to you."

"Oh yeah, that still stands. But, you've got to be the one to let everybody know that the Candy Shop is still open, but the shooting gallery is closed down for good. A'ight?"

"All right," I said. "But look, can you do me a favor?"

"What's up?" he asked.

"I haven't had shit to eat since y'all left yesterday morning, so I was hoping you can spare a few dollars so I can run out and get me something to put in my stomach."

"Yeah, here, take this five dollars and go get you something," he insisted and handed me the money.

Happy as a punk in jail, I shot outside and walked down to the corner store and got me a fried chicken dinner with a side of French fries.

And when I got back to the house I fucked it up in no time, so I was straight for the rest of the day. But, that full stomach didn't stop me from getting my high on. That shit is mandatory. 'Cause if I fuck around and can't get my shot, I will get sick as a fucking dog. Trust me, I don't look forward to the days when I've got uncontrollable diarrhea and major stomach cramps. I mean, that shit is unbearable. And anybody who has experienced it will tell you that it ain't shit to play with. So, it's kind of like a job when you have to get up every morning and try to figure out what is gonna be your next move to cop that pill of dope. And that's why desperate times calls for desperate measures.

Walt had been locked up for almost three months and believe me, shit has not been the same. Black changed the rules around here so many times it ain't funny. And then on top of that, he's now starting to treat me like the real dope fiend I am. I can't even get a few dollars from him anymore. So, I've offered to suck his dick for the five dollars but he clowned the hell outta me and said, "Bitch! I wouldn't let you suck my homeboy's dick, wit'cha' dirty ass!" And then he sent me right out of the room and laughed at me while I walked away.

Now I ain't gon' lie, it is pretty clear that I look like shit. My face is caving in around my bone structure and I lost about forty pounds, which means that I don't have that phat ass niggas use to run down behind me for. So, hey, what can I say? I guess, I am gonna have to use what I have to get what I want, which isn't much at all. And that's why I took it to the streets. Yeah, I am tricking now. And so what! Shit, I had to get down for mine, because I couldn't depend on no one else to go out and buy my dope. It's just not that type of party. Out here, you are on your motherfucking own and there's no ifs, ands, or buts about it.

Right now, I'm standing on Church Street near Tidewater Park, trying to pick up a decent trick and I've run across a couple of assholes who only want to give me two dollars for a dick suck. But, I told 'em if they ain't trying to shell out at least four or five dollars, we ain't got a whole lot to talk about. Like this fat, black, greasy-looking nigga name Paul that just pulled up in his old, beat-up Thunderbird. Now he has some game for a sista's ass but we gon' see whose gonna come out on top.

"So, whatcha' gon' do?" I asked him as I stood alongside his car.

"I told you what I had, but you ain't trying to give a nigga a free pass."

"Fuck that!" I said, "You think it's real easy for me to be standing out here all day and night, taking the constant shit I be getting from niggas like you?"

"I didn't say it was."

"Look Paul, or whatever your name is. If you ain't trying to give me four dollars, then you might as well carry your trifling ass!"

"You sure? 'Cause when I pull off, I'm going right down there to the next block and I betcha' dem hos will take my money."

"Well, carry your fat ass, then!" I yelled and then I kicked the side of his car.

"You stinking bitch!" he yelled back and sped off.

After Mr. Grease Ball pulled off, he drove his fat ass right down the block and picked up this bitch name Tracy. She's a gutter bucket ho that'll do anything for a couple dollars. But, I'm not because I have morals and standards. So, if a nigga can't abide by that, then he can carry his ass like ole fat ass just did.

Can you believe it? I've been standing out on this corner damn near all fucking night and I haven't snagged not one trick yet. But, what is really fucked up is that I am starting to get ill. And when I am ill, I act like a damn fool. I am a cranky bitch! And I'm always in the mood to fight somebody.

But, since that isn't gonna help me none, I see I'm gonna have to resort to plan B. So, the next trick that comes through, I'm gonna take whatever they give me, 'cause shit is getting really critical right now. And I'm the only chick standing out here who hadn't had no dope all day. I know them other hos are laughing at me. But, I ain't gonna worry about it 'cause I'll be back on real soon.

Chapter 32

When It Rains, It Pours

After sucking a handful of dicks, I finally got up enough money to cop me a pill of that Helter Skelter. But before I could get my shit together and head back out to the house, a car pulls up and stops right alongside the curb I was standing at. So, I put on my best smile and stooped down to get a look at the driver and hopefully get 'em to spend some money with me. And as soon as I laid eyes on this driver and realized that it was my husband, my heart damn neared jumped out of my chest.

"It's gotten that bad, huh?" he didn't hesitate to say.

Caught off guard and ashamed because my husband is seeing me at my worst, I couldn't do anything but just stand there. I honestly couldn't move a muscle in my entire body. But, that didn't deter him from humiliating me any further.

"How much does it cost for a blow job nowadays?" he asked and then he laughed.

"Whatcha' gotta resort to tricking because your new girlfriend ain't satisfying you?" I struck back without answering his question.

"No. Believe it or not, I've had a private investigator following you for weeks. And when he told me that you were downtown on this strip prostituting, I couldn't believe it. So, I had to come down here and see it for myself."

"Still getting other people to your dirty work for you, huh?"

"I needed pictures for court."

"And I'm sure you got 'em."

"Well actually, I got more than my money bargained for," he chuckled.

"Fuck off, asshole!" I belted out with rage and put one foot in front of the other and started walking away from his car. But, unfortunately Eric wasn't going to let me get off that easy, so he got out of his car and followed down the sidewalk behind.

"Hey, where you going?" he yelled. "I ain't done with you yet."

"Eric please, just leave me alone." I begged him.

"Why should I?" he said immediately after he grabbed a hold of my arm. "You need to be in somebody's rehab. I mean, look at you."

"I don't need you to remind me about how I look."

"Somebody should because you look like shit."

"Are you done?" I asked sarcastically.

"Nah, I'm not. I mean, what's gotten into you?"

"Look, I ain't got time for this!" I protested and stormed off.

"Well, you should." he snapped as he began to

storm down behind me once again. "Out here tricking for pennies so you can buy drugs. Looking a hot mess! I mean, don't you have an ounce of dignity?"

"Nah, I guess not." I replied in a nonchalant manner trying desperately not to show him my true emotions.

"Well, that's too bad, then," he commented and stopped dead in his tracks. Because I sure had hopes for you."

"You ain't have shit! All you came down here to do is humiliate me. And now that you've accomplished your mission, won't you hop back in your girlfriend's car and take your ass back on home to her." I yelled and kept right on walking.

"Don't let me wake up one morning and read about you in the obituaries," he yelled back.

Instead of responding to his outlandish comment, I ignored him and proceeded up the strip. Luckily for me, he got in the car and left. Because I would not have been able to take anymore of those blows he was throwing at me. I honestly would not have been able to handle it. I'm fragile, believe it or not. So, to have him stand over the top of me and belittle me like I'm some piece of trash wasn't working well with my heart, which is why I had to get away from him as fast as I could. I just hope I don't run into him like this ever again.

About a half of mile into my walk, I flag down another trick and ended up getting him to give me a lift back to the spot. But, when we pulled up, I wasn't expecting to find undercover narcs all over the damn place.

They had the Candy Shop surrounded with at least six or seven undercover police vehicles. And before I could barely get out of this man's car, I saw Black and one of his homeboys being carried out of the house in handcuffs. I was kind of happy that he finally got his due because of the way he'd been carrying me these last few months, but then I figured that it wasn't good to be glad about niggas going to jail. I heard that ain't a fun place to be.

Now after my trick dropped me off and left, I stood directly across the street and watched everything that moved in and out of that house. And while I was scoping the scenery out, Bootsey walked up to to me.

"You better count your lucky stars that you weren't in there when dem crackers rushed the place."

"I can see that," I said, not once taking my eyes off what was going on. "How long have they been in there?"

"Probably about fifteen minutes."

"Do you know who else was in there?"

"Yeah, they got two of Black's boys while they wuz' standing outside, handing out free testers."

"And where are they at now?"

"A couple of narcos took 'em downtown. So, you know what that was about?"

"Yeah, they're gonna try to get them to tell on the other two."

"Bingo," Bootsey replied and then he started coughing really bad.

So, I looked at him with concern and said, "Bootsey, you really need to take care of that."

"If I could, baby girl, I would. But, trust me when

I tell you that a muthafucka' ain't made a cure for the shit I got."

"Oh my, God! Bootsey, I'm sorry! I didn't know." I began to apologize after realizing he was sick with AIDS.

"Come on now, you ain't gotta' be sorry! I'm a big boy. I'm handing it," he tried assuring me, but that smile he put on his face wasn't convincing enough for me. So, I said, "How long have you been living with it?"

"Probably about ten years now."

"What does your family say about it?"

"Come on now, what family?" he began to say, "You know you ain't got no family when you out here on these streets."

"Well yeah, I know that. But, have you ever been married, or have any kids?"

"Yeah, I was married once. For fifteen years, as a matter of fact. Had two kids by my wife too, but they're all grown now with their own families."

"So, why did you and your wife split up?"

"These muthafucking streets split us up. Because as soon as I got turned on to dat dope, my whole world turned upside down." he started explaining, "I lost a good-ass job working as the lead foreman at a welding shop for the Norfolk Naval Shipyard, so that's ten years gone down the drain. And then I lost my house to a foreclosure and that's when my wife told me she had enough."

"What did she do?"

"Whatcha' think she did," he said, "she packed up her shit, took the kids back to her mother's house and filed for a divorce a year later, after she saw that I wasn't gon' let this life here go."

"Have you ever tried to stop before?"

"Hell yeah, I tried plenty of times. And I even went into detox a few times but as soon as I left, that urge to get another pill of that dope comes right back on you."

"You sure ain't fucking lying about that," I agreed.

"So, what's your story?" he asked.

"Well, mine is quite similar. I used to be an assistant principal at a performing arts school out in Virginia Beach. I'm still married, but I'm legally separated from my husband of ten years and we have a little girl named Kimora, whom I miss so much it kills me when I think about it."

"When is the last time you seen her?"

"It's been almost two years now."

"Have you tried to go and see her?"

"Her father won't let me come near her."

"Ahhh . . . man, I feel your pain. 'Cause my wife took me through the same exact thing. But now, when I look back on everything, I don't fault her for doing what she felt was right. I mean, look at us. Do we really want our children to see us like this?"

I thought for a moment and then I said, "You're right, I wouldn't want my baby to see me like this."

"Exactly. So, when you're ready to get yourself together and leave these streets alone, he'll see a change in you and when he does, trust me, he'll let you come back into her life."

"You think so?"

"Baby girl, I know so," he told me and then all of a sudden, our attention was shifted back over towards the house.

"Oh, shit! Look, who they got!" I blurted out, as I witnessed one of the narcotics officer escorting two familiar dope fiends out of the house in handcuffs.

.

"Ahhh . . . man, ain't dat' Zena and Pookie?" he asked.

"Yep, it sure is. And trust me, they gon' talk their asses off when they get downtown."

"Shit'd, look how long they been in there," he pointed out, "So, believe me when I tell you, that they already started telling dem crackers what they wanna know."

"I wouldn't doubt it," I replied.

Now it took the narcotics officers another thirty minutes to clear out all the drugs and guns they found doing that bust. They arrested six people in all, so I guess they felt like it was a job well done. I was just blessed that I hadn't been caught up in that mix. And since I still had my freedom, I was gonna take my ass out to Grandy Park to see if I could get me some of that penny candy or that Predator floating around there.

Chapter 33

Scheming Hard

Grandy Park was kind of deserted when I got out there. But, there were still a few fiends hanging around. And where there was dope fiends, there was dope. So, I approached this guy who looked like he had just had some good dope himself. I mean, you should have seen how this nigga was nodding and carrying on.

"Hey, you trying to share some of that dope that got that got you nodding like that?"

He started smiling and said, "Only if I had some left."

"What did you have? 'Cause I'm ill as hell right now," I told him.

"Dem young boys wit' dat Predator is 'round that building right there," he replied as he pointed to a building standing directly across the street from where we were standing.

"All right," I said and started walking that way.

And as soon as I bent that corner, I saw Papoose standing right beside two of his people, talking on a cellular phone. But, as soon as he recognized who I was, he told the caller on the other end that he'll call them back. And when he said that, I kind of felt really awkward. Humiliation engulfed my entire body while I was standing there. And all I could do was give him a cheesy-ass smile and ask could I cop one of his pills of dope.

"Damn, girl! I almost didn't recognize you," he said as he moved closer towards me.

So I handed him my ten dollars and waited for his homeboy to hand me my product. And in the meantime, Papoose had a lot of fucking questions for me. "So, where you been at?" he asked.

"Chilling out in Huntersville."

"Oh, so you been copping your dope from the Candy Shop, huh?"

"That's where I stay at," I told him.

"Oh, so you fucking wit' dat nigga Walt?"

"I was before he got locked up."

"When did he get locked up?"

"Almost four months ago."

"So, what, the police ran up in the spot and bagged him up?"

"No. He was hanging out by the corner store on Church Street when the police got him."

"What they catch him wit'?"

"Five caps."

"Have you talked to him?"

"Nope."

"So, whose been holding shit down while he's been gone?"

"Well, I had them Helter Skelter boys selling their dope out of there, but they're gone now."

"So, whose got heroin out there now?" Papoose wondered aloud.

"Nobody. That's why I came out here."

"Is there a lot of money out there?"

"Damn right, it is! That Helter Skelter dope used to keep motherfuckers lined up all day long."

"You bullshitting!"

"No, I'm not." I said with certainty.

"A'ight. Well, I'll tell you what," he said, "if you let me and my homeboys set up shop 'round there I'll hit cha' off with three pills a day."

Hearing Papoose give me an offer like that made me happy as a motherfucker. And before I gave him the okay, I broke down and told him about the narcs busting up in the spot. But, I neglected to tell him that it had just happened. I didn't want to deter him from coming by there and setting up shop, because it probably would've killed my chances of getting some free dope. And boy, you know I couldn't have that.

"So, whatcha' say? Can we do business?" he continued.

"Hell yeah!" I said, "But, just so you know, it's kind of hot out there right now. So, you might wanna wait a few days before you come through."

"Oh, we was gon' do dat anyway."

"Well, okay. I guess it's on, then."

"A'ight! Well, that's what's up. So here, take these two joints and come holler at me tomorrow," he told me as he handed me two caps of dope.

I looked down at my hand just to make sure I wasn't seeing things and when it finally registered that this nigga gave me a free cap of dope, I became giddy as hell.

"Good looking out!" I said and started walking away.

"Oh, you're a'ight! Just don't let nobody else come in that spot, 'cause I done already put my bid in."

"I ain't gon' let nobody else come up in there," I assured him and then I left.

Papoose and about five other niggas came through about three days later. They were suited up like fucking soldiers ready to go to war. He had two of his boys lined up out back as watch-outs, two in front of the house and one on the inside at the front door. But, what was really fascinating was when I saw Papoose install a steel door with a two-by-four latch to prolong the police from running in there at will. He also had a bucket of acid placed in the closet where he hid his stash of dope. Nobody was allowed in this room but him and the man he had holding up the front door.

Now, for the first month, shit was going really well. I was getting my dope like he had promised and he and I used to sneak around in the back to keep his homeboys from seeing me sucking his dick. He would've probably jumped out of a window if one of them caught us in the act. He was truly ashamed and didn't want them to think that he was a desperate nigga. But, then it all stopped. He found a bump on his dick one night and went the fuck off on me. He called me all kinds of dirty bitches! And he even beat my ass behind it, talking about I got a dripping mouth and that it fucked up his dick. But, when he went to the clinic and found out it was just a case of genital warts, I never got an apology from his ass, and I didn't expect one either. He's just that fucking arrogant.

But, I've got a trick for his motherfucking ass. And it's gonna be for all the old and new shit too. I can promise you that.

Chapter 34

Pointing Fingers

A couple of people from the city came by the house today and posted up "no trespassing" signs, deeming the building unfit to live in. They even had a maintenance worker board up the windows and the doors. Luckily, Papoose and his boys were nowhere in sight because these officials had the police to escort them on and off the property. And when everything was said and done, all my shit was put outside on the streets and I was right back to square one.

Papoose decided to show up back at the spot later that night, and got the surprise of his life. I was sitting outside on the stoop when him and his boys walked up to me and the first thing that came out of his mouth was, "What the fuck happened?" But, I didn't want to be the one to come right out and tell him that the Candy Shop was closed for good. So, I approached his question at a different angle.

"Some city service workers came by here early this morning and told me I had to leave." I told him.

"So, when did they board up the windows and shit?"

"Right after I got all my shit out of the house."

"Have you tried to get back in?"

"You know I did. But, they got their maintenance workers to nail them windows and doors shut real good."

"A'ight, well, this is what we gon' do," he began to say as he turned towards his homeboys, "we gon' go 'head and set up shop out here, since there's a lot of money to be made. But, I'm gon' need y'all niggas to work like soldiers and act like we used to act when we was on foot out in Grandy Park. That means we can't be all laid back and shit like we was when we was in the house. Y'all feel me?"

"Yeah," everybody said in unison.

"Good. Now, let's start grinding," he continued and they all went to work.

But before Papoose walked off, I got his attention by saying, "Can I get my three pills now?"

"Nah, I'm sorry but ain't no freebies jumping off tonight."

"Whatcha' mean?" I began to say, "But, you always give me three caps a day."

"Yeah, that was because we was using the spot, but we outside now. So, your services are no longer needed."

Choked up by his words, I wanted to just crawl under a rock and die because I had truly been looking forward to getting me some of that dope he had. In all honestly, I'd been waiting all day to get high, so you can imagine how sick I am. But, that nigga wouldn't care if I dropped dead right at his foot, which is really fucked up considering all the shit I've taken from him. But, I'll be all right and when it's all said and done he's gonna feel it.

Chapter 35

My Death Wish

I've been going through the motions all night, watching that motherfucker sell his shit in my face. Him and his homeboys have been through about four sandwich bags of his dope, so I know he's rolling in money. I also sat back and peeped out their stash spot. And from the looks of it, I think I might be able to snatch it up as soon as they went off to make the trade with whoever comes along. But, then the more I think about it, I knew the only way I would be able to execute this plan without getting caught, would be to get somebody I trust to be my decoy. And that's gonna be tough because there's not a soul out here I can rely on. So, I'll be better off doing the shit by my damn self. But, since I know it ain't gonna work, I'm gonna sit back and wait for the next opportunity to present itself.

Now while I was working my mind overtime, trying to figure out how I'm gonna get close enough to grab Papoose's stash without him noticing it, Boot-sey walked up behind me and said, "You don't look too good."

"That's because I'm ill," I told him.

"Ain't that dem Predator boys right there?" he asked.

"Yeah."

"Well, I thought they be looking out for you."

"Yeah, they did. But, when the city closed down the house, that nigga Papoose told me I didn't have shit coming."

"Damn, dat's fucked up!"

"Yeah, I know. But, it's cool though because as soon as I figure out a way to sting his ass, trust me I'm gonna do it."

"Whatcha' got in mind?" he asked me with an in-quisitive expression.

I hesitated for a moment before I answered his question. I wanted to make sure I was comfortable enough to tell him about my plan to snatch up Pa-poose's stash. But most importantly, will he be trust-worthy enough not to divulge a single word of this to Papoose for a trade off? Now, I don't know where Bootsey's loyalty lies, but I figure he couldn't hurt me no worse than what I was feeling right now. So, I finally got up the nerve and told him every detail in-volving my plan. I even told him that I preferred to go and do this thing alone, but I knew that this job re-quired a second person. And when heard me say that, he wanted in immediately.

"Are you sure, Bootsey? 'Cause, this will be a dangerous game we're about to play."

"Let me tell you something," he began to say, "I play Russian roulette with my life every muthafucking day, so this shit here ain't nothing but a walk in the park."

"Well, all right, this is what I need you to do." I began to tell him. And after I felt like he understood what needed to be done, he and I both sat back and waited for the perfect timing. And guess what? It finally came when we noticed Papoose laying down a fresh ziplock bag of his dope. And as soon as he did it, the four narc officers rolled up on him and his boys. So, they all started walking up the block to avoid being seen near the stash. But, not only that, they were all carrying heat on them, so they wanted to avoid getting a weapons charge, too.

Meanwhile, Bootsey and I were checking everything out. And as soon as we saw how the narc was fixated on harassing Papoose and his boys while they were being followed down the block, we made our move.

"Now, you know this is the perfect opportunity right now?" Bootsey pointed out. "So, if we gon' do something den we need to do it now."

"I'm ready," I assured him, my adrenaline pumping.

"A'ight. Well, I'ma sit right here and watch your back. So, I'ma need you to go around dat building right there and come back up through the alley."

"I know that. I've already got that part down in my head," I told him and then I skated off.

Now, the whole time I ducked and dodged behind every car and bush I came upon, my heart started racing faster and faster. Believe me, I was a nervous fucking wreck, but somewhere in my mind I knew that I was gonna be all right after I got my hands on the prize. So, immediately after I had gotten across the street and within a few feet from the bush where

Papoose had his drugs stashed, the narcotics had left the scene. And that meant Papoose and his homeboys were marching their asses right back down in my direction.

"Here they come," I heard Bootsey say in a loud whisper and then he disappeared on me.

Now, I had enough time to snatch the shit up, but getting away without being seen was another hurdle I had to jump. So, my first mind told me to leave it alone. But, my body was telling me something totally different. And after listening and feeling the effects of my ill body, I reached down behind the bush and grabbed the sandwich bag from underneath the rock placed on top of it, and sprinted off like Jackie Joyner-Kersee. But, it was too late, my timing was off because when Papoose saw my reflection from the light shining in the alleyway, he yelled out and said, "Bitch! I'm gon' kill you when I catch you!"

Hearing the tone of his voice and the speed at which he was running made me well aware that it was a matter of time before I would be begging him for mercy. So, I tried to speed up, but my body wouldn't allow me to. And then all of a sudden, it felt like I was running in slow motion. And as I looked around for an escape route, I noticed how all eyes were on me. It was two o'clock in the morning to be exact, so the eyes beaming from the sidelines of this dimly-lit street belonged to the local crackheads and dope fiends who migrated to this part of town. Some of them were silently cheering me on. So, when I looked back and noticed that this nigga was gaining on me, I nearly shitted on myself. I seriously had a good fifty-foot head start on him, but he quickly made up that distance in speed and now he's on my ass. So, as

I was about to crossover from one block to the next, I felt a hard blow hit me in the back of my head, forcing me headfirst to the pavement. And upon my fall, the bag of dope flew out of my hand and every pill of dope scattered all over the ground.

"Oh, bitch! You're dead now!" he screamed as he started kicking me in my side with his Timberland boots.

The intense pain from the blow of his boots sent me out of this world. He beat me to a fucking pulp. And when I thought he was going to let up on me, he took out his burner and cocked the hammer.

So, right then and there my life flashed before my eyes. And the images of my ex-husband and my daughter appeared right before me as I closed them and waited for the inevitable. But then out of nowhere, police sirens starts blaring uncontrollably and loud voices started roaring simultaneously, "Put the gun down now!"

Now, as I began to hear all of the commotion, I gradually opened my eyes and was instantly blinded by all the lights. But, that wasn't what I was concerned about. Because after I was able to focus in on Papoose's movements and noticed that those same narcotics officers that had came through a few minutes ago, had him pinned down on the ground, I knew then that I was safe. What a fucking relief that was. And after they carried his ass away from me, one of the officers approached me and said, "Don't move ma'am, because we have a paramedic unit on the way."

I wanted to respond, but I couldn't. Because all I could think about was how I would be able to pick up a few pills of that dope without the narcs noticing me. Shit, they're gonna go to waste anyway, so why not let me pump my veins up with that candy, since I just got my ass beat down behind them? I think that would be the most logical thing to do. What do you think?

Thankfully, that night I wasn't hauled off to jail for that stunt I pulled, because I overheard Papoose crying like a bitch to the police, telling them that it was my dope scattered all over the ground. But, them crackers wasn't buying into that lie. So, he wore that charge and that gun charge all by himself. I only walked away with a couple of bruises and a slap on the wrist. But, that didn't stop me, because three more years have gone by and I'm still out here on the grind everyday making moves so I can get the next best high. I've watched a few fiends 'round here OD right in front of me. And just the other day Bootsey fell out and got hauled off to the hospital. I heard he ain't doing so good. That virus he's got is full-blown now, so it's just a matter of time before he's put in a body bag. Believe it or not, but, I almost went out of here my damn self. Shit, if it won't for my Zena looking out for me, I probably would've OD'd off that horse tranquilizer dem young boys mix with their dope. But, luckily for me, God wasn't ready to take me out of here. But, being as my luck runs kind of funny, it's just a matter of time before I'm covered with a white sheet and carried on to a morgue too.

Speaking of which, my mother-in-law almost passed away from a heart attack. But, somehow she managed to cheat death too. And as far as my marriage goes, Eric ended up getting the divorce from me. He sold the house too. But, don't worry! I got $155,000 out of the deal. Can't say what I did with it, though. All I remember is that it only took me less than one month to spend every last dime of it.

Now as far as my daughter is concerned, I haven't seen or talked to her in years. And it doesn't effect me like it use to. I guess, I'm coming to terms with the fact that she's better off without me. Maybe, one day I'll be able to get up the strength and willpower to say the hell with these streets and get my life together, so she and I can be united. I mean, it ain't like I don't want to get clean. 'Cause I do. But, it's a battle trying to kick this dope habit. Especially when you shoot some dope up in your body and the shit don't even get you high, but you still inject that shit in you anyway so your body can function properly. Yeah, I know you're saying I'm talking crazy. But, any dope fiend you come across will tell you the exact same thing. 'Cause that's some real shit. So, believe it!

Enjoying the following excerpts from
Kiki Swinson's previous novels,

PLAYING DIRTY and
NOTORIOUS!

Available now wherever books are sold!

Playing Dirty

From the Beginning

"Okay, Yoshi, it's your time," I whispered to myself. I ran my hands over my Chanel pencil skirt to smooth out the wrinkles. Then I turned toward the large bathroom mirror and checked my ass—along with my silver tongue and beautiful face, it was one of my best assets. I stood in the old-fashioned marble courthouse bathroom, making sure I looked as stunning as always before I made my way to the courtroom. My assistant had just texted my BlackBerry to tell me the jury was back with a verdict. The jury had only deliberated for one day. For a defense attorney, that could spell disaster. But that rule stood for regular defense attorneys—and I'd like to think that I was in a class by myself.

The trial had had its moments, but through it all I shined like a star. On the second to last day, I had all but captured the jury in the palm of my hand. I used my half-Korean background and my native Korean tongue to appeal to the two second-generation Asian jurors. My mother would've been so proud. As a proud Korean, she always wanted me to forget that I was half Black. She spoke Korean all the time. It had everything to do with the volatile relationship she had with my father before he packed up and left New York to go back to his hometown in Virginia when I was only eight years old. Him leaving the family devastated my mother, but I was okay with it. I got tired of listening to them fuss and fight all the time. And it seemed like it always got worse on the weekends when he came home drunk.

That wasn't the life my mother's parents had in mind for her after they emigrated all the way from Korea to Brooklyn, New York. I'm sure they felt that if she was going to struggle, then she needed to struggle with her own kind. Not with some African-American scumbag, alcoholic, warehouse worker from Norfolk, Virginia, who only moved to New York City to pursue his dreams of making it big in the music industry. My mother, unfortunately, picked him to father me. When I got old enough to understand, my mother told me that as soon as my grandparents got wind of their relationship, they disowned her. But as soon as my dad packed his shit and left, they immediately came to her rescue and wrote her back into their will. They were so happy that nigga left, they got on their knees and started sending praises to Buddha.

I couldn't care one way or the other. I mean, it wasn't like we were close anyway. From as far back as I could remember, I pretty much did my own thing. After school I would always go to the library and find a book to read, which was why I excelled in grade school. After graduating from high school, I thought about nothing else but furthering my education in law. I had always aspired to be a TV court judge, so I figured the only way I could ever have my own show was to become an attorney first. So here I was defending my client, the alleged leader of the Fuc-Chang Korean mafia, who was on trial for murder, bribery, and racketeering. Now I knew he was guilty as hell, but I pulled every trick out of the bag to make the jury believe that he wasn't.

"Ms. Lomax, the jury returned its verdict after just one day of deliberation. Are you worried?" a reporter called out as I made my way down the hallway toward Judge Allen's courtroom. A swarm of reporters surrounded me, shoving microphones in my face. I never turned down an opportunity to show up on television.

"A fast verdict is just what I expected. My client is innocent." I smiled, flashing my perfect white teeth and shaking my long, jet black hair. And right after I entered the courtroom, I switched my ass as hard as I could down the middle aisle toward the defense table. All eyes turned toward me. I could feel the stares burning my entire body. My red Chanel suit was an eye-catcher. It showed off my curves and it made me look like a million bucks. When potential clients approach me for representation, they are not surprised to learn that I charge a minimum of $2,500 an hour. They don't even blink when the figure rolls off my tongue. The way they see it, you never put a price on freedom, and with my victory rate, how can they lose?

Right before I took my seat at the defense table, I looked at my client, Mr. Choo, who was shackled like an animal and guarded by courtroom officers. He appeared cool, calm, and collected, unlike the men in black across from him. The prosecutors sat at their table and fiddled with pens, bit nails, and adjusted ties. They looked nervous and frazzled, to say the least. I was just the opposite. In fact, I was laughing my ass off on the inside because I knew I had this case in the bag.

The senior court officer moved to the front of the jam-packed courtroom, ordered everyone to stand, and announced Judge Allen. I looked up at Judge Mark Allen, with his salt-and-pepper balding head and little beady eyes. Mark is what I call him when he's not in his black robe. As a matter of fact, it gets really personal when he and I get together for one of our so-called romantic interludes. Last week was the last time he and I got together, and it was in his chambers. It was so funny because I let him fuck me in his robe with his puny five-inch wrinkled dick. He thought he was the man, too. And when it was all said and done, I made sure I wiped my cum all over the crotch of his slacks. Shit, Monica Lewinsky ain't got nothing on me. I wanted him to know that I had no respect for his authority or his courtroom. After I let him get at me, and I bribed a few of the jurors, all of the calls in the courtroom went my way. The prosecutors never had a chance . . . . It was amusing to watch.

The judge cleared his throat and began to speak. The courtroom was "pin drop" quiet.

"Jury, what say you in the case of the State of Florida versus Haan Choo?" Judge Allen boomed.

The jury foreperson, a fair-skinned Black woman in her mid-fifties, stood up swiftly, her hands trembling. "'We, the jury, in the matter of the State of Florida versus Haan Choo, finds as follows: to the charge of first-degree murder . . . not guilty.'"

A gasp resounded through the courtroom. Then the scream of some victim's family members.

"Order!" Judge Allen screamed.

The foreperson continued without looking up from her paper. "'To the charge of racketeering . . . not guilty. To the charge of bribery . . . not guilty. And to the charge of conspiracy . . . not guilty.'"

Mr. Choo jumped up and grabbed me in a bear hug. "Yoshi, you greatest," he whispered in broken English.

"Order!" the judge screamed again. "Bailiff, take Mr. Choo back to booking so he can be released." He had to go through his motions to set Mr. Choo free. I looked over at the prosecutors' table and threw them a smile. I knew they all wished they could just jump across the table and kill me. Too bad they hadn't taken what I had offered them after the preliminary hearing. Both assistant district attorneys were new to the game and overeager to take on their first high-profile case. Out of the gate they wanted to prove to their boss that they both could take me on, but somebody should've warned them that I was no one to fuck with. With a smile still on my face, I strutted by them and said, "Idiots!" just loud enough for only them to hear. Then I threw my hair back and continued to strut my shit out the courtroom.

After I slid the city clerk's head administrator ten crisp one-hundred-dollar bills, it only took about an hour to process Mr. Choo's release papers. Money talks and bullshit runs the marathon! And before anyone knew it, Mr. Choo and I were walking outside to greet the press. He and I both were all smiles, because he was a free man and I knew that in an hour or so, I was going to be $2 million richer; that alone made me want to celebrate. But first, we needed to address the media.

Cameras flashed and microphones passed in front of us as we stepped into the sunlight. Mr. Choo rushed to the huddle of microphones that all but blocked his slim face from view. "Justice was served today. I am innocent and my lawyer proved that. I no crime boss, I am family man. I run my business and I love America," he rambled, his horrible English getting on my nerves. I waited patiently while he made his grandstand and then I took over the media show.

"All along I told everyone my client was innocent. Mr. Choo came to the United States from Korea to make an honest—" *Bang, bang, bang, bang, bang, bang!* The sound of shouts and then screams rang in my ears. Then I heard someone in the crowd yell in Korean, "You fucking snitch!" The shots stopped me dead in my tracks; my words tumbled back down my throat like hard marbles, choking me. I grabbed my arm as heat radiated up to my neck.

"Oh shit, I'm hit!" I screamed. I dropped to the ground, scrambling to hide . . . and saw Mr. Choo, his head dangling and his body slumped against the courthouse steps. His mouth hung open and blood dripped from his lips and chin. Before I could figure out what to do next, someone snatched me up from the ground. I didn't know where we were headed— my thoughts were on my throbbing arm and my racing heart. Then suddenly my vision became blurry and the world went black.

My career changed after Mr. Choo's trial. Shit, after having almost lost my damn life, I would not accept anything less than the best.

After the shooting, the law firm of Shapiro and

Witherspoon was thrown into the media spotlight like never before. I became known as the "ride-or-die bitch attorney" that would take a bullet to get a client off. I became the most sought-after criminal defense attorney in Florida. Sometimes I didn't know if that was good or bad. But one thing was sure, my life changed and my appetite for money and power grew more and more intense. I started living each day as if it were my last.

Years ago, I never thought I would have turned out to be the way I was today. When you look at it, I had become a heartless bitch! I could not care less about anyone, including my own damn mother. Even when having a nightcap with my flavor of the night, I never let my feelings get involved. Once I put the condom on him, I reminded myself that it was only business and that my client's freedom was on the line, so everything worked out fine. That's how I kept men in line. After the shooting, I vowed that my heart would remain in my pocket forever.

Notorious

Life in VA

I crossed a lot of state lines to get to my father's hometown, but I made it.

When I stepped foot into the state of Texas, I saw my picture plastered across the cover of several newspapers. Believe me when I tell you, I got the hell out of there really quick. I rented a Toyota Highlander from Enterprise, stuffed all my things into the back of it, and drove the rest of the way to Virginia. It took me approximately twenty-two hours to get to my destination. Along the way, I prayed that my father's people hadn't heard about my brush with the law and the reward that they were offering. It had been a long time since we had been together, so I was like a stranger to them, which would make it easy for any one of them to turn me in. I had to keep my eyes and ears open, and the first time I sensed that something wasn't right, I was going to haul ass without even looking back.

I had to admit that I was tired as hell when I arrived in Norfolk, so I stopped by the Marriott hotel downtown near Waterside Drive to get some rest. It was around three in the afternoon, so I was able to wear my sunshades in front of the hotel clerk without looking awkward. After I paid for my room with cash, I headed up to the fifth floor to unwind. I started to call my cousin Carmine right after I unpacked, but then decided to wait until I got me a nap.

When I woke up, it was a little after seven, so I got up from the bed and decided to make the call to my family. The only number I had was the number to my father's mother house. My grandmother had had that number for as long as I could remember, and it had never been disconnected. So I figured that when I called her I could get Carmine's number and make some arrangements to hook up.

The phone rang about four times before someone picked it up. I wasn't too familiar with the woman's voice, so I said hello and asked to speak with my grandmother.

"Can I ask who's calling?" the woman asked.

"This is her grandaughter, Yoshi," I replied.

"Wait a minute. Now I know this ain't my cousin Yoshi from New York."

"Yes . . . is this Carmine?"

"Oh my God! I can't believe it's you."

"How you been?"

"I've been doing okay. What about yourself?"

"Nothing has changed. I'm still a lawyer, trying to make a name for myself."

"Wow! When we were kids I remember how we used to talk about when we grew up that we were going to be lawyers. But you were the only one who stuck with it. Damn, that's so good."

"Trust me, Carmine, life as an attorney isn't a bowl of fucking cherries. Girl, you've got to constantly stay on the grind and stay away from the psycho-ass clients. They will try to kill you," I replied, reflecting on the shit I went through back in Miami with Haitian drug lord Sheldon Chisholm. He was part of the reason I was on the run from the law.

"Ahh, it can't be that bad. Shit, I would love to have your life any day."

"You can't be doing that bad."

"Yoshi, I am over thirty and working as a fucking waitress at the IHOP on 21st Street. I live with Grandma and I don't have a car. Now tell me I'm not in a fucked-up situation?"

I thought about it and the answer was clear. She was in a fucked-up situation. Not as fucked-up as mine, but she was on my tail. I never would have pictured Carmine's life like this. Back when we were kids, she was always the smarter one. She was prettier, too. All the boys wanted to be her boyfriend before they ever considered looking at me. There was no doubt that I was an attractive little girl growing up, but the boys couldn't get over my chinky eyes and the fact that I was boney as hell. Those little neighborhood bastards chose Carmine over me every single time because of her almond-shaped eyes and big butt. I dealt with their bullshit the entire time I was in Virginia visiting my dad. I wondered where those boys are now? Probably in jail on drug charges or deployed over in Iraq. Whatever their status was right now, it sure wasn't helping Carmine out, because the way she just laid out everything, shit was really messed up for her. I just hoped she didn't try to come at me with her hand out because I had only enough money to last me until I could make my next power move. Now, don't get me wrong, I'd help her as much as I could, but I would not purchase her a car. Instead of making any comments about her situation, I just told her that she was going to be alright.

"Easy for you to say. You're the big-time lawyer."

I sighed heavily. "That's what you think."

"So what's going on? Last time I heard, you moved on down to Florida."

"Yes, that was true. But I just took some time off and now I'm not too far from you."

"What do you mean, you're not too far from me? Where are you?" Carmine got excited.

"I'm in Norfolk at the downtown Marriott."

"Oh my God! Are you serious?"

"Yes, I'm serious. So let's get together in about another hour so we can continue to catch up."

"Are you driving?"

"Yes, I have a rental."

"Okay, well, you can come by the house and pick me up. That way you can see Grandma and the rest of the family."

"Does Grandma still live in the same house from when we were kids?"

"Yep, she sure does. Ain't nothing changed but our ages."

The thought of my grandmother still living in that old house made me cringe. I honestly couldn't imagine anyone living in a house for as long as she has. I thought back to when I used to visit her and how the floor used to crackle because the hardwood flooring was old and had never been maintained. I also remembered her having wooden paneling on her walls, space heaters in every room of the house during the winter season, and one big air conditioner in the living room during the summer months. Everybody used to pile up in that small-ass room when it was hot. That was the only way to stay cool. I just hoped conditions for them had gotten a little bit better.

After I told Carmine to get ready and that I would be out there to get her in about an hour, she said okay and then we hung up. It took me only thirty minutes to hop in the shower and get dressed. Even though I was a fugitive, I didn't need to look sloppy, so I slid on a pair of dark blue Chip & Pepper jeans, a black wool Ellen Tracy turtleneck sweater, and a black pair of Fendi riding boots. It was kind of nippy outside, so I also threw on a wool blazer with patches on the elbow. Right before I left La La's estate in South America, I had gotten some hair extensions put in my hair, so I was back to my normal-looking self. I planned to have Carmine point me in the direction of a good hairstylist because I was overdue for a full makeover.